THE
WARLOCK LORD

By Terry Brooks

The Sword of Shannara
1. THE WARLOCK LORD
2. THE DRUIDS' KEEP
3. THE SECRET OF THE SWORD

The Shannara saga continues with:
THE ELFSTONES OF SHANNARA
THE WISHSONG OF SHANNARA

The Heritage of Shannara
THE SCIONS OF SHANNARA
THE DRUID OF SHANNARA
THE ELF QUEEN OF SHANNARA
THE TALISMANS OF SHANNARA

The Magic Kingdom of Landover
MAGIC KINGDOM FOR SALE – SOLD!
THE BLACK UNICORN
WIZARD AT LARGE
THE TANGLE BOX
WITCHES' BREW

The Word and the Void
RUNNING WITH THE DEMON
A KNIGHT OF THE WORD
ANGEL FIRE EAST

THE
WARLOCK LORD

Volume One of
THE SWORD OF SHANNARA

Terry Brooks

www.atombooks.co.uk

An *Atom* Book

First published in Great Britain as part of The Sword of Shannara by
Futura Publications Limited in 1978
Reprinted 1983 (twice), 1985, 1986, 1987, 1988, 1989, 1990
Reprinted by Orbit 1992 (twice), 1993, 1995, 1996, 1997, 1998,
1999, 2000

First published in this edition by Atom 2004

A CIP catalogue record for this book is available from the British Library.

ISBN 1 904233 340 6

Printed and bound in Great Britain
by Bookmarque Ltd, Croydon, Surrey

Atom
An imprint of
Time Warner Books UK
Brettenham House
Lancaster Place
London WC2E 7EN

for my parents,
who believed

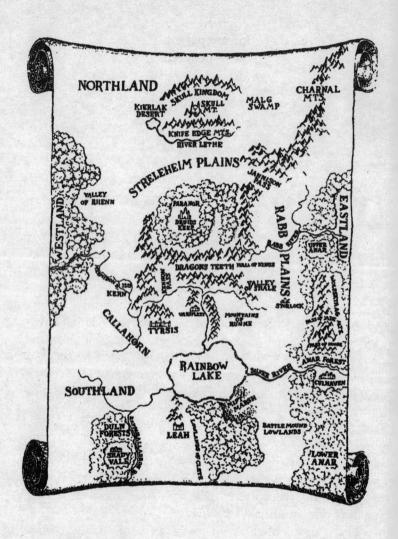

CHAPTER

1

The sun was already sinking into the deep green of the hills to the west of the valley, the red and gray-pink of its shadows touching the corners of the land, when Flick Ohmsford began his descent. The trail stretched out unevenly down the northern slope, winding through the huge boulders which studded the rugged terrain in massive clumps, disappearing into the thick forests of the lowlands to reappear in brief glimpses in small clearings and thinning spaces of woodland. Flick followed the familiar trail with his eyes as he trudged wearily along, his light pack slung loosely over one shoulder. His broad, windburned face bore a set, placid look, and only the wide gray eyes revealed the restless energy that burned beneath the calm exterior. He was a young man, though his stocky build and the grizzled brown hair and shaggy eyebrows made him look much older. He wore the loose-fitting work clothes of the Vale people and in the pack he carried were several metal implements that rolled and clanked loosely against one another.

There was a slight chill in the evening air, and Flick clutched the collar of his open wool shirt closer to his neck. His journey ahead lay through forests and rolling flatlands, the latter not yet visible to him as he passed into the forests, and the darkness of the tall oaks and somber hickories reached upward to overlap and blot out the cloudless night sky. The sun had set, leaving only the deep blue of the heavens pinpointed by thousands of friendly stars. The huge trees shut out even these, and Flick was left alone in the silent darkness as he moved slowly along the beaten path. Because he had traveled this same route a hundred times, the young man noticed immediately the unusual stillness that seemed to have captivated the entire valley this evening. The familiar buzzing and chirping of insects normally present in the quiet of the night, the cries of the birds that awoke with the setting of the sun to fly in search of food – all were missing. Flick listened intently for some sound of life, but his keen ears could detect nothing. He shook his head uneasily. The deep silence was unsettling, particularly in view of the rumors of a frightening black-winged creature sighted in the night skies north of the valley only days earlier.

He forced himself to whistle and turned his thoughts back to his day's work in the country just to the north of the Vale, where outlying families farmed and tended domestic livestock. He traveled to their homes every week, supplying various items that they required and bringing bits of news on the happenings of the Vale and occasionally the distant cities of the deep Southland. Few people knew the surrounding countryside as well as he did, and fewer still cared to travel beyond the comparative safety of their homes in the valley. Men were more inclined to remain in isolated communities these days and let the rest of the world get along as best it could. But Flick liked to travel outside the valley from time to time, and the outlying homesteads were in need of his services and were willing to pay him for the trouble. Flick's father was not one to let an opportunity pass him by where there was money to be made, and the arrangement seemed to work out well for all concerned.

A low-hanging branch brushing against his head caused

Flick to start suddenly and leap to one side. In chagrin, he straightened himself and glared back at the leafy obstacle before continuing his journey at a slightly quicker pace. He was deep in the lowland forests now and only slivers of moonlight were able to find their way through the thick boughs overhead to light the winding path dimly. It was so dark that Flick was having trouble finding the trail, and as he studied the lay of the land ahead, he again found himself conscious of the heavy silence. It was as if all life had been suddenly extinguished, and he alone remained to find his way out of this forest tomb. Again he recalled the strange rumors. He felt a bit anxious in spite of himself and glanced worriedly around. But nothing stirred on the trail ahead nor moved in the trees about him, and he felt embarrassingly relieved.

Pausing momentarily in a moonlit clearing, he gazed at the fullness of the night sky before passing abruptly into the trees beyond. He walked slowly, picking his way along the winding path that had narrowed beyond the clearing and now seemed to disappear into a wall of trees and bushes ahead. He knew that it was merely an illusion, but found himself glancing about uneasily all the same. A few moments later, he was again on a wider trail and could discern bits of sky peeking through the heavy trees. He was almost to the bottom of the valley and about two miles from his home. He smiled and began whistling an old tavern song as he hurried on. He was so intent on the trail ahead and the open land beyond the forest that he failed to notice the huge black shadow that seemed to rise up suddenly, detaching itself from a great oak tree on his left and moving swiftly toward the path to intercept him. The dark figure was almost on top of the Valeman before Flick sensed its presence looming up before him like a great, black stone which threatened to crush his smaller being. With a startled cry of fear he leaped aside, his pack falling to the path with a crash of metal, and his left hand whipped out the long thin dagger at his waist. Even as he crouched to defend himself, he was stayed by a commanding arm raised above the figure before him and a strong, yet reassuring voice that spoke out quickly.

'Wait a moment, friend. I'm no enemy and have no wish to harm you. I merely seek directions and would be grateful if you could show me the proper path.'

Flick relaxed his guard a bit and tried to peer into the blackness of the figure before him in an effort to discover some semblance of a human being. He could see nothing, however, and he moved to the left with cautious steps in an attempt to catch the features of the dark figure in the tree-shadowed moonlight.

'I assure you, I mean no harm,' the voice continued, as if reading the Valeman's mind. 'I did not mean to frighten you, but I didn't see you until you were almost upon me, and I was afraid you might pass me by without realizing I was there.'

The voice stopped and the huge black figure stood silently, though Flick could feel the eyes following him as he edged about the path to put his own back to the light. Slowly the pale moonlight began to etch out the stranger's features in vague lines and blue shadows. For a long moment the two faced one another in silence, each studying the other, Flick in an effort to decide what it was he faced, the stranger in quiet anticipation.

Then suddenly the huge figure lunged with terrible swiftness, his powerful hands seizing the Valeman's wrists, and Flick was lifted abruptly off the solid earth and held high, his knife dropping from nerveless fingers as the deep voice laughed mockingly up at him.

'Well, well, my young friend! What are you going to do now, I wonder? I could cut your heart out on the spot and leave you for the wolves if I chose, couldn't I?'

Flick struggled violently to free himself, terror numbing his mind to any thought but that of escape. He had no idea what manner of creature had subdued him, but it was far more powerful than any normal man and apparently prepared to dispatch Flick quickly. Then abruptly, his captor held him out at arm's length, and the mocking voice became icy cold with displeasure.

'Enough of this, boy! We have played our little game and still you know nothing of me. I'm tired and hungry and have no wish to be delayed on the forest trail in the chill of the evening while you decide if I am man or beast. I will set you down that you may show me the path. I warn you – do not try to run from me or it will be the worse for you.'

The strong voice trailed off and the tone of displeasure disappeared as the former hint of mockery returned with a short laugh.

'Besides,' the figure rumbled as the fingers released their iron grip and Flick slipped to the path, 'I may be a better friend than you realize.'

The figure moved back a step as Flick straightened himself, rubbing his wrists carefully to restore the circulation to his numbed hands. He wanted to run, but was certain that the stranger would catch him again and this time finish him without further thought. He leaned over cautiously and picked up the fallen dagger, returning it to his belt.

Flick could see the fellow more clearly now, and a quick scrutiny of him revealed that he was definitely human, though much larger than any man Flick had ever seen. He was at least seven feet tall, but exceptionally lean, though it was difficult to be certain about this, since his tall frame was wrapped in a flowing black cloak with a loose cowl pulled close about his head. The darkened face was long and deeply lined, giving it a craggy appearance. The eyes were deep-set and almost completely hidden from view by shaggy eyebrows that knotted fiercely over a long flat nose. A short, black beard outlined a wide mouth that was just a line on the face – a line that never seemed to move. The overall appearance was frightening, all blackness and size, and Flick had to fight down the urge building within him to make a break for the forest's edge. He looked straight into the deep, hard eyes of the stranger, though not without some difficulty, and managed a weak smile.

'I thought you were a thief,' he mumbled hesitantly.

'You were mistaken,' was the quiet retort. Then the voice softened a bit. 'You must learn to know a friend from an enemy. Sometime your life may depend upon it. Now then, let's have your name.'

'Flick Ohmsford.'

Flick hesitated and then continued in a slightly braver tone of voice.

'My father is Curzad Ohmsford. He manages an inn in Shady Vale a mile or two from here. You could find lodging and food there.'

'Ah, Shady Vale,' the stranger exclaimed suddenly. 'Yes, that is where I am going.' He paused as if reflecting on his own words. Flick watched him cautiously as he rubbed his craggy face with crooked fingers and looked beyond the forest's edge to the rolling grasslands of the valley. He was still looking away when he spoke again.

'You . . . have a brother.'

It was not a question; it was a simple statement of fact. It was spoken so distantly and calmly, as if the tall stranger were not at all interested in any sort of a reply, that Flick almost missed hearing it. Then suddenly realizing the significance of the remark, he started and looked quickly at the other.

'How did . . .?'

'Oh, well,' the man said, 'doesn't every young Valeman like yourself have a brother somewhere?'

Flick nodded dumbly, unable to comprehend what it was that the other was trying to say and wondering vaguely how much he knew about Shady Vale. The stranger was looking questioningly at him, evidently waiting to be guided to the promised food and lodging. Flick quickly turned away to find his hastily discarded pack, picked it up and slung it over his shoulder, looking back at the figure towering over him.

'The path is this way.' He pointed, and the two began walking.

They passed out of the deep forest and entered rolling, gentle hills which they would follow to the hamlet of Shady Vale at the far end of the valley. Out of the woods, it was a bright night; the moon was a full white globe overhead, its glow clearly illuminating the landscape of the valley and the path which the two travelers were following. The path itself was a vague line winding over the grassy hills and distinguishable only by occasional rain-washed ruts and flat, hard patches of earth breaking through the heavy grass. The wind had gathered strength and rushed at the two men with quick gusts that whipped at their clothing as they walked, forcing them to bow their heads slightly to shield their eyes. Neither spoke a word as they proceeded, each concentrating on the lay of the land beyond, as new hills and small depressions appeared with the passing of each traveled knoll. Except for the rushing of the wind, the night remained silent. Flick listened intently, and once he thought he heard a sharp cry far to the north, but an instant later it was gone, and he did not hear it again. The stranger appeared to be unconcerned with the silence. His attention seemed to be focused on a constantly changing point on the ground some six feet in front of them. He did not look up and he did not look at his young guide for directions as they went. Instead, he seemed to know exactly where the other was going and walked confidently beside him.

After a while, Flick began to have trouble keeping pace with the tall man, who traveled the path with long, swinging strides that dwarfed Flick's shorter ones. At times, the Valeman almost had to run to keep up. Once or twice the other man glanced down at his smaller companion and, seeing the difficulty he was having in trying to match strides, slowed to an easier pace. Finally, as the southern slopes of the valley drew near, the hills began to level off into shrub-covered grasslands that hinted at the appearance of new forests. The terrain began to dip downward at a gentle slope, and Flick located several familiar landmarks that bounded the outskirts of Shady Vale. He felt a surge of relief in spite of himself. The hamlet and his own warm home were just ahead.

The stranger did not speak a single word during the brief journey, and Flick was reluctant to attempt any conversation. Instead, he tried to study the giant in quick glimpses as they walked, without permitting the other to observe what he was doing. He was understandably awed. The long, craggy face, shaded by the sharp black beard, recalled the fearful Warlocks described to him by stern elders before the glowing embers of a late evening fire when he was only a child. Most frightening were the stranger's eyes – or rather the deep, dark caverns beneath the shaggy brows where his eyes should be. Flick could not penetrate the heavy shadows that continued to mask that entire area of his face. The deeply lined countenance seemed carved from stone, fixed and bowed slightly to the path before it. As Flick pondered the inscrutable visage, he suddenly realized that the stranger had never even mentioned his name.

The two were on the outer lip of the Vale, where the now clearly distinguishable path wound through large, crowded bushes that almost choked off human passage. The tall stranger stopped suddenly and stood perfectly still, head bowed, listening intently. Flick halted beside him and waited quietly, also listening, but unable to detect anything. They remained motionless for seemingly endless minutes, and then the big man turned hurriedly to his smaller companion.

'Quickly! Hide in the bushes ahead. Go now, run!'

He half pushed, half threw Flick in front of him as he raced swiftly toward the tall brush. Flick scurried fearfully for the sanctuary of the shrubbery, his pack slapping wildly against his back and the metal implements clanging. The stranger turned on him and snatched the pack away, tucking it beneath the long robe.

'Silence!' he hissed. 'Run now. Not a sound.'

They ran quickly to the dark wall of foliage some fifty feet ahead, and the tall man hurriedly pushed Flick through the leafy branches that whipped against their faces, pulling him roughly into the middle of a large clump of brush, where they stood breathing heavily. Flick glanced at his companion and saw that he was not looking through the brush at the country around them, but instead was peering upward where the night sky was visible in small, irregular patches through the foliage. The sky seemed clear to the Valeman as he followed the other's intense gaze, and only the changeless stars winked back at him as he watched and waited. Minutes passed; once he attempted to speak, but was quickly silenced by the strong hands of the stranger, gripping his shoulders in warning. Flick remained standing, looking at the night and straining his ears for some sound of the apparent danger. But he heard nothing save their own heavy breathing and a quiet rush of wind through the weaving branches of their cover.

Then, just as Flick prepared to ease his tired limbs by sitting, the sky was suddenly blotted out by something huge and black that floated overhead and then passed from sight. A moment later it passed again, circling slowly without seeming to move, its shadow hanging ominously above the two hidden travelers as if preparing to fall upon them. A sudden feeling of terror raced through Flick's mind, trapping it in an iron web as it strained to flee the fearful madness penetrating inward. Something seemed to be reaching downward into his chest, slowly squeezing the air

9

from his lungs, and he found himself gasping for breath. A vision passed sharply before him of a black image laced with red, of clawed hands and giant wings, of a thing so evil that its very existence threatened his frail life. For an instant the young man thought he would scream, but the hand of the stranger gripped his shoulder tightly, pulling him back from the precipice. Just as suddenly as it had appeared, the giant shadow was gone and the peaceful sky of the patched night was all that remained.

The hand on Flick's shoulder slowly relaxed its grip, and the Valeman slid heavily to the ground, his body limp as he broke out in a cold sweat. The tall stranger seated himself quietly next to his companion and a small smile crossed his face. He laid one long hand on Flick's and patted it as he would a child's.

'Come now, my young friend,' he whispered, 'you're alive and well, and the Vale lies just ahead.'

Flick looked up at the other's calm face, his own eyes wide with fear as he shook his head slowly.

'That thing! What was that terrible thing?'

'Just a shadow,' the man replied easily. 'But this is neither the place nor the time to concern ourselves with such matters. We will speak of it later. Right now, I would like some food and a warm fire before I lose all patience.'

He helped the Valeman to his feet and returned his pack to him. Then with a sweep of his robed arm, he indicated that he was ready to follow if the other was ready to lead. They left the cover of the brush, Flick not without misgivings as he glanced apprehensively at the night sky. It almost seemed as if the whole business had been the result of an overactive imagination. Flick pondered the matter solemnly and quickly decided that whatever the case, he had had enough for one evening: first this nameless giant and then that frightening shadow. He silently vowed that he would think twice before traveling again at night so far from the safety of the Vale.

Several minutes later, the trees and brush began to thin out and the flickering of yellow light was visible through the darkness. As they drew closer, the vague forms of buildings began to take shape as square and rectangular bulks in the gloom. The path widened into a smoother dirt road that led straight into the hamlet, and Flick smiled gratefully at the lights that shone in friendly greeting through the windows of the silent buildings. No one moved on the road ahead; if it had not been for the lights, one might well have wondered if anyone at all lived in the Vale. As it was, Flick's thoughts were far from such questions. Already he was considering how much he ought to tell his father and Shea, not wishing to worry them about strange shadows that could easily have been the product of his imagination and the gloomy night. The stranger at his side might shed some light on the subject at a later time, but so far he had not proved to be much of a conversationalist. Flick glanced involuntarily at the tall figure walking silently beside him. Again he was chilled by the blackness of the man. It seemed to reflect from his cloak and hood over his bowed head and lean hands, to shroud the entire figure in hazy gloom. Whoever he was, Flick felt certain that he would be a dangerous enemy.

They passed slowly between the buildings of the hamlet, and Flick could see torches burning through the wooden frames of the wide windows. The houses themselves were long, low structures, each containing only a ground floor beneath a slightly sloping roof, which in most instances tapered off on one side to shelter a small veranda, supported by heavy poles affixed to a long porch. The buildings were constructed of wood, with stone foundations and stone frontings on a few. Flick glanced through the curtained windows, catching glimpses of the inhabitants, the sight of familiar faces reassuring to him in the darkness outside. It had been a frightening night, and he was relieved to be home among people he knew.

The stranger remained oblivious to everything. He did not bother with more than a casual glance at the hamlet and had not spoken once since they had entered the Vale. Flick remained incredulous at the way in which the other followed him. He wasn't following Flick at all, but seemed to know exactly where the Valeman was going. When the road branched off in opposite directions amid identical rows of houses, the tall man had no difficulty in determining the correct route, though he never once looked at Flick nor even raised his head to study the road. Flick found himself trailing along while the other guided.

The two quickly reached the inn. It was a large structure consisting of a main building and lounging porch, with two long wings that extended out and back on either side. It was constructed of huge logs, cut and laced on a high stone foundation and covered with the familiar wood shingle roof, this particular roof much higher than those of the family dwellings. The central building was well lighted, and muffled voices could be heard from within, interspersed with occasional laughter and shouts. The wings of the inn were in darkness; it was there that the sleeping quarters of the guests were located. The smell of roasting meat permeated the night air, and Flick quickly led the way up the wooden steps of the long porch to the wide double doors at the center of the inn. The tall stranger followed without a word.

Flick slid back the heavy metal door latch and pulled on the handles. The big door on the right swung open to admit them into a large lounging room, filled with benches, high-backed chairs, and several long, heavy wooden tables set against the wall to the left and rear. The room was brightly lit by the tall candles on the tables and wall racks and by the huge fireplace built into the center of the wall on the left; Flick was momentarily blinded as his eyes adjusted to this new light. he squinted sharply, glancing past the fireplace and lounging furniture to the closed double doors at the back of the room and over to the long serving bar running down the length of the wall to his right. The men gathered about the bar looked up idly as the pair entered the room, their faces registering undisguised amazement at the appearance of the tall stranger. But Flick's silent companion did not seem to see them, and they quickly returned to their conversation and evening drinks, glancing back at the newcomers once or twice to see what they were going to do. The pair remained standing at the door for a few moments more as Flick looked around a second time at the faces of the small crowd to see if his father were present. The stranger motioned to the lounging chairs on the left.

'I will have a seat while you find your father. Perhaps we can have dinner together when you return.'

Without further comment, he moved quietly away to a small table at the rear of the room and seated himself with his back to the men at the bar, his face slightly bowed and turned away from Flick. The Valeman watched him for a moment, then moved quickly to the double doors at the rear of the room and pushed through them to the hallway beyond. His father was probably in the kitchen, having dinner with Shea. Flick hurried down the hall past several closed doors before reaching the one that opened into the inn kitchen. As he entered, the two cooks who were working at the rear of the room greeted the young man with a cheerful good evening. His father was seated at the end of a long counter at the left. As Flick had anticipated, he was in the process of finishing his dinner. He waved a brawny hand in greeting.

'You're a bit later than usual, son,' he growled pleasantly. 'Come over here and have dinner while there's still something to eat.'

Flick walked over wearily, lowered the traveling pack to the floor with a slight clatter, and perched himself on one of the high counter stools. His father's large frame straightened itself as he shoved back the empty plate and looked quizzically at the other, his wide forehead wrinkling.

'I met a traveler on the road coming into the valley,' Flick explained hesitantly. 'He wants a room and dinner. Asked us to join him.'

'Well, he came to the right place for a room,' the elder Ohmsford declared. 'I don't see why we shouldn't join him for a bite to eat – I could easily do with another helping.'

He raised his massive frame from the stool and signaled the cooks for three dinners. Flick looked about for Shea, but he was nowhere in sight. His father lumbered over to the cooks to give some special instructions on preparing the meal for the small party, and Flick turned to the basin next to the sink to wash off the dirt and grime from the road. When his father came over to him, Flick asked where his brother had gone.

'Shea has gone out on an errand for me and should return on the moment,' his father replied. 'By the way, what's the name of this man you brought back with you?'

'I don't know. He didn't say.' Flick shrugged.

His father frowned and mumbled something about close-mouthed strangers, rounding off his muffled comment with a vow to have no more mysterious types at his inn. Then motioning to his son, he led the way through the kitchen doors, his wide shoulders brushing the wall beyond as he swung to his left toward the lounging area. Flick followed quickly, his broad face wrinkled in doubt.

The stranger was still sitting quietly, his back to the men gathered at the serving bar. When he heard the rear doors swing open, he shifted about slightly to catch a glimpse of the two who entered. The stranger studied the close resemblance between father and son. Both were of medium height and heavy build, with the same broad, placid faces and grizzled brown hair. They hesitated in the doorway and Flick pointed toward the dark figure. He could see the surprise in Curzad Ohmsford's eyes as the innkeeper

14

regarded him for a minute before approaching. The stranger stood up courteously, towering over the other two as they came up to him.

'Welcome to my inn, stranger,' the elder Ohmsford greeted him, trying vainly to peer beneath the cloak hood that shadowed the other's dark face. 'My name, as my boy has probably told you, is Curzad Ohmsford.'

The stranger shook the extended hand with a grip that caused the stocky man to grimace and then nodded to Flick.

'Your son was kind enough to show me to this pleasant inn.' He smiled with what Flick could have sworn was a mocking grin. 'I hope you will join me for dinner and a glass of beer.'

'Certainly,' answered the innkeeper, lumbering past the other to a vacant chair where he seated himself heavily. Flick also pulled up a chair and sat down, his eyes still on the stranger, who was in the process of complimenting his father on having such a fine inn. The elder Ohmsford beamed with pleasure and nodded in satisfaction to Flick as he signaled one of the men at the serving bar for three glasses. The tall man still did not pull back the hood of the cloak shading his face. Flick wanted to peer beneath the shadows, but was afraid the stranger would notice, and one such attempt had already earned him sore wrists and a healthy respect for the big man's strength and temper. It was safer to remain in doubt.

He sat in silence as the conversation between his father and the stranger lengthened from polite comments on the mildness of the weather to a more intimate discussion of the people and happenings of the Vale. Flick noticed that his father, who never needed much encouragement anyway, was carrying the entire conversation with only casual questions interjected by the other man. It probably did not matter, but the Ohmsfords knew nothing about the stranger. He had not even told them his name. Now he was quite subtly drawing out information on the Vale from the unsuspecting innkeeper. The whole situation bothered Flick, but he was uncertain what he should do. He began to wish that Shea would appear and see what was happening. But his brother remained absent, and the long-awaited dinner was served and entirely consumed before one of the wide double doors at the front of the lobby swung open, and Shea appeared from out of the darkness.

For the first time, Flick saw the hooded stranger take more than a passing interest in someone. Strong hands gripped the table as the black figure rose silently, towering over the Ohmsfords. He seemed to have forgotten they were there, as the lined brow furrowed more deeply and the craggy features radiated an intense concentration. For one frightening second, Flick believed that the stranger was somehow about to destroy Shea, but then the idea disappeared and was replaced with another. The man was searching his brother's mind.

He stared intently at Shea, his deep, shaded eyes running quickly over the young man's slim countenance and slight build. He noted the telltale Elven features immediately – the hint of slightly pointed ears beneath the tousled blond hair, the pencil-like eyebrows that ran straight up at a sharp angle from the bridge of the nose rather than across the brow, and the slimness of the nose and jaw. He saw intelligence and honesty in that face, and now as he faced Shea across the room, he saw determination in the penetrating blue eyes – determination that spread in a flush over the youthful features as the two men locked their gazes on one another. For a moment Shea hesitated in awe of the huge, dark apparition across the room. He felt unexplainably trapped but, bracing himself with sudden resolve, he walked toward the forbidding figure.

Flick and his father watched Shea approach them, his eyes still on the tall stranger and then, as if suddenly realizing who he was, the two rose from the table. There was a moment of awkward silence as they faced one another, and then all the Ohmsfords began greeting each other at once in a sudden jumble of words that relieved the initial tension. Shea smiled at Flick, but could not take his eyes off the imposing figure before him. Shea was slightly shorter than his brother and was therefore even more in the shadow of the stranger than Flick had been, though he was less nervous about it as he faced the man. Curzad Ohmsford was talking to him about his errand, and his attention was momentarily diverted while he replied to his father's insistent questions. After a few preliminary remarks, Shea turned back to the newcomer to the Vale.

'I don't believe we have met; yet you seem to know me from somewhere, and I have the strangest feeling that I should know you.'

The dark face above him nodded as the familiar mocking smile crossed it fleetingly.

'Perhaps you should know me, though it is not surprising that you do not remember. But I know who you are; indeed, I know you well.'

Shea was dumbfounded at this reply and, unable to respond, stood staring at the stranger. The other raised a lean hand to his chin to stroke the small dark beard, glancing slowly around at the three men who waited for him to continue. Flick's open mouth was framing the question on the minds of all the Ohmsfords, when the stranger reached up and pulled back the cowl of his cloak to reveal clearly the dark face, now framed by long black hair, cut nearly shoulder length and shading the deep-set eyes, which still showed only as black slits in the shadows beneath the heavy brows.

'My name is Allanon,' he announced quietly.

There was a long moment of stunned silence as the three listeners stared in speechless amazement. Allanon – the mysterious wanderer of the four lands, historian of the races, philosopher and teacher, and, some said, practitioner of the mystic arts. Allanon – the man who had been everywhere from the darkest havens of the Anar to the forbidden heights of the Charnal Mountains. His was a name familiar to the people of even the most isolated Southland communities. Now he stood unexpectedly before the Ohmsfords, none of whom had ventured outside their valley home more than a handful of times in their lives.

Allanon smiled warmly for the first time, but inwardly he felt pity for them. The quiet existence they had known for so many years was finished, and, in a way, it was his responsibility.

'What brings you here?' Shea asked at last.

The tall man looked sharply at him and uttered a deep, low chuckle that caught them all by surprise.

'You, Shea,' he murmured. 'I came looking for you.'

CHAPTER

2

S hea was awake early the next morning, rising from
the warmth of his bed to dress hastily in the damp
cold of the morning air. He had arisen so early, he
discovered, that no one else in the entire inn, guest or
family, was yet awake. The long building was silent as
he moved quietly from his small room in the rear of the
main section to the large lobby, where he quickly started a fire in the great stone hearth, his fingers almost
numb with cold. The valley was always strikingly cold in
the early-morning hours before the sun reached the rim
of the hills, even during the warmest seasons of the year.
Shady Vale was well sheltered, not only from the eyes of
men, but from the fury of perverse weather conditions
that drifted down from the Northland. Yet while the
heavy storms of the winter and spring passed over the
valley and Shady Vale, the bitter cold of early morning
all year round settled into the high hills, holding until
the warmth of the noonday sun filtered down to chase
away the chill.

The fire crackled and snapped at the wood as Shea
relaxed in one of the high, straight-backed chairs and pondered the events of the previous evening. He leaned back,
folded his arms for warmth, and hunched down into the
hard wood. How could Allanon have known him? He had

seldom been out of the Vale and would certainly have remembered the other man if he had met him while on one of his infrequent journeys. Allanon had refused to say more on the subject after that one declaration. He had finished his dinner in silence, concluding that further talk should wait until the next morning, and he became once again the forbidding figure he had first appeared when Shea entered the inn that evening. His meal completed, he had asked to be shown to his room so that he might sleep, and then excused himself. Neither Shea nor Flick could get him to say one word further about the trip to Shady Vale and his interest in Shea. The two brothers had talked alone later that night, and Flick had related the story of his encounter with Allanon and the incident with the terrifying shadow.

Shea's thoughts drifted back to his initial question – how could Allanon have known him? Mentally he retraced the events of his life. His early years were a vague memory. He did not know where he had been born, although sometime after the Ohmsfords had adopted him, he had been told that his place of birth was a small Westland community. His father had died before he was old enough to form a lasting impression, and now he could recall almost nothing of him. For a time his mother had kept him, and he could recall bits and pieces of his years with her, playing with Elven children, surrounded by great trees and deep green solitude. He was five when she became suddenly ill and decided to return to her own people in the hamlet of Shady Vale. She must have known then that she was dying, but her first concern was for her son. The journey south was the finish for her, and she died shortly after they reached the valley.

The relatives his mother had left when she married were gone, all but the Ohmsfords, who were no more than distant cousins. Curzad Ohmsford had lost his wife less than a year earlier, and was raising his son Flick while he managed the inn. Shea became a part of their family, and the two boys had grown up as brothers, both bearing the name Ohmsford. Shea had never been told his true name, nor did he care to ask. The Ohmsfords were the only family that meant anything to him, and they had accepted him as their own. There were times that being a half-blood bothered him, but Flick had stoutly insisted that it was a distinct advantage because it gave him the instincts and character of two races to build upon.

Yet nowhere could he remember an encounter with Allanon. It was as if the event had never really occurred. Perhaps it never had. He shifted around in the chair and gazed absently into the fire. There was something about the grim wanderer that frightened him. Perhaps it was his imagination, but he could not shake off the feeling that the man could somehow read his thoughts, could see right through him whenever he chose to do so. It seemed ridiculous, but the thought had lingered with the Valeman since the meeting in the lobby of the inn. Flick had remarked on it too. And he had gone further than that, whispering in the darkness of their sleeping room to his brother, fearful that he might in some way be overheard, that he felt Allanon was dangerous.

Shea stretched himself and sighed deeply. Already it was becoming light outside. He rose to add some more wood to the fire, and heard the sound of his father's voice in the hallway, grumbling loudly about matters in general. Sighing in resignation, Shea put aside his thoughts and hastened to the kitchen to help with the morning preparations.

It was almost noon before Shea saw any sign of Allanon, who had evidently kept to his room for the duration of the morning. He appeared quite suddenly from around one corner of the inn as Shea relaxed beneath a huge shade tree at the rear of the building, absently munching on a quick luncheon he had prepared for himself. His father was occupied within, and Flick was off somewhere on an errand. The dark stranger of the previous night seemed no less forbidding in the noon sun, still a shadowed figure of tremendous height, though he appeared to have changed his cloak from black to a light gray. The lean face was slightly bowed to the path before him as he walked toward Shea and seated himself on the grass next to the Valeman, gazing absently at the hilltops to the east which appeared above the trees of the hamlet. Both men were silent for several long minutes, until at last Shea could stand it no longer.

'Why did you come to the vale, Allanon? Why were you looking for me?'

The dark face turned toward him and a slight smile played across the lean features.

'A question, my young friend, that cannot be as easily answered as you would like. Perhaps the best way in which to answer you is first to question you. Have you read anything of the history of the Northland?'

He paused.

'Do you know of the Skull Kingdom?'

Shea stiffened at the mention of the name – a name that was synonymous with all the terrible things in life, real and imagined, a name used to frighten little children who had been bad or to send shivers down the spines of grown men when stories were told before the dying coals of a late evening fire. It was a name that hinted of ghosts and goblins, of the sly forest Gnomes of the east and the great Rock Trolls of the far north. Shea looked at the grim visage before him and nodded slowly. Again Allanon paused before continuing.

'I am a historian, Shea, among other things – perhaps the most widely traveled historian alive today, since few besides myself have entered the Northland in over five hundred years. I know much about the race of Man that none now suspect. The past has become a blurred memory, and

22

just as well perhaps; for the history of Man has not been particularly glorious in the last two thousand years. Men today have forgotten the past; they know little of the present and less of the future. The race of Man lives almost solely in the confines of the Southland. It knows nothing at all of the Northland and its peoples, and little of the Eastland and Westland. A pity that Men have developed into such a shortsighted people, for once they were the most visionary of the races. But now they are quite content to live apart from the other races, isolated from the problems of the rest of the world. They remain content, mind you, because those problems have not as yet touched them and because a fear of the past has persuaded them not to look too closely at the future.'

Shea felt slightly irritated by these sweeping accusations, and his reply was sharp.

'You make it sound like a terrible thing to want to be left alone. I know enough history – no, I know enough life – to realize that Man's only hope for survival is to remain apart from the races, to rebuild everything he has lost over the last two thousand years. Then perhaps he will be smart enough not to lose it a second time. He almost destroyed himself entirely in the Great Wars by his persistent intervention in the affairs of others and his ill-conceived rejection of an isolation policy.'

Allanon's dark face turned hard.

'I am well aware of the catastrophic consequences brought about by those wars – the products of power and greed that the race of Man brought down on its own head through a combination of carelessness and remarkable shortsightedness. That was long ago – and what has changed? You think that Man can start again, do you, Shea? Well, you might be quite surprised to learn that some things never change, and the dangers of power are always present, even to a race that almost completely obliterated itself. The Great Wars of the past may be gone – the wars

23

of the races, of politics and nationalism, and the final ones of sheer energy, of ultimate power. But we face new dangers today, and these are more of a threat to the existence of the races than were any of the old! If you think Man is free to build a new life while the rest of the world drifts by, then you do not know anything of history!'

He paused suddenly, his grim features lined with anger. Shea stared back defiantly, though within he felt small and frightened.

'Enough of this,' Allanon began again, his face softening as one strong hand reached up to grip Shea's shoulder in friendship. 'The past is behind us, and it is with the future that we must concern ourselves. Let me refresh your memory for a moment on the history of the Northland and the legend of the Skull Kingdom. As you know, I'm sure, the Great Wars brought an end to an age where Man alone was the dominant race. Man was almost completely destroyed and even the geography he had known was completely altered, completely restructured. Countries, nations, and governments all ceased to exist as the last members of the human race fled south to survive. It was nearly a thousand years before Man had once again raised himself above the standard of the animals he hunted for food and established a progressive civilization. It was primitive, to be sure, but there was order and a semblance of government. Then Man began to discover there were other races besides himself inhabiting the world – creatures who had survived the Great Wars and developed their own races. In the mountains were the huge Trolls, powerful and ferocious, but quite content with what they had. In the hills and forests were the small and cunning creatures we now call Gnomes. Many a battle was fought between Men and Gnomes for the rights to land during the years following the Great Wars, and the battles hurt both races. But they fought to survive, and reason has no place in the mind of a creature fighting for its life.

'Man also discovered that there was another race – a race of men who had fled beneath the earth to survive the effects of the Great Wars. Years of living in the huge caverns beneath the earth's crust away from the sunlight altered their appearance. They became short and stocky, powerful in the arms and chest, with strong, thick legs for climbing and scrambling underground. Their sight in the dark became superior to that of other creatures, yet in the sunlight they could see little. They lived beneath the earth for many hundreds of years, until at last they began to emerge to live again on the face of the land. Their eyes were very bad at first, and they made their homes in the darkest forests of the Eastland. They developed their own language, though they later reverted to the language of Man. When Man first discovered remnants of this lost race, they called them Dwarfs, after a fictional race of the old days.'

His voice trailed off and he remained silent for a few minutes staring out at the tips of the hills showing brilliant green in the sunlight. Shea considered the historian's comments. He had never seen a Troll, and only one or two Gnomes and Dwarfs, and those he did not remember very well.

'What about the Elves?' he asked finally.

Allanon looked back thoughtfully and bowed his head a little more.

'Ah, yes, I had not forgotten. A remarkable race of creatures, the Elves. Perhaps the greatest people of all, though no one has ever fully realized it. But the tale of the Elven people must wait for another time; suffice to say that they were always there in the great forests of the Westland, though the other races seldom encountered them at this stage of history.

'Now we shall see how much you know of the history of the Northland, my young friend. Today, it is a land inhabited by almost no one other than the Trolls, a barren and forbidding country where few people of any race care to travel, let alone settle. The Trolls, of course, are bred to survive there. Today, Men live in the warmth and comfort of the Southland's mild climate and green lands. They have forgotten that once the Northland, too, was settled by creatures of all the races, not only the Trolls in the mountain regions, but Men, Dwarfs, and Gnomes in the lowlands and forests. This was in the years when all the races were just beginning to rebuild a new civilization with new ideas, new laws, and many new cultures. It was a very promising future, but Men today have forgotten that those times ever existed – forgotten that they are more than a beaten race trying to live apart from those who defeated them and crippled their pride. There was no division of countries then. It was an earth reborn, where each race was being given a second chance at building a world. Of course, they did not realize the significance of the opportunity. They were too concerned with holding what they considered theirs and building their own private little worlds. Each race was certain that it was destined to be the dominant power in the years ahead – gathered together like a pack of angry rats guarding a stale, sorry piece of cheese. And Man, oh, yes, in all his glory, was groveling and snapping at the chance just like the others. Did you know that, Shea?'

The Valeman shook his head slowly, unable to believe that what he was hearing could be the truth. He had been told that Man had been a persecuted people ever since the Great Wars, fighting to keep alive his dignity and honor, to protect the little land that was his in the face of complete savagery on the part of the other races. Man had never been the oppressor in these battles; always he was the oppressed. Allanon smiled grimly, his lips curling with mocking satisfaction as he saw the effect of his words.

'You didn't realize that it was this way, I see. No matter – it will be the least of the surprises I have in store for you. Man has never been the great people he has fancied himself. In those days Men fought like the rest, although I will concede that perhaps they had a higher sense of honor and a clearer purpose to rebuild than some of the others, and they were slightly more civilized.' He twisted the word meaningfully as he spoke it, lacing it with undisguised sarcasm. 'But all this commentary has little to do with the main point of our discussion, which I hope to make clear to you shortly.

'It was about this same time, when the races had discovered one another and were fighting for dominance, that the Druid Council first opened the halls of Paranor in the lower Northland. History is rather vague about the origins and purposes of the Druids, though it is believed they were a group of highly knowledgeable men from all the races, skilled in many of the lost arts of the old world. They were philosophers and visionaries, students of the arts and science all at once, but more than this, they were the teachers of the races. They were the givers of power – the power of new knowledge in the ways of life. They were led by a man named Galaphile, a historian and philosopher like myself, who called the greatest men of the land together to form a council to establish peace and order. He relied on their learning to hold sway over the races, their ability to give knowledge to gain the people's confidence.

'The Druids were a very powerful force during those years and the plan of Galaphile seemed to be working as anticipated. But as time passed, it became apparent that some of the members of the Council had powers far surpassing those of the others, powers that had lain dormant and gathered strength in a few phenomenal, genius minds. It would be difficult to describe those powers to you without taking quite some time – more time than we have available to us. What is important for our purposes is to recognize that some among the Council who possessed the very greatest minds became convinced that they were destined to shape the future of the races. In the end, they broke from the Council to form their own group and for some time disappeared and were forgotten.

'About one hundred and fifty years later, there occurred a terrible civil war within the race of Man, which eventually widened into the First War of the Races, as the historians named it. Its cause was uncertain even then, and has now almost been forgotten. In simple terms, a small sector of the race of Man revolted against the teachings of the Council and formed a very powerful and highly trained army. The proclaimed purpose of the uprising was the subjugation of the rest of Man under a central rule for the betterment of the race and the furthering of its pride as a people. Eventually, almost all segments of the race rallied to the new cause and war was begun upon the other races, ostensibly to accomplish this new goal. The central figure behind the war was a man called Brona – an archaic Gnome term for "Master." It was said that he was the leader of the Druids of the first Council who had broken away and disappeared into the Northland. No reliable source ever reported seeing him or talking with him, and in the end it was concluded that Brona was merely a name, a fictitious character. The revolt, if you care to call it such, was finally crushed by the combined power of the Druids and the other allied races. Did you know of this, Shea?'

The Valeman nodded and smiled slightly.

'I have heard of the Druid Council, of its purposes and work – all ancient history since the Council died out long ago. I have heard of the First War of the Races, though not in the same way as you tell it. Prejudiced, I believe you would call my version. The war was a bitter lesson for Man.'

Allanon waited patiently and did not speak as Shea paused to reflect on his own knowledge of the past before continuing.

'I know that the survivors of our race fled south after the war was over and have remained there ever since, rebuilding again the homes and cities lost, trying to create life rather than destroy it. You seem to think of it as an isolation born of fear. But I believe it was and still is the best way to live. Central governments have always been the greatest danger to mankind. Now there are none – small communities are the new rule of life. Some things are better left alone by everyone.'

The tall man laughed, a deep mirthless chuckle that made Shea feel suddenly foolish.

'You know so little, though what you say is true enough. Truisms, my young friend, are the useless children of hindsight. Well, I don't propose to argue with you now on the fine points of social reform, let alone political activism. That will have to wait until another time. Tell me what you know of the creature called Brona. Perhaps . . . no, wait a moment. Someone is coming.'

The words were scarcely out of his mouth before the stocky figure of Flick appeared around the corner of the inn. The Valeman stopped abruptly as he saw Allanon and hesitated until Shea waved to him. He came over slowly and remained standing, his eyes on the dark face as the big man smiled slowly down at him, the familiar enigmatic twist at the corners of his mouth.

'I was just wondering where you had gone,' Flick began, speaking to his brother, 'and didn't mean to interrupt . . .'

'You are not interrupting anything,' Shea replied quickly. But Allanon seemed to disagree.

'This conversation was for your ears alone,' he declared flatly. 'If your brother chooses to stay, he will have decided his own fate in the days to come. I would strongly suggest that he not remain to hear the rest of our discussion, but forget that we ever talked. Still, it is his own choice.'

The brothers looked at each other, unable to believe that the tall man was serious. But his grim face indicated that he was not joking, and for a moment both men hesitated, reluctant to say anything. Finally Flick spoke.

'I have no idea what you're talking about, but Shea and

I are brothers and what happens to one must happen to both. If he's in any trouble, I should share it with him – it's my own choice, I'm sure.'

Shea stared at him in amazement. He had never heard Flick sound more positive about anything in his entire life. He felt proud of his brother and smiled up at him gratefully. Flick winked back quickly and sat down, not looking at Allanon. The tall traveler stroked his small, dark beard with a lean hand and smiled quite unexpectedly.

'Indeed, the choice is your own, and you have proven yourself a brother by your words. But it is deeds that make the difference. You may regret the choice in the days to come . . .'

He trailed off, lost in thought as he studied the bowed head of Flick for several long moments before turning to Shea.

'Well, I cannot begin my story again just for your brother. He will have to follow as best he can. Now tell me what you know of Brona.'

Shea thought silently for a few minutes and then shrugged.

'I really don't know much of anything about him. He was a myth, as you said, the fictional leader of the uprising in the First War of the Races. He was supposed to have been a Druid who left the Council and used his own evil power to master the minds of his followers. Historically, he was never seen, never captured, or killed in the final battle. He never existed.'

'Historically accurate, I'm sure,' muttered Allanon. 'What do you know of him in connection with the Second War of the Races?'

Shea smiled briefly at the question.

'Well, legend has it that he was the central force behind that war also, but it turned out to be just another myth. He was supposed to be the same creature who had organized the armies of Man in the first war, except in this one he was called the Warlock Lord – the evil counterpart to the Druid Bremen. I believe Bremen was supposed to have killed him in the second war, however. But all that was only fantasy.'

Flick hastened to nod his agreement, but Allanon said nothing. Shea waited for some form of confirmation, openly amused by the whole subject.

'Where is all this talk taking us anyway?' he asked after a moment.

Allanon glanced down at him sharply, cocking one dark eyebrow in wonder.

'Your patience is remarkably limited, Shea. After all, we have just covered in a matter of minutes the history of a thousand years. However, if you think you can restrain yourself for a few moments longer, I believe I can promise you that your question will be answered.'

Shea nodded, feeling no little mortification at the reprimand. It was not the words themselves that hurt; it was the way Allanon said them – with that mocking smile and ill-concealed sarcasm. The Valeman regained his composure quickly, though, and shrugged his willingness to allow the historian to continue at his own pace.

'Very well,' the other acknowledged. 'I shall try to complete our discussion quickly. What we have spoken of up to this point has been background history to what I will tell you now – the reason why I came to find you. I recall to your memory the events of the Second War of the Races – the most recent war in the new history of Man, fought less than five hundred years ago in the Northland. Man had no part in this war; Man was the defeated race of the first, living deep in the heart of the Southland, a few small communities trying hard to survive the threat of total extinction. This was a war of the great races – the Elven people and the Dwarfs fighting against the power of the savage Rock Trolls and the cunning Gnomes.

'After the completion of the First War of the Races, the

known world partitioned into the existing four lands, and the races were at peace for quite a long time. During this period, the power and influence of the Druid Council diminished greatly as the apparent need for its assistance seemed to have ceased. It is only fair to add that the Druids had grown lax in their attention to the races, and over a period of years the new members lost sight of the Council's purposes and turned away from the peoples' problems to more personal concerns, leading a more isolated existence of study and meditation. The Elven people were the most powerful race, but confined themselves to their isolated homeland deep in the west where they were content to remain in relative isolation – a mistake they were to regret deeply. The other peoples scattered and developed into smaller, less unified societies, primarily in the Eastland, though some groups did settle in parts of the Westland and Northland in the border countries.

'The Second War of the Races began when a huge army of Trolls came down out of the Charnal Mountains and seized all of the Northland, including the Druid fortress at Paranor. The Druids had been betrayed from within by several of their own people who had been won over by promises and offers from the enemy commander, who at this time was unknown. The remaining Druids, except for a very few who escaped or were away, were captured and thrown into the dungeons of the Keep and never seen again. Those who had escaped the fate of their brothers scattered about the four lands and went into hiding. The Troll army immediately moved against the Dwarf people in the Eastland with the obvious intent of crushing all resistance as quickly as possible. But the Dwarfs gathered deep within the huge forests of the Anar, which only they know well enough to survive in for any length of time, and there held firm against the advances of the Troll armies despite the aid being given by a few of the Gnome tribes who had joined the invasion force. The Dwarf King,

Raybur, recorded in his own peoples' history whom he had discovered the real enemy to be – the rebel Druid, Brona.'

'How could the Dwarf King believe this?' Shea interjected quickly. 'If it were true, the Warlock Lord would be over five hundred years old! At any rate, I should think that some ambitious mystic must have suggested the idea to the king with the thought of reviving an old, outdated myth – perhaps to better his own position in the court or something.'

'That is a possibility,' Allanon conceded. 'But let me continue the story. After long months of fighting, the Trolls were evidently led to believe that the Dwarfs had been beaten, so they turned their war legions to the west and began to march against the powerful Elven kingdom. But during the months the Trolls had battled the Dwarf people, the few Druids who had escaped from Paranor had been assembled by the famous mystic Bremen, an old and highly esteemed elder of the Council. He led them to the Elven kingdom in the Westland to warn the people there of this new threat and to prepare for the almost certain invasion of the Northlanders. The Elven King in that year was Jerle Shannara – the greatest of all the Elven kings, perhaps, with the exception of Eventine. Bremen warned the King of the probable assault on his lands, and the Elven ruler quickly prepared his armies before the advancing Troll hordes had reached their borders. I'm sure that you know your history well enough to remember what happened when the battle was fought, Shea, but I want you to pay attention to the particulars of what I tell you next.'

Both Shea and an excited Flick nodded.

'The Druid Bremen gave to Jerle Shannara a special sword for the battle against the Trolls. Whoever held the sword was supposed to be invincible – even against the awesome power of the Warlock Lord. When the Troll legions entered the Valley of Rhenn in the borderlands of the Elven kingdom, they were attacked and trapped by the armies of the Elven people fighting from higher ground and were badly beaten in a two-day, pitched battle. The Elves were led by the Druids and Jerle Shannara, who carried the great sword given him by Bremen. They fought together against the Troll armies, who were said to have had the added might of beings from the spirit world under the domination of the Warlock Lord. But the courage of the Elven King and the power of the fabulous sword overwhelmed the spirit creatures and destroyed them. When the remainder of the Troll army attempted to escape back to the safety of the Northland across the Plains of Streleheim, it was caught between the pursuing army of Elves and an army of Dwarfs approaching from the Eastland. There was a terrible battle fought in which the Troll army was destroyed almost to the last man. During the battle, Bremen disappeared while in combat at the side of the Elven King, facing the Warlock Lord himself. It was recorded that both Druid and Warlock were lost in the fighting and neither was ever seen again. Not even the bodies were found.

'Jerle Shannara carried the famous sword given him until his death some years later. His son gave the weapon to the Druid Council at Paranor, where the blade was set in a huge block of Tre-Stone and placed in a vault in the Druid's Keep. I'm sure you are quite familiar with the legend of the sword and what it stands for, what it means to all the races. The great sword rests today at Paranor just as it has for five hundred years. Have I been sufficiently lucid in my narration, Valemen?'

Flick nodded in dumbfounded wonder, still caught up in the excitement of the history. But Shea suddenly decided that he had heard enough. Nothing that Allanon had told them of the history of the races was fact – not if he was to believe what he had been taught by his own people since he was a child. The big man had simply related to them a childhood fantasy that had been passed down through the ages from parents to small children. He had listened patiently to everything Allanon had falsely represented to be the truth about the races, humoring him out of respect for his reputation. But the entire tale of the sword was ridiculous, and Shea was through being played for a fool.

'What has all this got to do with your coming to Shady Vale?' he persisted, a faint smile betraying his disgust. 'We've heard all about a battle that took place some five hundred years ago – a battle that did not even concern Man, but Trolls and Elves and Dwarfs and goodness knows what else, as you tell it. Did you say there were spirits or something? I'm sorry if I sound incredulous, but I find this whole tale a little hard to swallow. The story of the Sword of Jerle Shannara is well known to all the races, but it's only fiction, not fact – a glorified story of heroism created to stir up a sense of loyalty and duty in the races that have a part in its history. But the legend of Shannara is a tale for children that adults must outgrow as they accept the responsibilities of manhood. Why did you waste time relating this fairy tale when all I want is a simple answer to a simple question? Why are you looking for . . . me?'

Shea stopped short as he saw Allanon's dark features tighten and grow black with anger, the great brows knitting over sudden pinpoints of light in the deep shadows that hid the eyes. The tall man seemed to be fighting to contain some terrible fury within, and for a moment it appeared to Shea that he was about to be strangled by the huge hands that locked before his face as the man glared in open rage. Flick moved back hastily and tripped over his own feet in the process, fear welling up inside.

'Fool . . . you fool,' rasped the giant in barely controlled fury. 'You know so little . . . children! What does the race of Man know of truth – where has Man been but hiding, creeping in terror under pitecus shelters in the deepest regions of the Southland like frightened rabbits? You dare to tell me that I speak of fairy tales – you, who have never known strife, safe here in your precious Vale! I came to find the bloodline of kings, but I have found a little boy who hides himself in falsehoods. You are nothing but a child!'

Flick was fervently wishing he could sink into the ground beneath his feet or perhaps simply vanish, when to his utter astonishment he saw Shea leap to his feet before the tall man, his lean features flushed in fury and his hands knotted into fists as he braced himself. The Valeman was so overcome with anger that he could not speak, and stood before his accuser, shaking with rage and humiliation. But Allanon was not impressed and his deep voice sounded again.

'Hold, Shea. Do not be a greater fool! Pay attention to what I tell you now. All that I told you has come down through the ages as legend and was so told to the race of Man. But the time for fairy tales is ended. What I have told you is not legend; it is the truth. The sword is real; it rests today at Paranor. But most important of all, the Warlock Lord is real. He lives today and the Skull Kingdom is his domain!'

Shea started, suddenly realizing that the man was not deliberately lying after all – that he did not believe this to be a fairy tale. He relaxed and sat down slowly, his gaze still riveted on the dark face. Abruptly he recalled the historian's words.

'You said king . . . you were looking for a king . . .?'

'What is the legend of the Sword of Shannara, Shea? What does the inscription carved into the block of Tre-Stone read?'

Shea was dumbfounded, unable to recall any legend at all.

'I don't know . . . I can't remember what it said. Something about the next time . . .'

'A son!' spoke up Flick suddenly from the other side. 'When the Warlock Lord appeared again in the Northland, a son of the House of Shannara would come forth to take up the Sword against him. That was the legend!'

Shea looked over at his brother, remembering then what the inscription was supposed to read. He looked back at Allanon, who was watching him intently.

'How does this concern me?' he asked quickly. 'I'm not a son of the House of Shannara – I'm not even Elven. I'm a half-blood, not an Elf, not a king. Eventine is the heir to the House of Shannara. Are you telling me that I'm a lost son – a missing heir? I don't believe it!'

He looked quickly to Flick for support, but his brother appeared to be completely lost, staring in bewilderment at the face of Allanon. The dark man spoke quietly.

'You do have Elven blood in you, Shea, and you are not the true son of Curzad Ohmsford. That you must know. And Eventine is not directly of the blood of Shannara.'

'I have always known that I was an adopted son,' the Valeman admitted, 'but surely I could not have come from . . . Flick, tell him!'

But his brother just stared at him in astonishment, unable to frame an answer to the question. Shea stopped speaking abruptly, shaking his head in disbelief. Allanon nodded.

'You are a son of the House of Shannara – a half son only, however, and far removed from the direct line of descent that can be traced down through the last five hundred years. I knew you as a child, Shea, before you were taken into the Ohmsford household as their own son. Your father was Elven – a very fine man. Your mother was of the race of Man. They both died when you were still very young, and you were given to Curzad Ohmsford to raise as his own son. But you are a son of Jerle Shannara, albeit a distant son and not of pure Elven blood.'

Shea nodded absently at the tall man's explanation, confused and still suspicious. Flick was looking at his brother as if he had never seen him before.

'What does all this mean?' he asked Allanon eagerly.

'What I have told you is known also to the Lord of

Darkness, though he does not yet know where you live or who you are. But his emissaries will find you sooner or later, and when they do, you will be destroyed.'

Shea's head jerked up, and he looked at Flick fearfully, remembering the tale of the huge shadow seen near the lip of the Vale. His brother, too, felt a sudden chill, recalling that awful feeling of terror.

'But why?' asked Shea quickly. 'What have I done to deserve that?'

'You must understand many things, Shea, before you can understand the answer to that question,' replied Allanon,' and I have not the time to explain them all now. You must believe me when I tell you that you are descended from Jerle Shannara, that you are of Elven blood, and that the Ohmsfords are a foster family to you. You were not the only son of the House of Shannara, but you are the only son who survives today. The others were Elven, and they were easily found and destroyed. That is what prevented the Dark Lord from finding you for so long – he was unaware that there was a half son alive in the Southland. The Elven kin he knew of from the first.

'But know this, Shea. The power of the Sword is unlimited – it is the one great fear with which Brona lives, the one power he may not withstand. The legend of the Sword is a powerful amulet in the hands of the races, and Brona means to put an end to the legend. He will do this by destroying the entire house of Shannara, so that no son will come forth to draw the Sword against him.'

'But I did not even know of the Sword,' protested Shea. 'I did not even know who I was, or anything about the Northland or about . . .'

'It does not matter!' cut in Allanon sharply. 'If you are dead, there can be no doubt about you.'

His voice died away in a weary murmur, and he turned to look again at the distant mountaintops beyond the fringe of tall elms. Shea lay back slowly on the soft grass, staring at the pale blue of the late winter sky laced with small, soft wisps of white cloud that drifted from the tall hills. For a few pleasant moments the presence of Allanon and the threat of death were submerged in the sleepy warmth of the afternoon sun and the fresh smell of the lofty trees towering over him. He closed his eyes and thought of his life in the Vale, of the plans that he had made with Flick, of their hopes for the future. They would all go up in smoke if what he had been told were true. He lay quietly considering these things, and finally sat up, his arms braced behind him.

'I'm not sure what to think,' he began slowly. 'There are so many questions I have to ask you. I feel confused by the whole idea of being someone other than an Ohmsford – someone threatened with death at the hands of a . . . a myth. What do you suggest that I do?'

Allanon smiled warmly for the first time.

'For the moment, do nothing. There is no immediate danger to you. Think about what I have told you and we will speak further of the implications another time. I shall be glad to answer all your questions then. But do not talk about this to anyone else, not even your father. Act as if this conversation had never taken place until we have a chance to work out the problems further.'

The young men looked at each other and nodded in agreement, though it would be difficult to pretend that nothing had happened. Allanon rose silently, stretching his tall frame to relieve cramped muscles. The brothers rose with him and stood quietly as he looked down at them.

'Legends and myths that did not exist in yesterday's world will exist in tomorrow's. Things of evil, ruthless and cunning, after lying dormant for centuries, will now awaken. The shadow of the Warlock Lord begins to fall across the four lands.'

He trailed off abruptly.

'I did not mean to be harsh with you,' he smiled gently,

quite unexpectedly, 'but if this is the worst thing that happens in the days to come, you should be glad indeed. You are faced with a very real threat, not a fairy tale that can be laughed away. Nothing about any of this will be fair to you. You will learn much about life that you will not like.'

He paused, a tall gray shadow against the green of the distant hills, his robes gathered carefully about his gaunt frame. One great hand reached over to grip firmly Shea's lean shoulder, and for an instant bound them together as one person. Then he turned away and was gone.

CHAPTER

3

Allanon's plan for further discussions at the inn did not work out. He left the brothers sitting in hushed conversation behind the inn and returned to his room. Shea and Flick finally went back to their chores and shortly thereafter were dispatched on an errand by their father that took them out of the Vale to the north end of the valley. It was dark by the time they returned, and they hastened to the dining room, hoping to question the historian further, but he did not appear. They ate dinner hurriedly, unable to speak to each other about the afternoon while their father was present. After eating, they waited almost an hour, but still he did not appear and eventually, long after their father had departed for the kitchen, they decided to go to Allanon's room. Flick was reluctant to go looking for the dark stranger, especially after his meeting with him on the Vale road the previous night. But Shea was so insistent that at last his brother agreed to go along, hoping that there might be safety in numbers.

When they reached his room, they found the door unlocked and the tall wanderer gone. The room looked as if no one had even used it recently. They made a hasty search of the inn and the surrounding premises, but Allanon was not to be found. At last they were forced to conclude that for some unknown reason he had departed from Shady Vale. Shea was openly angered that Allanon had left without even a parting word, yet at the same time he began to experience a growing apprehension that he was no longer under the historian's protective wing. Flick, on the other hand, was just as happy that the man was gone. As he sat with Shea in the tall, hard-backed chairs before the fire in the big lounge room of the inn, he tried to assure his brother that everything was working out for the best. He had never completely believed the historian's wild tale of the Northland wars and the Sword of Shannara, he argued, and even if some of it were true, certainly the part about Shea's lineage and the threat from Brona was completely exaggerated – a ridiculous fairy tale.

Shea listened in silence to Flick's muddled rationalization of the possibilities, offering only an occasional nod of acquiescence, his own thoughts concentrated on deciding what he should do next. He had serious doubts about the credibility of Allanon's tale. After all, what purpose did the historian have in coming to him in the first place? He had appeared conveniently, it seemed, to tell Shea about his strange background, and to warn him that he was in danger, then had disappeared without a word about his own interest in this business. How could Shea be sure that Allanon had not come on some hidden purpose of his own, hoping to use the Valeman as his cat's-paw? There were too many questions that he didn't have the answers to.

Eventually, Flick grew tired of offering advice to the silent Shea and finally ceased to speak of the matter, slumping down in his chair and gazing resignedly into the crackling fire. Shea continued to ponder the details of Allanon's story, trying to decide what he should do now. But after an hour of quiet deliberation, he threw up his hands in disgust, feeling as confused as before. Stalking out of the lounge, he headed for his own room, the faithful Flick close behind. Neither felt inclined to discuss it further. Upon reaching their small bedroom in the east wing, Shea dropped into a chair in moody silence. Flick collapsed heavily on the bed and stared disinterestedly at the ceiling.

The twin candles on the small bedside table cast a dim glow over the large room, and Flick soon found himself on the verge of drifting off to sleep. He hastily jerked awake and, stretching his hands above his head, encountered a long piece of folded paper which had partially slipped down between the mattress and headboard. Curiously, he brought it around in front of his eyes and saw that it was addressed to Shea.

'What's this?' he muttered and tossed it across to his prostrate brother.

Shea ripped open the sealed paper and hurriedly scanned it. He had scarcely begun before he let out a low whistle and leaped to his feet. Flick sat up quickly, realizing who must have left the note.

'It's from Allanon,' Shea confirmed his brother's suspicion. 'Listen to this, Flick:

I have no time to find you and explain matters further. Something of the greatest importance has occurred, and I must leave immediately – perhaps even now I am too late. You must trust me and believe what I told you, even though I will not be able to return to the valley.

You will not long be safe in Shady Vale, and you must be prepared to flee quickly. Should your safety be threatened, you will find shelter at Culhaven in the forests of the Anar. I will send a friend to guide you. Place your trust in Balinor.

Speak with no one of our meeting. The danger to you is extreme. In the pocket of your maroon travel cloak, I have placed a small pouch which contains three Elfstones. They will provide you with guidance and protection when nothing else can. Be cautioned – they are for Shea alone and to be used only when all else fails.

The sign of the Skull will be your warning to flee. May luck be with you, my young friend, until we meet again.

Shea looked excitedly at his brother, but the suspicious Flick shook his head in disbelief and frowned deeply.

'I don't trust him. Whatever is he talking about anyway – Skulls and Elfstones? I never even heard of a place called Culhaven, and the Anar forests are miles from here – days and days. I don't like it.'

'The stones!' Shea exclaimed, and leaped for the traveling cloak which hung in the long corner closet. He rummaged through his clothes for several minutes while Flick watched anxiously, then carefully stepped back with a small leather pouch balanced gently in his right hand. He held it up and tested its weight, displaying it to his brother, and then hurried back to the bed and sat down. A moment later he had the drawstrings open and was emptying the contents of the pouch into his open palm. Three dark blue stones tumbled out, each the size of an average pebble, finely cut and glowing brightly in the faint candlelight. The brothers peered curiously at the stones, half expecting that they would immediately do something wondrous. But nothing happened. They lay motionless in Shea's palm, shimmering like small blue stars snatched from the night, so clear that it was almost possible to see through them, as if they were merely tinted glass. Finally, after Flick had summoned enough courage to touch one, Shea dropped them back into the pouch and stuffed it into his shirt pocket.

'Well, he was right about the stones,' ventured Shea a moment later.

'Maybe yes, maybe no – maybe they're not Elfstones,' suggested Flick suspiciously. 'How do you know – ever see one? What about the rest of the letter? I never heard of anyone named Balinor and I never heard of Culhaven. We ought to forget the whole business – especially that we ever saw Allanon.'

Shea nodded doubtfully, unable to answer his brother's questions.

'Why should we worry now? All we have to do is to keep our eyes open for the sign of the Skull, whatever that may be, or for Allanon's friend to appear. Maybe nothing will happen after all.'

Flick continued to voice his distrust of the letter and its author for several minutes more before losing interest. Both brothers were weary and decided to call it a night. As the candles were extinguished, Shea's last act was to place the pouch carefully beneath his pillow where he could feel its small bulk pressing against the side of his face. No matter what Flick might think, he had resolved to keep the stones close at hand in the days ahead.

The next day, it began to rain. Huge, towering black clouds rolled in from the north quite suddenly and settled over the entire valley, blotting out all traces of sun and sky as they released torrents of shattering rain which swept through the tiny hamlet with unbelievable ferocity. All work in the fields came to an abrupt halt and travel to and from the valley ceased entirely – first for one, then two, and finally three complete days. The downpour was a tremendous spectacle of blinding streaks of lightning lacing the darkly clouded sky and deeply rolling thunder breaking over the valley with earthshaking blasts that followed one after the other and died into slower, more ominous distant rumblings from somewhere beyond the blackness to the north. For the entire three days it rained, and the Vale people began to grow fearful that flash floods from the hills all about them would wash down with devastating effect on their small homes and unprotected fields. The men gathered daily in the Ohmsford inn and chatted worriedly over their mugs of beer, casting apprehensive glances at the sheets of rain falling steadily beyond the dripping windows. The Ohmsford brothers watched in silence, listening to the conversation and scanning the worried faces of the anxious Valemen huddled together in small groups about the crowded lounge. At first they held out hope that the storm would pass over, but after three days there was still little sign of clearing in the weather.

Near midday on the fourth day, the rain lessened from a steady downpour to a muggy drizzle mixed with heavy fog and a sticky, humid heat that left everyone thoroughly disgruntled and uncomfortable. The crowd at the inn began to thin out as the men left to return to their jobs, and soon Shea and Flick were occupied with repairs and general cleaning chores. The storm had smashed shutters and torn the wooden shingles from the roof, scattering them all about the surrounding premises. Large leaks had developed in the roof and walls of the inn wings, and the small tool shed in the rear of the Ohmsford property had been all but flattened by a falling elm, uprooted by the force of the storm. The young men spent several days patching up leaks, repairing the roof, and replacing lost or broken shingles and shutters. It was tedious work, and time dragged by slowly.

After ten days, the rains ceased altogether, the huge clouds rolled on, and the dark sky cleared and brightened into a friendly light blue streaked with trailing white clouds. The expected floods did not come, and as the Valemen returned to their fields, the warm sun reappeared and the land of the valley began to dry from soggy mud to solid earth, spattered here and there by small puddles of murky water that sat defiantly upon an always thirsty land. Eventually even the puddles disappeared and the valley was as it had been – the fury of the passing storm only a dim memory.

Shea and Flick, in the process of rebuilding the smashed tool shed, their other repair work on the inn complete, heard snatches of conversation from Valemen and inn guests about the heavy rain. No one could ever remember a storm of such ferocity at that particular time of the year in the Vale. It was equivalent to a winter windstorm, the kind that caught unsuspecting travelers in the great mountains to the north and swept them from the passes and the cliff trails, never to be seen again. Its sudden appearance caused everyone in the hamlet to pause and reflect once again on the continuing rumors of strange happenings far to the North.

The brothers paid close attention to such talks, but they learned nothing of interest. Often they spoke quietly together about Allanon and the strange tale he had told them of Shea's heritage. A pragmatic Flick had long since dismissed the whole business as either foolishness or a bad joke. Shea listened tolerantly, though he was less willing than his brother to shrug the matter off. Yet while he was unwilling to dismiss the tale, he was at the same time unable to accept it. He felt there was too much still hidden from him, too much about Allanon that neither Flick nor he knew. Until he had all the facts, he was content to let the matter lie. He kept the pouch containing the Elfstones close to him at all times. While Flick mumbled on, usually several times a day, about his foolishness in carrying the stones and believing that anything Allanon had told them was true, Shea carefully watched all strangers passing through the Vale, eagerly perusing their belongings for any sign of a Skull marking. But as time passed, he observed nothing and eventually felt obliged to scratch the whole matter off as an experience in the fine art of gullibility.

Nothing occurred to change Shea's mind on the matter until one afternoon more than three weeks after Allanon's abrupt departure. The brothers had been out all day cutting shingles for the inn roof, and it was almost evening by the time they returned. Their father was sitting in his favorite seat at the long kitchen counter when they entered, his broad face bent over a steaming plate of food. He greeted his sons with a wave of his hand.

'A letter came for you while you were gone, Shea,' he informed them, holding out a long, white folded sheet of paper. 'It's marked Leah.'

Shea let out an exclamation of surprise and reached eagerly for the letter. Flick groaned audibly.

'I knew it, I knew it; it was too good to be true,' he muttered. 'The biggest wastrel in the entire Southland has decided it's time we suffered some more. Tear up the letter, Shea.'

But Shea had already opened the sealed sheet of paper and was scanning its contents, totally disregarding Flick's comments. The latter shrugged in disgust and collapsed on a stool next to his father, who had returned to his evening meal.

'He wants to know where we've been hiding,' laughed Shea. 'He wants us to come see him as soon as we can.'

'Oh, sure,' muttered Flick. 'He's probably in trouble and needs someone to blame it on. Why don't we just jump off the nearest cliff? You remember what happened the last time Menion Leah invited us to visit? We were lost in the Black Oaks for days and nearly devoured by wolves! I'll never forget that little adventure. The Shades will get me before I accept another invitation from him!'

His brother laughed and clapped an arm around Flick's broad shoulders.

'You are envious because Menion is the son of kings and able to live any way he chooses.'

'A kingdom the size of a puddle,' was the quick retort. 'And royal blood is cheap stuff these days. Look at your own . . .'

He caught himself and clamped his mouth shut quickly. Both shot hurried glances at their father, but he apparently hadn't heard and was still absorbed in eating. Flick shrugged apologetically, and Shea smiled at his brother encouragingly.

'There's a man in the inn looking for you, Shea,' Curzad

48

Ohmsford announced suddenly, looking up at him. 'He mentioned that tall stranger that was here several weeks back when he asked for you. Never seen him before in the Vale. He's out in the main lounge now.'

Flick stood up slowly, fear gripping at him. Shea was momentarily caught off balance by the message, but motioned hurriedly to his brother, who was about to speak. If this new stranger were an enemy, he had to find out quickly. He clutched at his shirt pocket, reassuring himself that the Elfstones were still there.

'What does the man look like?' he asked quickly, unable to think of any other way of finding out about the Skull mark.

'Can't really say, son,' was the muffled reply as his father continued to chew on his dinner, face bent to the plate. 'He's wrapped in a long green forest cloak. Just rode in this afternoon – beautiful horse. He was very anxious to find you. Better go see what he wants right away.'

'Did you see any markings?' asked the exasperated Flick.

His father stopped chewing and looked up with a puzzled frown.

'What are you talking about? Would you be satisfied if I presented you with a chalk drawing? What's wrong with you anyway?'

'It's nothing, really,' interjected Shea quickly. 'Flick was just wondering if . . . if the man looked anything like Allanon . . . You remember?'

'Oh, yes,' his father smiled knowingly, as Flick suppressed a swallow of relief. 'No, I didn't notice any real similarity, though this man is big, too. I did see a long scar running down the right cheek – probably from a knife cut.'

Shea nodded his thanks and quickly pulled Flick after him as he moved out to the hallway and started for the main lounge. They hurried to the wide double doors and halted breathlessly. Cautiously, Shea pushed one door open a crack and peered into the crowded lounge area.

For a moment he saw nothing but the ordinary faces of the usual customers and average Vale travelers, but a moment later he started back, and let the door swing shut as he faced the anxious Flick.

'He's out there, near the front corner by the fireplace. I can't tell who he is or what he looks like from here; he's wrapped in the green cloak, just as Father said. We've got to get closer.'

'Out there?' gasped Flick. 'Have you lost your mind? He would spot you in a second if he knows who he's looking for.'

'Then you go,' Shea ordered firmly. 'Make some pretense of putting logs on the fire and get a quick look at him. See if he bears the markings of a Skull.'

Flick's eyes went wide, and he turned to escape, but Shea caught his arm and pulled him back, forcibly shoving him through the doors into the lounge and quickly ducking back out of sight. A moment later he opened one door a crack and peeped out to see what was happening. He saw Flick move uncertainly across the room to the fireplace and begin to poke the glowing embers idly, finally adding another log from the woodbox. The Valeman was taking his time, apparently trying to get in a position where he could catch a glimpse of the man wrapped in the green cloak. The stranger was seated at a table several feet away from the fireplace, his back to Flick but turned slightly toward the door behind which Shea had concealed himself.

Suddenly, just as it appeared that Flick was ready to return, the stranger moved slightly in his seat and made a quick comment and Flick went stiff. Shea saw his brother turn toward the stranger and reply, glancing hurriedly toward Shea's place of concealment. Shea slipped back further into the shadows of the hall and let the door swing shut. Somehow, they had given themselves away. As he pondered whether to flee, Flick abruptly pushed through the double doors, his face white with fear.

'He saw you at the door. The man has the eyes of a hawk! He told me to bring you out.'

Shea thought a moment and finally nodded hopelessly. After all, where could they run to that they wouldn't be found in a matter of minutes?

'Maybe he doesn't know everything,' he suggested hopefully. 'Maybe he thinks we know where Allanon has gone. Be careful what you tell him, Flick.'

He led the way through the wide, swinging doors and across the lounge to the table where the stranger sat. They stopped just behind him and waited, but without turning, he beckoned them to seats around the table with a sweep of his hand. They reluctantly obeyed the unspoken command and the three sat in silence for a few moments looking at one another. The stranger was a big man with a broad frame, though he did not have Allanon's height. The cloak covered all of his body, and only his head was visible to them. His features were rugged and strong, pleasant to the eye except for the dark scar that ran from the outside tip of the right eyebrow down across the cheek just above the mouth. The eyes seemed curiously mild to Shea as they studied the young Valemen, a hazel color that hinted at a gentleness beneath the hard exterior. The blond hair was cut short and lay scattered loosely about the broad forehead and around the small ears. As Shea viewed the stranger, he found it hard to believe that this man could be the enemy Allanon had warned might come to the valley. Even Flick seemed relaxed in his presence.

'There is no time for games, Shea,' the newcomer spoke suddenly in a mild, but weary voice. 'Your caution is well advised, but I am not a bearer of the Skull mark. I am a friend of Allanon. My name is Balinor. My father is Ruhl Buckhannah, the King of Callahorn.'

The brothers recognized his name instantly, but Shea was not taking any chances.

'How do I know that you are who you say you are?' he demanded quickly.

The stranger smiled.

'The same way I know you, Shea. By the three Elfstones you carry in your shirt pocket – the Elfstones given you by Allanon.'

The Valeman's startled nod was barely perceptible. Only someone sent by the tall historian could have known about the stones. He leaned forward cautiously.

'What has happened to Allanon?'

'I cannot be sure,' the big man replied softly. 'I have not seen nor heard from him in over two weeks. When I left him, he was traveling to Paranor. There was rumor of an attack against the Keep; he was afraid for the safety of the Sword. He sent me here to protect you. I would have reached you sooner, but I was delayed by the weather – and by those who sought to follow me to you.'

He paused and looked directly at Shea, his hazel eyes suddenly hard as they bored into the young man.

'Allanon revealed to you your true identity and told you of the danger you would someday face. Whether you believed him or not is of no consequence now. The time has come – you must flee the valley immediately.'

'Just pick up and leave?' exclaimed the astounded Shea. 'I can't do that!'

'You can and you will if you wish to stay alive. The bearers of the Skull suspect you are in the valley. In a day, perhaps two, they will find you and that will be the end if you are still here. You must leave now. Travel quickly and lightly; stick with trails you know and the shelter of the forest when you can. If you are forced to travel in the open, travel only by day when their power is weaker. Allanon has told you where you are to go, but you must trust to your own resourcefulness to get you there.'

The astonished Shea stared at the speaker for a moment and then turned to Flick who was speechless at this new turn of events. How could the man expect him just to pack up and run? It was ridiculous.

'I have to leave,' the stranger rose suddenly, his great cloak wrapped tightly about his broad frame. 'I would take you with me if I could, but I have been followed. Those who seek to destroy you will expect me to give you away eventually. I will serve you better as a decoy; perhaps they will follow me still farther, and I will be able to give you a chance to slip away without being noticed. I will ride south for a while, and then swing back toward Culhaven. We will meet again there. Remember what I said. Do not linger in the Vale – flee now, tonight! Do as Allanon has said and guard the Elfstones with care. They are a powerful weapon.'

Shea and Flick rose with him and shook the extended hand, noticing for the first time that the exposed arm was covered with gleaming chain mail. Without further comment, Balinor moved swiftly across the room and disappeared through the front door into the night.

'Well, now what?' Flick asked as he collapsed back into his seat.

'How should I know?' replied Shea wearily. 'I'm no fortune-teller. I don't have the vaguest idea if what he told us was the truth any more than what Allanon said! If he is right, and I have an uneasy suspicion that there is at least some truth in what he says, then for the sake of everyone concerned, I've got to get out of the valley. If someone is after me, we cannot be sure that others, like yourself and Father, won't be hurt if I stay.'

He gazed despondently across the room, hopelessly entangled by the tales he had been told, unable to decide what his best move would be. Flick watched him silently, knowing he could not help, but sharing his brother's confusion and worry. Finally, he leaned across and put his hand on Shea's shoulder.

'I'm going with you,' he announced softly.

Shea looked around at him, plainly startled.

'I can't have you doing that. Father would never understand. Besides, I may not be going anywhere.'

'Remember what Allanon said – I'm in this with you,' Flick insisted stubbornly. 'Besides, you're my brother. I can't let you go alone.'

Shea stared at him wonderingly, then nodded and smiled his thanks.

'We'll talk about it later. At any rate, I can't leave until I decide where I am going and what I will need – if I even go. I've got to leave some kind of note for Father – I can't just walk out, despite what Allanon and Balinor think.'

They left the table and retired to the kitchen for dinner. The remainder of the evening was spent restlessly wandering about the lounge and kitchen area, with several side trips to the sleeping quarters, where Shea rifled through his personal belongings, absently noting what he owned and setting aside stray items. Flick followed him about silently, unwilling to leave him alone, inwardly afraid that his brother might decide to depart for Culhaven without telling him. He watched Shea push clothing and camping equipment into a leather pack, and when he asked his brother why he was packing, he was told that this was just a precaution in case he did have to flee suddenly. Shea assured him that he would not leave without telling him, but the reassurance did not make Flick any easier in his mind, and he watched Shea all the more closely.

It was pitch black when Shea was awakened by the hand on his arm. He had been sleeping lightly, and the cold touch woke him instantly, his heart pounding. He struggled wildly, unable to see anything in the darkness, and his free hand reached out to clutch his unseen attacker. A quick hiss reached his ears, and abruptly he recognized Flick's broad features vaguely outlined in the dim light of the cloud-masked stars and a small crescent moon that shone through the curtained window. The fear eased, replaced by sudden relief at the familiar sight of his brother.

'Flick! You scared . . .'

His relief was cut short as Flick's strong hand clamped over his open mouth and the warning hush sounded again. In the gloom, Shea could see deep lines of fear in his brother's face, the pale skin drawn tightly with the cold of the night air. He started up, but the strong arms holding him grasped him tighter and drew his face near tightly clenched lips.

'Don't speak,' the whisper sounded in his ears, the voice trembling with terror. 'The window – quietly!'

The hands loosened their grip and gently, hastily pulled him from the bed and down along the floor until both brothers were crouched breathlessly on the hard wooden planks deep within the shadows of the room. Then Shea crawled with Flick toward the partly open window, still crouching, not daring even to breathe. When they reached the wall, Flick pulled Shea to one side of the window with hands that were now shaking.

'Shea, by the building – look!'

Frightened beyond description, he raised his head to the windowsill and carefully peered over the wooden frame into the blackness beyond. He saw the creature almost immediately – a huge, terrible black shape, stooped in a half-crouch as it crawled, dragging itself slowly through the shadows of the buildings across from the inn, its humped back covered by a cloak that rose and billowed softly as something beneath pushed and beat against it. The hideous rasping sound of its breathing was plainly audible even from that distance, and its feet emitted a curious scraping sound as it moved across the dark earth. Shea clutched the sill tightly, his eyes locked on the approaching creature, and in the instant before he ducked below the open window, he caught a clear glimpse of a silver pendant fashioned in the shape of a gleaming Skull.

CHAPTER

4

Shea collapsed wordlessly next to the dark form of his brother, and they sat huddled together in the blackness. They could hear the creature moving, the scraping sound growing louder as the seconds passed, and they were certain they had heeded Balinor's warning too late. They waited, not daring to speak, even to breathe as they listened. Shea wanted to run, torn by the knowledge that the thing outside would kill him if it found him now, but afraid that if he moved he would be heard and caught on the spot. Flick sat rigid beside him, shaking in the cool of the blowing night wind that whipped the curtains about the window frame.

Suddenly they heard the sharp bark of a dog sound again and again, then shift to a hoarse growl of mingled fear and hatred. Cautiously, the brothers raised their heads above the windowsill and looked out, squinting in the dim light. The creature bearing the Skull mark was crouched against the wall of the building directly across from their window. Some ten feet away was a huge wolf dog, a hunter for one of the Valemen, its white fangs bared and gleaming as it watched the intruder. The two shapes faced each other in the night shadows, the creature breathing in the same slow, rasping wheeze, and the dog growling low and snapping the air before it, inching forward in a half crouch. Then, with a snarl of rage, the big wolf dog sprang at the intruder, its jaws open and reaching for the blackened head. But the dog was caught suddenly in midair by a clawlike limb that whipped out from beneath the billowing cloak and jerked at the throat of the hapless animal, smashing him lifeless to the ground. It happened in an instant, and the brothers were so astonished that they almost forgot to duck down again to avoid being seen. A moment later, they heard the strange scraping sound as the creature began to drag itself along the wall of the adjacent building – but the sound grew fainter and appeared to be moving away from the inn.

Long moments passed as the brothers waited breathlessly in the shadows of the room, shivering uncontrollably. The night grew quiet around them, and they strained their ears for some indication of the creature's position. Eventually Shea worked up enough courage to peer once more over the edge of the windowsill into the darkness beyond. By the time he ducked down again, the frightened Flick was ready to scramble for the nearest exit, but a hurried shake of Shea's head assured him that the creature was gone. He hastened back from the window to the warmth of his bed, but caught himself halfway under the covers as he saw Shea begin to dress hurriedly in the darkness. He tried to speak, but Shea raised a finger to his lips. Immediately, Flick began pulling on his own clothes. Whatever Shea had in mind, wherever he was going, Flick was determined to follow. When they were both dressed, Shea pulled his brother close and whispered softly in his ear.

'Everyone in the Vale will be in danger as long as we remain. We must get out tonight – now! Are you determined to go with me?'

Flick nodded emphatically and Shea continued.

'We'll go to the kitchen and pack some food to take with us – just enough to get by on for a few days. I'll leave a note for Father there.'

Without another word, Shea picked up his small bundle of clothing from inside the closet and disappeared noiselessly into the pitch-black hallway that led to the kitchen. Flick hurriedly followed, groping his way from the bedroom behind his brother. It was impossible to see anything in the hallway, and it took them several minutes to feel their way along the walls and around the corners to the broad kitchen door. Once inside the kitchen, Shea lit a candle and motioned Flick over to the foodstuffs while he scratched out a note for his father on a small sheet of paper and stuck it under a beer mug. Flick finished his job in a few minutes and came back to his brother, who quickly extinguished the small candle and moved to the rear door where he stopped and turned.

'Once we're outside, don't speak at all. Just follow me closely.'

Flick nodded doubtfully, more than a little concerned about what might be waiting for them beyond the closed door – waiting to rip out their throats as it had the wolf dog's a few minutes before. But there was no time for hesitation now, and Shea swung open the wooden door carefully and peered out into a brightly moonlit yard bordered by heavy clumps of trees. A moment later, he motioned to Flick, and they stepped cautiously from the building into the cool night air, closing the door carefully behind them. It was brighter outside the building in the soft light of the moon and stars, and a quick glance revealed that no one was around. There was only an hour or two until dawn, when the hamlet would begin to awaken. The brothers paused next to the building as they listened for any sound that would warn of danger. Hearing nothing, Shea led the way across the yard, and they disappeared into the shadows of an adjacent hedgerow, Flick casting a last, wistful glance back at the home he might never see again.

Shea silently picked his way through the buildings of the

hamlet. The Valeman knew that the Skull Bearer was uncertain who he was or it would have caught them at the inn. But it was a good bet that the creature suspected he lived within the valley and so had come into the sleeping town of Shady Vale on an exploratory search for the missing half son of the house of Shannara. Shea ran back over the plan of travel he had hastily formed at the inn. If the enemy had discovered where he was, as Balinor had warned, then all the possible escape routes would be watched. Moreover, once they discovered he was missing, they would lose no time in tracking him down. He had to assume that there was more than one of these frightening creatures, and that they were probably watching the whole valley. Flick and he would have to seize the advantage of stealth and secrecy to get out of the valley and the country immediately surrounding it within the next day or so. That meant a forced march with very few hours' sleep. This would be tough enough, but the real problem was where they would flee. They had to have supplies within a few days, and a trip to the Anar would take weeks. The country beyond the Vale was unfamiliar to both brothers, except for a few well-traveled roads and hamlets that the Skull Bearers would certainly be watching. Given their present situation, it would be impossible to do much more than choose a general direction. But which way should they run? Which direction would the prowling creatures least expect them to go?

Shea considered the alternatives carefully, though he had already made up his mind. West of the Vale was open country except for a few villages, and if they went that way, they would be moving away from the Anar. If they traveled south, they would eventually reach the comparative safety of the larger Southland cities of Pia and Zolomach where there were friends and relatives. But this was the logical route for them to take to escape the Skull Bearers, and the creatures would be carefully watching roads south of the Vale. Moreover, the country beyond the Duln forests was broad and open, offering little cover for the fugitives and promising a long journey to the cities, during which they could be easily caught and killed. North of the Vale and beyond the Duln was a broad sweep of land encompassing the Rappahalladran River and the huge Rainbow Lake and miles of wild, unsettled land that led eventually to the kingdom of Callahorn. The Skull Bearers would have passed through it on their journey from the Northland. They would in all likelihood know it far better than the brothers and would be watching it closely if they suspected that Balinor had come to the Vale from Tyrsis.

The Anar lay northeast of the Vale, through miles and miles of the roughest, most treacherous country in all of the vast Southland. This direct route was the most dangerous one, but the one in which the enemy searchers would least expect him to run. It wound through murky forests, treacherous lowlands, hidden swamps and any number of unknown dangers that claimed the lives of unwary travelers every year. But there was something else that lay east of the Duln forests that even the Skull Bearers could not know about – the safety of the highlands of Leah. There the brothers could seek the aid of Menion Leah, Shea's close friend and, despite Flick's fears, the one person who might be able to show them a way through the dangerous lands that led to the Anar. For Shea, this seemed the only reasonable alternative.

The brothers reached the southeast edge of town and halted breathlessly beside an old woodshed, their backs to the coarse boarding. Shea looked cautiously ahead. He had no idea where the prowling Skull creature might be by this time. Everything was still hazy in the clouded moonglow of the dying night. Somewhere off to their left, several dogs barked furiously, and scattered lights appeared in the windows of nearby houses as sleepy owners peered out curiously into the blackness. Dawn was only a little over an hour away, and Shea knew they would have to chance discovery and run for the lip of the valley and the concealment of the Duln forests. If they were still in the valley when it became light, the creature searching for them would see them climbing the slopes of the open hills, and they would be caught trying to escape.

Shea clapped Flick on the back and nodded, breaking into a slow jog as he moved away from the shelter of the Vale homes into the heavy clumps of trees and brush that dotted the valley floor. The night was silent around them except for the muffled sound of their feet padding on the long grass that was wet with early-morning dew. Leafy branches whipped at them as they ran, slapping their unprotected hands and faces in small, stinging swipes that left the dew clinging to their skin. They ran hurriedly for the gentle, brush-covered eastern slope of the Vale, dodging in and out of the heavy oaks and hickories, bounding over loose nut shells and fallen twigs that were scattered beneath the wide limbs ribbing the deep sky overhead. They reached the slope and scampered up the open grassland as quickly as their legs would carry them, not pausing to look back or even down in the darkness, but only ahead to the ground that rushed by them in sudden bounds and disappeared into the Vale behind. Slipping frequently on the damp grass, they reached the lip of the Vale, where their eyes were greeted with a clear view of the great valley walls to the east, studded with shapeless boulders and sparse shrubbery, looming like a great barrier to the world beyond.

Shea was in excellent physical condition, and his light form flew across the uneven ground, moving agilely among the clumps of brush and small boulders that blocked his path. Flick followed doggedly, the stout muscles of his legs working tirelessly to keep his heavier frame even with the fleet figure ahead. Only once did he risk a quick glance back, and his eyes recorded only a blurred image of mingled treetops that rose above the now hidden town and were outlined in the glow of the fading night stars and clouded moon. He watched Shea run ahead of him, bounding lightly over small rises and scattered rocks, apparently intent on reaching the small wooded area near the base of the eastern slope of the valley about a mile ahead. Flick's legs were beginning to tire, but his fear of the creature somewhere behind them kept him from lagging. He wondered what would happen to them now, fugitives from the only home they had known, pursued by an incredibly vicious enemy that would snuff out their lives like a small candle's flame if they were caught. Where could they go that they wouldn't be found? For the first time since Allanon had departed, Flick wished fervently that the mysterious wanderer would reappear.

The minutes passed quickly and the small woods ahead grew closer as the brothers ran on wearily, silently through the chill night. No sound reached their ears; nothing moved in the land ahead. It was as if they were the only living creatures in a vast arena, alone except for the watchful stars winking solemnly overhead in quiet contentment. The sky was growing lighter as the night came to a wistful close, and the vast audience above slowly disappeared one by one into the morning light. The brothers ran on, oblivious to everything but the need to run faster – to escape being caught in the revealing light of a sunrise only minutes away.

When the runners finally reached the wooded area, they collapsed breathlessly on the twig-covered ground beneath a stand of tall hickories, their ears and hearts pounding wildly from the strain of running. They lay motionless for several minutes, breathing heavily in the stillness. Then Shea dragged himself to his feet and looked back in the direction of the Vale. Nothing was moving either on the ground or in the air, and it appeared the brothers had gotten this far without being spotted. But they were still not out of the valley. Shea reached over and forcibly dragged

Flick to his feet, pulling him along as he moved through the trees and began to ascend the steep valley slope. Flick followed wordlessly, no longer even thinking, but concentrating his ebbing willpower on putting one foot before the other.

The eastern slope was rugged and treacherous, its surface a mass of boulders, fallen trees, prickly shrubbery, and uneven ground that made the climb a long and difficult one. Shea set the pace, moving over the large obstacles as fast as he could, while Flick followed in his footsteps. The young men scrambled and clawed their way up the slope. The sky began to grow lighter and the stars disappeared altogether. Ahead of them, above the lip of the valley, the sun was sending its first faint glow into the night sky with tinges of orange and yellow that reflected vaguely the outline of the distant horizon. Shea was beginning to tire, his breath coming in short gulps, as he stumbled on. Behind him, Flick forced himself to crawl, dragging his exhausted body after his lighter brother, his hands and forearms scratched and cut by the sharp brush and rocks. The climb seemed endless. They moved at a snail's pace over the rugged terrain, the fear of discovery alone forcing their tired legs to continue moving. If they were caught here, in the open, after all this effort . . .

Suddenly, as they reached the three-quarter mark of their climb, Flick cried out sharply in warning and fell gasping against the slope. Shea whirled around fearfully, his eyes instantly catching sight of the huge black object that rose slowly from the distant Vale – climbing like a great bird into the dimness of the morning sunrise in widening spirals. The Valeman dropped flat amid the rocks and brush, motioning his fallen brother to crawl quickly from sight and praying the creature had not seen them. They lay unmoving on the mountainside as the awesome Bearer of the Skull rose higher, its circle of flight growing wider, its path carrying it closer to where the brothers lay. A sudden chilling cry burst from the creature, draining from the two young men the last faint hope that they might escape. They were gripped by the same unexplainable feeling of horror that had immobilized Flick, hidden in the brush with Allanon beneath the huge black shadow. Only this time there was no place to hide. Their terror grew rapidly into the beginning stages of hysteria as the creature soared directly toward them, and in that fleeting moment they knew they were going to die. But in the next instant, the black hunter wheeled in flight and glided north in an unaltering line, receding steadily into the horizon until it was lost from their sight.

The Valemen lay petrified, buried in the scant brush and loose rock for endless minutes, afraid the creature would come winging back to destroy them the minute they tried to move. But when the terrible, unreasoning fear had ebbed away, they climbed shakenly to their feet and in exhausted silence resumed the weary climb to the summit of the valley. It was a short distance to the lip of the rugged slope, and they hurried across the small, open field beyond to the concealment of the Duln forest. Within minutes they were lost in the great trees, and the rising morning sun in its first glow found the land that stretched back to the Vale country silent and empty.

The young men slowed their pace as they entered the Duln, and finally Flick, who still had no idea where they were going, called ahead to Shea.

'Why are we going this way?' he demanded. His own voice sounded strange after the long silence. 'Where are we going anyway?'

'Where Allanon told us – to the Anar. Our best chance is to go the way the Skull Bearers least expect us to take. So we'll go east to the Black Oaks and from there travel northward and hope we can find help along the way.'

'Wait a minute!' exclaimed Flick in sudden understanding. 'What you mean is we're going east through Leah

64

and hope Menion can help us. Are you completely out of your mind? Why don't we just give ourselves up to that creature? It would be quicker that way!'

Shea threw up his hands and turned wearily to face his brother.

'We do not have any other choice! Menion Leah is the only one we can turn to for help. He's familiar with the country beyond Leah. He may know a way through the Black Oaks.'

'Oh, sure,' nodded Flick gloomily. 'Are you forgetting that he got us lost there last time? I wouldn't trust him any farther than I could throw him, and I doubt I can even lift him!'

'We have no choice,' repeated Shea. 'You didn't have to come on this trip, you know.'

He trailed off suddenly and turned away.

'Sorry I lost my temper. But we have to do this thing my way, Flick.'

He started walking again in dejected silence, and Flick followed glumly, shaking his head in disapproval. The whole idea of running away was a bad one to begin with, even though they knew that monstrous creature was prowling the valley. But the idea of going to Menion Leah was worse still. That cocky idler would lead them right into a trap if he didn't get them lost first. Menion was only interested in Menion, the great adventurer, off on another wild expedition. The whole idea of asking him for help was ridiculous.

Flick was admittedly biased. He disapproved of Menion Leah and everything he represented – he had done so from the time they met five years earlier. The only son of a family that for centuries had governed the little highland kingdom, Menion had spent his entire life involving himself in one wild escapade after another. He had never worked for a living and, as far as Flick could tell, he had never done anything worthwhile. He spent most of his time hunting or fighting, pursuits that hardworking Valemen would consider idle recreation. His attitude was equally disturbing. Nothing about his life, his family, his homeland, or his country seemed to be of very great importance to him. The highlander seemed to float through life very much the same as a cloud in an empty sky, touching nothing, leaving no trace of his passing. It was this careless approach to life that had nearly got them killed a year ago in the Black Oaks. Yet Shea was drawn to him; and in his flippant way, the highlander seemed to respond with genuine affection. But Flick had never been convinced that it was a friendship he could depend upon, and now his brother proposed to entrust their lives to the care of a man who did not know the first thing about responsibility.

He mulled the situation over in his mind, wondering what could be done to prevent the inevitable. Finally he concluded that his best chance would be to watch Menion carefully and warn Shea as tactfully as possible when he suspected they were doing the wrong thing. If he alienated his brother now, he would have no chance later of contradicting the bad advice of the Prince of Leah.

It was late afternoon when the travelers finally reached the banks of the great Rappahalladran. Shea led the way down the riverbank for about a mile until they reached a place where the far bank cut toward them and the channel began to narrow considerably. Here they stopped and gazed across at the forests beyond. The sun would be down in another hour or so, and Shea did not want to be caught on the near bank that night. He would feel safer with the water between him and any pursuers. He explained to Flick, who agreed, and they set about making a small raft, using their hand axes and hunting knives. The raft was necessarily a small one, its only purpose to carry their packs and clothing. There was no time to construct a raft large enough to carry them, and they would have to swim the river, towing their belongings. They completed the job in short order and, stripping off their packs and clothes, tied them down in the middle of the raft and slipped into the chilling waters of the Rappahalladran. The current was swift, but not dangerous at this time of the year, the spring thaws having already passed. The only problem was finding a suitable landing place along the high banks of the other shore after their swim was over. As it happened, the current swept them along for almost half a mile as they struggled to tow the cumbersome raft, and when the crossing had finally been completed, they found they were close to a narrow inlet in the far bank that offered an easy landing. They scrambled out of the cold water, shivering in the early evening air, and after dragging the raft out after them, quickly dried off and dressed again. The entire operation had taken a little over an hour, and the sun was now lost from sight beneath the tall trees, leaving only a dull reddish glow to light the afternoon sky in the minutes that remained before darkness.

The brothers were not ready to quit for the day, but Shea suggested they sleep for several hours to regain their strength and then resume their journey during the night to avoid any chance of being seen. The sheltered inlet seemed safe, so they curled up in their blankets beneath a great elm and were quickly asleep. It was not until midnight that Shea woke Flick with a light shake, and they quickly packed their gear and prepared to resume their hike through the Duln. At one point, Shea thought he heard something prowling about on the far shore and hurriedly warned Flick. They listened in silence for long minutes, but could detect nothing moving in the blackness of the massive trees and finally concluded that Shea must have been mistaken. Flick was quick to point out that nothing could be heard anyway above the sound of the surging river, and the Skull creature was probably still looking for them in the Vale. His confidence had been bolstered considerably by the mistaken belief that they had momentarily outsmarted any pursuers.

They walked until sunrise, trying to move in an easterly direction, but unable to see much from their low vantage point. Any clear view of the stars was masked by a confusing network of heavy branches and rustling leaves interlocked above them. When they finally stopped, they were still not clear of the Duln, and had no idea how much farther they had to walk before reaching the borders of Leah. Shea was relieved at the appearance of the sun rising directly before them; they were still heading in the right direction. Finding a clearing nestled in a cluster of great elms sheltered on three sides by thick brush, the young men tossed down their packs and quickly fell asleep, totally exhausted from the strenuous flight. It was late afternoon before they awoke and began preparations for the night walk. Unwilling to start a fire that might attract attention, they contented themselves with munching on dried beef and raw vegetables, completing the meal with some fruit and a little water. As they ate, Flick again brought up the question of their destination.

'Shea,' he began cautiously, 'I don't want to dwell on the matter, but are you sure this is the best way to go? I mean, even if Menion wants to help, we could easily get lost in the swamps and hills that lie beyond the Black Oaks and never get out.'

Shea nodded slowly and then shrugged.

'It's that or go farther north where there is less cover and the country would be unfamiliar even to Menion. Do you think we have a better choice?'

'I suppose not,' Flick responded unhappily. 'But I keep thinking about what Allanon told us – you remember, about not telling anyone and being careful about trusting anyone. He was very definite about that.'

'Let's not start that again,' Shea flared up. 'Allanon isn't here and the decision is mine. I don't see how we can hope to reach the Anar forests without the help of Menion. Besides, he's always been a good friend, and he's one of the finest swordsmen I have ever seen. We'll need his experience if we're forced to stand and fight.'

'Which we are certain to have to do with him along,' Flick finished pointedly. 'Besides, what chance do we have against something like that Skull creature? Why, it would tear us to bits!'

'Don't be so gloomy,' Shea laughed, 'we aren't dead yet. Don't forget – we have the protection of the Elfstones.'

Flick was not particularly convinced by this argument, but felt that the whole matter was best left alone for the present. He had to admit that Menion Leah would be a good man to have around in a fight, but at the same time he was not sure whose side the unpredictable fellow would decide to take. Shea trusted Menion because of the instinctive liking he had developed for the flashy adventurer during trips to Leah with his father over the past few years. But Flick did not feel that his brother was entirely rational in his analysis of the Prince of Leah. Leah was one of the few remaining monarchies in the Southland, and Shea was an outspoken advocate of decentralized government, an opponent of absolute power. Nevertheless, he claimed friendship with the heir to a monarch's throne – facts which in Flick's opinion seemed entirely inconsistent. Either you believed in something or you didn't – you couldn't have it both ways and be honest with yourself.

The meal was finished in silence as the first shadows of evening began to appear. The sun had long since disappeared from view and its soft golden rays had changed slowly to a deep red mingling with the green boughs of the giant trees. The brothers quickly packed their few belongings and began the slow, steady march eastward, their backs to the fading daylight. The woods were unusually still, even for early evening, and the wary Valemen walked in uneasy silence through the shrouded gloom of the forest night, the moon a distant beacon that appeared only at brief intervals through the dark boughs overhead.

Flick was particularly disturbed by the unnatural silence of the Duln, a silence strange to this huge forest – but uncomfortably familiar to the stocky Valeman. Occasionally, they would pause in the darkness, listening to the deep stillness; then, hearing nothing, they would quickly resume the tiring march, searching for a break in the forest ahead that would open onto the highlands beyond. Flick hated the oppressive silence and once began whistling softly to himself, but was quickly stilled by a warning motion from Shea.

Sometime during the early hours of the morning, the brothers reached the edge of the Duln and broke through into the shrub-covered grasslands that stretched beyond for miles to the highlands of Leah. The morning sun was still several hours away, so the travelers continued their journey eastward. Both felt immensely relieved to be free of the Duln, away from the stifling closeness of its monstrous trees and from the unpleasant silence. They may have been safer within the concealing shadows of the forest, but they felt considerably better equipped to deal with any danger that threatened them on the open grasslands. They even began to speak again in low voices as they walked. About an hour before daybreak, they reached a small, brush-covered vale where they stopped to eat and rest. They were already able to see the dimly lighted highlands of Leah to the east, a journey of yet another day. Shea estimated that if they started walking again at sundown they could easily reach their destination before another sunrise. Then everything would depend on Menion Leah. With this unspoken thought in mind, he quickly fell asleep.

Only minutes passed and they were awake again. It was not something moving that caused them to rise in sudden apprehension, but a deathly quiet that settled ominously over the grasslands. Immediately they sensed the unmistakable presence of another being. The feeling struck them

70

at the same instant and both came to their feet with a start, without a word, their drawn daggers gleaming in the faint light as they looked cautiously about their small cover. Nothing moved. Shea motioned his brother to follow as he crawled up the shrub-covered slope of the little vale to where they could view the land beyond. They lay motionless in the brush, peering into the early-morning gloom, eyes straining to detect what lurked beyond. They did not question the fact that something was out there. There was no need – both had known the feeling before the window of their bedroom. Now they waited, scarcely daring to breathe, wondering if the creature had found them at last, praying they had been careful enough to conceal their movements. It seemed impossible that they could be found now after their hard struggle to escape, wrong that death should come when the safety of Leah was only a few hours away.

Then with a sudden rush of wind and leaves, the black shape of the Skull Bearer rose soundlessly from a long line of scrub trees far to their left. Its dim bulk seemed to rise and hang heavily above the earth for several long moments, as if unable to move, silhouetted against the faint light of an approaching dawn. The brothers lay flat against the edge of the rise, as silent as the brush about them, waiting for the creature to move. How it had tracked them this far – if indeed it had – they could only guess. Perhaps it was only blind luck that had brought them all together in this single, empty piece of grassland, but the fact remained that the Valemen were hunted creatures and their death had become a very real possibility. The creature hung motionless against the sky a moment longer, then slowly, sluggishly, the great wings reaching outward, it began to move toward their place of concealment. Flick gave an audible gasp of dismay and sank farther back into the surrounding brush, his face ashen in the gray light, his hand gripping Shea's slim arm. But before reaching them, while still several hundred feet away, the creature dropped into a small grove of trees and was momentarily lost from sight. The brothers peered desperately in the hazy light, unable to see their pursuer.

'Now,' Shea's determined voice whispered urgently in his brother's ear, 'while the creature can't see us. Make for that line of brush ahead!'

Flick did not need to be told twice. Once the black monster finished with the trees that now occupied its attention, the next stop would be their hiding place. The Valeman scampered fearfully from his place of conceal-ment, half running, half crawling along the wet morning grass, his touseled head jerking in quick glimpses over his shoulder, expecting the Skull Bearer to rise any moment from the grove and spy him. Behind him ran Shea, his lithe body bent close to the ground as he darted across the open grassland, zigzagging his way silently behind his brother's stocky figure. They reached the brush without mishap, and then Shea remembered they had forgotten their packs – the packs that now lay at the bottom of the vale they had just left. The creature could not miss seeing them and, when it did, the chase would be over and there would be no more guessing which way they had gone. Shea felt his stomach sink. How could they have been so stupid? He grabbed Flick's shoulder in desperation, but his brother had also realized their error and slumped heavily to the ground. Shea knew he had to go back for the telltale packs, even if he were seen – there was no other choice. But even as he rose hesitantly, the black shape of the hunter appeared, hanging motionless in the brightening sky. The chance was gone.

Once again they were saved by the coming of dawn. As the Skull Bearer poised silently above the grasslands, the golden rim of the morning sun broke from its resting place in the eastern hills and sent its first emissaries of the approaching day shooting forth to light the land and sky in their warm glow. The sunlight broke over the dark bulk of the night creature, and seeing that its time was gone, it rose abruptly into the sky, wheeling about the land in great, widening circles. It screamed its deathlike cry with chilling hatred, freezing for one quick moment all the gentle sounds of morning; then turning north, it flew swiftly from sight. A moment later it was gone, and two grateful, unbelieving Valemen were left staring mutely into the distant, empty morning sky.

CHAPTER

5

By late afternoon of that same day, the Valemen had reached the highland city of Leah. The stone and mortar walls that bounded the city were a welcome haven to the weary travelers, even though the bright afternoon sun made their hot, dull-gray mass appear as unfriendly as low-heated iron. The very size and bulk of the walls were repugnant to the Valemen, who preferred the freedom of the more pregnable forest lands surrounding their own home, but exhaustion quickly pushed any dislikes aside and they passed without hesitating through the west gates and into the narrow streets of the city. It was a busy hour, with people pushing and shoving their way past the small shops and markets that lined the entryway to the walled city and ran inward toward Menion's home, a stately old mansion screened by trees and hedges that bordered carefully manicured lawns and fragrant gardens. Leah appeared to be a great metropolis to the men of Shady Vale, though it was in fact comparatively small when one considered the size of the great cities of the deep Southland or even the border city of Tyrsis. Leah was a city set apart from the rest of the world, and travelers passed through its gates only infrequently. It was self-contained, existing primarily to serve the needs of its own people. The monarchy that governed the land was the

74

oldest in the Southland. It was the only law that its subjects knew – perhaps the only one they needed. Shea had never been convinced of this, though the highland people for the most part were content with the government and the way of life it provided.

As the Valemen maneuvered their way through the crowds, Shea found himself reflecting on his improbable friendship with Menion Leah. It would have to be termed improbable, he mused, because on the surface they seemed to have so little in common. Valeman and highlander, with backgrounds so completely dissimilar as to defy any meaningful comparison. Shea, the adopted son of an innkeeper, hardheaded, pragmatic, and raised in the tradition of the workingman. Menion, the only son of the royal house of Leah and heir to the throne, born into a life filled with responsibilities he pointedly ignored, possessed of a brash self-confidence that he tried to conceal with only moderate success, and blessed with an uncanny hunter's instinct that merited grudging respect even from so severe a critic as Flick. Their political philosophies were as unlike as their backgrounds. Shea was staunchly conservative, an advocate of the old ways, while Menion was convinced that the old ways had proved ineffective in dealing with the problems of the races.

Yet for all their differences, they had formed a friendship that evidenced mutual respect. Menion found his small friend to be anachronistic in his thinking at times, but he admired his conviction and determination. The Valeman, contrary to Flick's oft-expressed opinion, was not blinded to Menion's shortcomings, but he saw in the Prince of Leah something others were inclined to overlook – a strong, compelling sense of right and wrong.

At the present time, Menion Leah was pursuing life without any particular concern for the future. He traveled a good deal, he hunted the highland forests, but for the most part he seemed to spend his time finding new ways to get into trouble. His hard-earned expertise with the long bow and as a tracker achieved no useful purpose. On the contrary, it merely served to aggravate his father, who had repeatedly but unsuccessfully attempted to interest his son and only heir in the problems of governing his kingdom. One day, Menion would be a king, but Shea doubted that his lighthearted friend ever gave the possibility more than a passing thought. This was foolish, if somewhat expected. Menion's mother had died several years ago, shortly after Shea had first visited the highlands. Menion's father was not an old man, but the death of a king did not always come with age, and many former rulers of Leah had died suddenly and unexpectedly. If something unforeseen should befall his father, Menion would become king whether he was prepared or not. There would be some lessons learned then, Shea thought and smiled in spite of himself.

The Leah ancestral home was a wide, two-story stone building nestled peacefully amid a cluster of spreading hickories and small gardens. The grounds were screened away from the surrounding city by high shrubbery. A broad park lay directly across from a small walkway fronting the home, and as the Valemen crossed wearily to the front gates, children splashed playfully through a small pond at the hub of the park's several paths. The day was still warm, and people hurried past the travelers on their way to meet friends or to reach their homes and families. In the west, the late afternoon sky was deepening into a soft golden haze.

The tall iron gates were ajar, and the Valemen walked quickly toward the front door of the home, winding through the long stone walkway's high shrubbery and garden borders. They were still approaching the stone threshold at the front of the home, when the heavy oak door opened from within, and there, unexpectedly, was Menion Leah. Dressed in a multicolored cloak and vest of

76

green and pale yellow, his lean, whiplike frame moved with the graceful ease of a cat. He was not a big man, though several inches taller than the Valemen, but he was broad through the shoulders and his long arms gave him a rangy look. He was on his way down a side path, but when he caught sight of the two ragged, dusty figures approaching along the main walk, he stopped short. A moment later his eyes went wide with surprise.

'Shea!' he exclaimed sharply. 'What in the name of all . . . what happened to you?'

He rushed over quickly to his friend and gripped the slim hand warmly.

'Good to see you, Menion,' Shea said with a smile.

The highlander stepped back a pace, and his gray eyes studied them shrewdly.

'I never expected that my letter would get results this quickly . . .' He trailed off and studied the other's weary face. 'It hasn't, has it? But don't tell me – I don't want to hear it. I'd rather assume for the sake of our friendship that you came just to visit me. And brought distrustful old Flick, too, I see. This is a surprise.'

He grinned quickly past Shea at the scowling Flick, who nodded curtly.

'This wasn't my idea, you may be sure.'

'I wish that our friendship alone were the reason for this visit.' Shea sighed heavily. 'I wish I didn't have to involve you in any of this, but I'm afraid that we're in serious trouble and you are the one person who might be able to help us.'

Menion started to smile, then changed his mind quickly as he caught the mood reflected in the other's drawn face and nodded soberly.

'Nothing funny about this, is there? Well, a hot bath and some dinner are the first order of business. We can discuss what brought you here later. Come on in. My father's engaged on the border, but I'm at your disposal.'

Once inside, Menion directed the servants to take charge of the Valemen, and they were led off to a welcome bath and a change of clothes. An hour later, the three friends gathered in the great hall for a dinner that would ordinarily have fed twice their number, but on this night barely satisfied them. As they ate, Shea related to Menion the strange tale behind their flight from Shady Vale. He described Flick's meeting with the mysterious wanderer Allanon and the involved story behind the Sword of Shannara. It was necessary, despite Allanon's order of secrecy, if he must ask Menion's help. He told of the coming of Balinor with his terse warning, of their narrow escape from the black Skull creature, and finally of their flight to the highlands. Shea did all the talking. Flick was unwilling to enter into the conversation, resisting the temptation he felt to elaborate on his own part in the events of the past few weeks. He chose to keep quiet because he was determined not to trust Menion. He was convinced that it would be better for the Valemen if at least one of them kept his guard up and his mouth closed.

Menion Leah listened quietly to the long tale, evincing no visible surprise until the part about Shea's background, with which he appeared immeasurably pleased. His lean brown face remained for the most part an inscrutable mask, broken only by that perpetual half smile and the small wrinkles at the corners of the sharp gray eyes. He recognized quickly enough why the Valemen had come to him. They could never expect to make it from Leah through the lowlands of Clete and from there through the Black Oaks without assistance from someone who knew the country – someone they could trust. Correction, Menion thought, smiling inwardly – someone Shea could trust. He knew that Flick would never have agreed to come to Leah unless his brother had insisted. There had never been much of a friendship between Flick and himself. Still, they were both here, both willing to seek his help, whatever the reason, and he would never be able to refuse anything to Shea, even where there was risk to his own life.

Shea finished his story and waited patiently for Menion's response. The highlander seemed lost in thought, his eyes fixed on the half-filled glass of wine at his elbow. When he spoke, his voice was distant.

'The Sword of Shannara. I haven't heard that story in years – never really believed it was true. Now out of complete obscurity it reappears with my old friend Shea Ohmsford as the heir apparent. Or are you?' His eyes snapped up suddenly. 'You could be a red herring, a decoy for these Northland creatures to chase and destroy. How can we be sure about Allanon? From the tale you've told me, he seems almost as dangerous as the things hunting you – perhaps even one of them.'

Flick started noticeably at this suggestion, but Shea shook his head firmly.

'I can't bring myself to believe that. It doesn't make any sense.'

'Maybe not,' continued Menion slowly, inwardly musing over the prospect. 'Could be I'm getting old and suspicious. Frankly, this whole story is pretty improbable. If it's true, you are fortunate to have gotten this far on your own. There are a great many tales of the Northland, of the evil that dwells in the wilderness above the Streleheim Plains – power, they say, beyond the understanding of any mortal being . . .'

He trailed off for a moment, then sipped gingerly at his wine.

'The Sword of Shannara . . . just the possibility that the legend might be true is enough to . . .' He shook his head and grinned openly. 'How can I deny myself the chance to find out? You'll need a guide to get you to the Anar, and I'm your man.'

'I knew you would be.' Shea reached over and gripped

his hand in thanks. Flick groaned softly, but managed a feeble smile.

'Now then, let's see where we stand.' Menion took charge quickly, and Flick went back to drinking wine. 'What about these Elfstones? Let's have a look at them.'

Shea quickly produced the small leather pouch and emptied the contents into his open palm. The three stones sparkled brightly in the torchlight, their blue glow deep and rich. Menion touched one gently and then picked it up.

'They are indeed beautiful,' he acknowledged approvingly. 'I don't know when I've seen their like. But how can they help us?'

'I don't know that yet,' admitted the Valeman reluctantly. 'I only know what Allanon told us – that the stones were only to be used in emergencies, and that they were very powerful.'

'Well, I hope that he was right,' snorted the other. 'I would hate to discover the hard way that he was mistaken. But I suppose we'll have to live with that possibility.'

He paused for a moment and watched as Shea placed the stones back in the pouch and tucked the leather container into his tunic front. When the Valeman looked up again, he was staring blankly into his wineglass.

'I do know something of the man called Balinor, Shea. He is a fine soldier – I doubt we could find his equal in the whole of the Southland. We might be better off to seek the aid of his father. You would be better protected by the soldiers of Callahorn than by the forest-dwelling Dwarfs of the Anar. I know the roads to Tyrsis, all of them safe. But almost any path to the Anar will run directly through the Black Oaks – not the safest place in the Southland, as you know.'

'Allanon told us to go to the Anar,' persisted Shea. 'He must have had a reason, and until I find him again, I'm not taking any chances. Besides, Balinor himself advised us to follow his instructions.'

Menion shrugged.

'That's unfortunate, because even if we manage to get through the Black Oaks, I really don't know much about the land beyond. I'm told that it's relatively unsettled country all the way to the Anar forests. The inhabitants are mostly South-landers and Dwarfs, who should not prove dangerous to us. Culhaven is a small Dwarf village on the Silver River in the lower Anar – I don't think we'll have much trouble finding it, if we get that far. First, we have to navigate the Lowlands of Clete, which will be especially bad with the spring thaws, and then the Black Oaks. That will be the most dangerous part of the trip.'

'Can't we find a way around . . .?' Shea asked him hopefully.

Menion poured himself another glass of wine and passed the decanter to Flick who accepted it without blinking.

'It would take weeks. North of Leah is the Rainbow Lake. If we go that way, we have to circle the entire lake to the north through the Runne Mountains. The Black Oaks stretch south from the lake for a hundred miles. If we try to go south and come north again on the other side, it will take us at least two weeks – and that's open coun-try all the way. No cover at all. We have to go east through the lowlands, then cut through the oaks.'

Flick frowned, recalling how on their last visit to Leah, Menion had succeeded in losing them for several days in the dreaded forest, where they were menaced by wolves and ravaged by hunger. They had barely escaped with their lives.

'Old Flick remembers the Black Oaks,' laughed Menion as he caught the other's dark expression. 'Well, Flick, this time we shall be better prepared. It's treacherous country, but no one knows it better than I do. And we aren't like-ly to be followed there. Still, we'll tell no one where we're going. Simply say that we are off for an extended hunting trip. My father has his own problems anyway – he won't even miss me. He's used to having me gone, even for weeks at a time.'

He paused for a moment and looked to Shea to see if he had forgotten anything. The Valeman grinned at the highlander's undisguised enthusiasm.

'Menion, I knew we could count on you. It will be good to have you along.'

Flick looked openly disgusted; and Menion, catching the look, could not allow the opportunity for a little fun at the other's expense to pass.

'I think we ought to talk for a minute about what's in this for me,' he declared suddenly. 'I mean, what do I get out of all this if I do guide you safely to Culhaven?'

'What do you get?' exclaimed Flick without thinking. 'Why should you . . .'

'It's all right,' the other interrupted quickly. 'I had forgotten you, old Flick, but you don't need to worry; I don't intend to take anything from your share.'

'What are you talking about, sly one?' raged Flick. 'I did not mean ever to take anything . . .'

'That's enough!' Shea leaned forward, his face flushed. 'This cannot continue if we are to travel together. Menion, you must cease your attempts to bait my brother into anger; and you, Flick, must put aside, once and for all, your pointless suspicions of Menion. We must have some faith in one another – and we must be friends!'

Menion looked down sheepishly, and Flick was biting his lip in disgust. Shea sat back quietly as the anger drained out of him.

'Well spoken,' acknowledged Menion after a moment. 'Flick, here is my hand on it. Let us make a temporary truce, at least – for Shea.'

Flick looked at the extended hand and then slowly accepted it.

'Words come easily for you, Menion. I hope you mean them this time.'

The highlander accepted the rebuke with a smile.

'A truce, Flick.'

He released the Valeman's hand and drained his wine-glass. He knew he had convinced Flick of nothing.

It was growing late now, and all three were eager to complete their plans and retire for the night. They quickly decided that they would leave early the following morning. Menion arranged to have them outfitted with light camping gear, including backpacks, hunting cloaks, provisions, and weapons. He produced a map of the country east of Leah, but it was poorly detailed because the lands were so little known. The Lowlands of Clete, which spread from the highlands eastward to the Black Oaks, was a dismal, treacherous moor – yet on the map, it was no more than a blank white area with the name written in. The Black Oaks stood out prominently, a dense mass of forest land running from the Rainbow Lake southward, standing like a great wall between Leah and the Anar. Menion discussed briefly with the Valemen his knowledge of the terrain and weather conditions at this time of the year. But like the map, his information was sketchy. Most of what the travelers would find could not be accurately anticipated, and the unexpected could be most dangerous.

By midnight, the three were in bed, their preparations for the journey to the Anar complete. In the room he was sharing with Flick, Shea lay back wearily in the softness of the bedding and studied for a moment the darkness beyond his open window. The night had clouded over, the sky a mass of heavy, rolling blackness that settled ominously about the misty highlands. Gone was the heat of the day, blown east by the cooling night breezes, and throughout the sleeping city there was a peaceful solitude. In the bed next to him, Flick was already asleep, his breathing heavy and regular. Shea watched him thoughtfully. His own head was heavy and his body weary from the struggle to reach Leah, yet he remained awake. He was beginning to realize for the first time the truth about his predicament. The flight to reach Menion was only the first step in a journey that might very possibly go on for years. Even if they managed to reach the Anar safely, Shea knew that eventually they would be forced to run again. The search to find them would continue until the Warlock Lord was destroyed – or Shea was dead. Until then, there would be no going back to the Vale, to the home and father he had left, and wherever they were, their safety would last only until the winged hunters found them once again.

The truth was terrifying. In the silent darkness, Shea Ohmsford was alone with his fear, and deep within himself, he fought back against a rising knot of terror. He took a long time finally to fall asleep.

It was a dull, sunless day that followed, a day damp and chilling to human flesh and bone. Shea and his two companions found it devoid of any warmth and comfort as they journeyed eastward through the misty highlands of Leah and began a slow descent toward the cheerless climate of the lowlands beyond. There was no talking among them as they hiked in single file down the narrow footpaths which wound tediously about gray, hulking boulders and clumps of dying, formless brush. Menion led, his keen eyes carefully picking out the often obscure traces of a trail, his stride long and relaxed as he moved almost gracefully over the gradually roughening terrain. Across his lean back he carried a small pack to which he had attached a great ash bow and arrows. In addition, beneath the pack and fastened to his body by a long leather strap was the ancient sword which his father had given him when he had reached the age of manhood – the sword which was the birthright of the Prince of Leah. Its cold, gray iron glimmered faintly in the dim light; and Shea, who followed several paces back, found himself wondering if it was at all like the fabled

84

Sword of Shannara. His Elven eyebrows lifted quizzically as he tried to peer into the endless gloom of the land ahead. Nothing seemed alive. It was a dead land for dead things, and the living were trespassers here. Not a very stimulating idea; he grinned faintly to himself as he forced his mind to turn to other matters. Flick brought up the rear, his sturdy back bearing the bulk of the provisions that would have to sustain them until they were through the Lowlands of Clete and the forbidding Black Oaks. Once they had gotten that far – if they got that far – they would be forced to buy or trade for food from the few scattered inhabitants of the country beyond, or as a last resort, seek nourishment from the land itself, a prospect that Flick did not particularly relish. Although he felt somewhat more secure in his mind now that Menion was genuinely interested in helping them on this journey, he was nevertheless still unconvinced of the highlander's ability to do so. The events of their last trip were still fresh in his mind, and he wanted no part of another hair-raising experience like that one.

The first day wore on quickly as the three traveled past the boundaries of the kingdom of Leah and by nightfall had reached the fringes of the dismal Lowlands of Clete. They found shelter for the night in a small vale under the negligible protection of a few scruffy trees and some heavy brush. The dampness of the mist had soaked their clothing completely through, and the chill of the descending night left them shivering with cold. A brief attempt was made to start a fire in an effort to gain some small warmth and dryness, but the wood in the area was so thoroughly saturated with moisture that it was impossible to get it to burn. Eventually, they gave up on the fire and settled for some cold rations while wrapped in blankets which had carefully been waterproofed at the start of the journey. Little was said because no one felt much like talking beyond mumbling curses upon the general weather conditions. There was no sound from the darkness beyond where they sat huddled within the brush; it was a penetrating stillness that prodded the mind with sudden, unexpected apprehension, forcing it to listen in a frightened effort to catch some faint, reassuring rustle of life. But there was only the silence and the blackness, and not even the wisp of a brief wind touched their chilled faces as they lay quietly in the blankets. Eventually the weariness of the day's march stole over them, and one by one they dropped uneasily off to sleep.

The second and third day were unimaginably worse than the first. It rained the entire time – a slow, chilling drizzle that soaked first the clothing, then penetrated into the skin and bone, and finally reached the very nerve centers, so that the only feeling the weary body would permit was one of thorough, discomforting wetness. The air was damp and cold in the day, dropping off to a near freeze at night. Everything around the three travelers seemed totally beaten down by this lingering coldness; what little brush and small foliage could be seen was twisted and dying, formless clumps of wood and withered leaves that silently waited to crumble and disappear altogether. No human or animal lived here – even the smallest rodent would have been swallowed up and consumed by the clutching softness of an earth seeped through with the chilling dampness of long, sunless, lifeless days and nights. Nothing moved, nothing stirred as the three walked eastward through shapeless country where there was no trail, no hint that anyone or anything had ever passed that way before, or would ever do so again. The sun never appeared during their march, no faint trace of its direct rays flickering downward to show that somewhere beyond this dead, forgotten land was a world of life. Whether it was the perpetual mist or the heavy clouds or a combination of both that so completely blotted out the sky remained an unanswered question. Their only world was that cheerless, hateful gray land through which they walked.

By the fourth day, they began to despair. Even though there had been no further sign of the winged hunters of the Warlock Lord and it appeared that any pursuit had been abandoned, the possibility offered little solace as the hours dragged by and the silence grew deeper, the land more sullen. Even Menion's great spirit began to waver and doubt wormed its stealthy way into his usually confident mind. He began to wonder if they had lost the direction, if perhaps they had even traveled in a circle. He knew the land would never tell them, that once lost in this bleak country, they were lost forever. Shea and Flick felt the fear even more deeply. They knew nothing of the lowlands and lacked the hunter's skill and instinct that Menion possessed. They relied completely on him, but sensed that something was wrong even though the highlander had purposely kept silent about his own doubts so as not to worry them. The hours passed, and the cold and the wet and the hateful deadness of the land remained unchanged. They felt their last shred of confidence in one another and in themselves begin to slip slowly, agonizingly away. Finally, as the fifth day of the journey drew to a close and still the lowland bleakness stretched on with no visible sign of the desperately-sought-after Black Oaks, Shea wearily called a halt to the endless march and dropped heavily to the ground, his questioning eyes on the Prince of Leah.

Menion shrugged and looked absently at the misty lowlands about them, his handsome face drawn with the chill of the air.

'I won't lie to you,' he murmured. 'I can't be sure that we have kept our sense of direction. We may have traveled in a circle; we may even be hopelessly lost.'

Flick dropped his pack disgustedly and looked at his brother with his own special 'I told you so' look. Shea glanced at him and turned hurriedly back to Menion.

'I can't believe we're completely lost! Isn't there any way we can get our bearings?'

'I'm open to suggestions.' His friend smiled humorlessly, stretching as he, too, dropped his pack to the rough ground and sat down beside the brooding Flick. 'What's the trouble, old Flick? Have I gotten you into it again?'

Flick glanced over at him angrily; but looking into the gray eyes, he quickly reconsidered his dislike of the man. There was genuine concern there, and even a trace of sadness at the thought that he had failed them. With rare affection, Flick reached over and placed a comforting hand on the other's shoulder, nodding silently. Suddenly, Shea leaped up and flung off his own pack, hastily rummaging through its contents.

'The stones can help us,' he cried.

For a moment the other two looked blankly at him and then in sudden understanding rose expectantly to their feet. A moment later, Shea produced the small leather pouch with its precious contents. They all stared at the worn container in mute anticipation that the Elfstones would at last prove their value, that they would somehow aid them in escaping the wasteland of Clete. Eagerly Shea opened the drawstrings and carefully dropped the three small, blue stones into his upturned palm. They lay there twinkling dimly as the three watched and waited.

'Hold them up, Shea,' urged Menion after a moment. 'Perhaps they need the light.'

The Valeman did as he was told, watching the blue stones anxiously. Nothing happened. He waited a moment longer before lowering his hand. Allanon had cautioned him against use of the Elfstones except in the gravest of emergencies. Perhaps the stones would only come to his aid in special situations. He began to despair. Whatever the case, he was faced with the hard fact that he had no idea how the stones were to be used. He looked desperately at his friends.

'Well, try something else!' exclaimed Menion heatedly.

Shea took the stones between his hands and rubbed them together sharply, then shook them and cast them like dice. Still nothing happened. Slowly he retrieved them from the damp earth and carefully wiped them clean. Their deep blue color seemed to draw him to them, and he peered closely into their clear, glasslike core as if somehow the answer might be found there.

'Maybe you should talk to them or something . . .' Flick's voice trailed off hopefully.

A mental picture of Allanon's dark face, bowed and locked in deep concentration, flashed sharply in Shea's mind. Perhaps the secret of the Elfstones could be unlocked in a different way, he thought suddenly. Holding them out in his open palm, the little Valeman closed his eyes and concentrated his thoughts on reaching into the deep blueness, searching for the power that they so desperately needed. Silently, he urged the Elfstones to help them. Long moments passed, seemingly hours. He opened his eyes and the three friends watched and waited while the stones rested in Shea's palm, their blue gleam dull in the darkness and damp of the mist.

Then, with ferocious suddenness, they flared up in a blinding blue glare that caused the travelers to reel back from the brightness, shielding their unprotected eyes. So powerful was the aura that Shea nearly dropped the small gems in astonishment. The sharp glow became steadily brighter, lighting up the dead land about them as the sun had never been able to do. The brightness intensified from the deep blue to a bright blue so dazzling that the awestruck watchers were actually hypnotized. It grew, steadied, and abruptly shot forward like a huge beacon, traveling to their left, cutting effortlessly through the mist-covered grayness to rest at last, some hundreds, perhaps thousands of yards ahead upon the great gnarled boles of the ancient Black Oaks. The light held for one brief moment, and then it was gone. The gray mist returned with its chill dampness and the three small blue stones gleamed quietly as they had before.

89

Menion recovered quickly, clapping Shea sharply on the back and grinning broadly. In one quick motion, he had his pack back in place and was ready to travel, his eyes already scanning the now-invisible spot through which the vision of the Black Oaks had appeared. Shea hastily returned the Elfstones to the pouch, and the Valemen strapped on their packs. Not a word was spoken as they walked rapidly in the direction the beacon had flashed, each watching eagerly for the long-expected forest. Gone was the chill of the gray darkness and slow drizzle of the past five days. Gone was the despair they had felt so strongly only minutes before. There was only the conviction that escape from these dreaded lowlands was at last at hand. They did not question, did not doubt the vision the stones had revealed to them. The Black Oaks was the most dangerous forest in the Southland, but at this particular moment, it seemed a haven of hope compared to the land of Clete.

The time seemed endless as they pushed ahead. It could have been hours or perhaps only minutes later when suddenly the graying mist grudgingly gave way to huge, moss-covered trunks which rose hulkingly into the air to be lost in the haze above. The exhausted trio halted together, their tired eyes gazing joyfully on the cheerless monsters that stood evenly, endlessly before them, their great mass an impenetrable wall of damp, scarred bark on wide, deep-rooted bases that had stood there for countless ages of man and would very likely be there until the destruction of the land itself. It was an awesome sight, even in the dim light of the misty lowlands, and the watchers felt the undeniable presence of a life-force in those woods so incredibly ancient that it almost commanded a deep, grudging respect for its years. It was as if they had stepped into another age, another world, and all that stood so silently before them had the magic of an enticingly dangerous fairy tale.

'The stones were right,' murmured Shea softly, a slow smile spreading over his tired, but happy face. He breathed deeply with relief and flashed a quick grin.

'The Black Oaks,' pronounced Menion in admiration.

'Here we go again,' sighed Flick.

CHAPTER

6

They spent that night camped within the protective fringes of the Black Oaks in a small clearing, sheltered by the great trees and dense shrubbery which blotted out the dreariness of the lowlands of Clete less than fifty yards to the west. The heavy mist dissipated within the forest, and it was possible to look skyward to the magnificent canopy of interlocking boughs and leaves several hundred feet above them. Where there had been no sign of life in the deathly lowlands, within the giant oaks the mingled sounds of insect and animal life whispered through the night. It was pleasant to hear living things again, and the three weary travelers felt at ease for the first time in days. But lingering in the back of their minds was the memory of their prior journey to this deceptively peaceful haven, when they had been lost for several long days and nearly devoured by the ravenous wolves that prowled deep within its confines. Moreover, the tales of unfortunate travelers who had attempted to pass through this same forest were too numerous to be disregarded.

However, the young Southlanders felt reasonably secure at the edge of the Black Oaks and gratefully made preparations to start a fire. Wood was plentiful and dry. They stripped to the skin and hung their soggy garments on a line near the small blaze. A meal was quickly prepared – the first hot one in five days – and devoured in minutes. The floor of the forest was soft and smooth, a comfortable bed compared to the dampened earth of the lowlands. As they lay quietly on their backs gazing skyward at the gently swaying treetops, the bright light of the fire seemed to shoot upward in faint streaks of orange that gave the impression of an altar burning in some great sanctuary. The light danced and glittered against the rough bark and the soft, green moss that clung in dark patches to the massive trees. The forest insects maintained their steady hum in contentment. Occasionally one would fly into the flames of the fire and extinguish its brief life with a dazzling flash. Once or twice they heard the rustle of some small animal outside the light of the fire, watching from the protective blackness.

After a while, Menion rolled over on his side and looked curiously at Shea.

'What is the source of the power of those stones, Shea? Can they grant any wish? I'm still not sure . . .'

His voice trailed off and he shook his head vaguely. Shea continued to lie motionless on his back, staring upward for a few moments as he thought back on the events of that afternoon. He realized that none of them had spoken of the Elfstones since the mysterious vision of the Black Oaks in that awesome display of incomprehensible power. He glanced over at Flick, who was watching him closely.

'I don't think that I have that much control over them,' he announced abruptly. 'It was almost as if *they* made the decision . . .' He paused, and then added absently, 'I don't think I can control them.'

Menion nodded thoughtfully and lay back again. Flick cleared his throat.

'What's the difference? They got us out of that dismal swamp, didn't they?'

Menion glanced sharply at Flick and shrugged.

'It might be helpful to know when we can count on that

kind of support, don't you think?' He breathed deeply and clasped his hands behind his head, his keen gaze shifting to the fire at his feet. Flick stirred uneasily across from him, glancing from Menion to his brother and back again. Shea said nothing, his gaze focused on some imaginary point overhead.

Long moments passed before the highlander spoke again.

'Well, at least we've made it this far,' he declared cheerfully. 'Now for the next leg of the trip!'

He sat up and began to sketch a quick map of the area in the dry earth. Shea and Flick sat up with him and watched quietly.

'Here we are,' Menion pointed to a spot on the dirt map representing the fringe of the Black Oaks. 'At least that's where I think we are,' he added quickly. 'To the north is the Mist Marsh and farther north of that the Rainbow Lake, out of which runs the Silver River east to the Anar Forests. Our best bet is to travel north tomorrow until we reach the edge of the Mist Marsh. Then we'll skirt the edge of the swamp,' he traced a long line, 'and come out on the other side of the Black Oaks. From there, we can travel due north until we run into the Silver River, and that should get us safely to the Anar.'

He paused and looked over at the other two. Neither seemed to be happy with the plan.

'What's the matter?' he asked in bewilderment. 'The plan is designed to get us past the Black Oaks without forcing us to go directly through them, which was the cause of all the trouble the last time we were here. Don't forget those wolves are still in there somewhere!'

Shea nodded slowly and frowned.

'It's not the general plan,' he began hesitantly, 'but we've heard tales of the Mist Marsh . . .'

Menion clapped his hand to his forehead in amazement.

'Oh, no! Not the old wives' tale about a Mist Wraith

that lurks on the edges of the marsh waiting to devour stray travelers? Don't tell me you believe that!'

'That's fine, coming from you,' Flick blazed up angrily. 'I suppose you've forgotten who it was that told us how safe the Black Oaks were just before that last trip!'

'All right,' soothed the lean hunter. 'I'm not saying that this is a safe part of the country and that some very strange creatures don't inhabit these woods. But no one has ever seen this so-called creature of the marsh, and we have seen the wolves. Which do you choose?'

'I suppose that your plan is the best one,' interjected Shea hastily. 'But I would prefer it if we could cut as far east as possible while traveling through the forest to avoid as much of the Mist Marsh as possible.'

'Agreed!' exclaimed Menion. 'But it may prove to be a bit difficult when we haven't seen the sun in three days and can't really be sure which way is east.'

'Climb a tree,' Flick suggested casually.

'Climb a . . .' stuttered the other in unabashed amazement. 'Why, of course! Why don't I think of that? I'll just climb two hundred feet of slick, damp, moss-covered tree bark with my bare hands and feet!' He shook his head in mock wonderment. 'Sometimes you appall me.'

He glanced wearily over at Shea for understanding, but the Valeman had bounded excitedly to his brother's side.

'You brought the climbing equipment?' he demanded in astonishment; when the other nodded, he clapped him heartily on his broad back.

'Special boots and gloves and rope,' he explained quickly to a bewildered Prince of Leah. 'Flick is the best climber in the Vale, and if anyone can make it up one of these monsters, he can.'

Menion shook his head uncomprehendingly.

'The boots and gloves are coated with a special substance just before use that makes the surface rough enough to grip even damp, mossy bark. He'll be able to climb one of these oaks tomorrow and check the position of the sun.'

Flick grinned smugly and nodded.

'Yes, indeed, wonder of wonders.' Menion shook his head and looked over at the stocky Valeman. 'Even the slow-witted are starting to think. My friends, we may make it yet.'

When they awoke the following morning, the forest was still dark, with only faint traces of daylight filtering through at the tops of the great oaks. A thin mist had drifted in off the lowlands which, when glimpsed from the edges of the forest, appeared as sunless and dismal as ever. It was cold in the woods – not the damp, penetrating chill of the lowland country, but rather the brisk, crisp cool of a forest's early morn. They ate a quick breakfast, and then Flick prepared to climb one of the towering oaks. He pulled on the heavy, flexible boots and gloves, which Shea then coated with a thick pasty substance from a small container. Menion looked on quizzically, but his curiosity changed to astonishment as the stocky Valeman grasped the base of the great tree and, with a dexterity that belied both his bulky size and the difficulty of the task, proceeded to climb rapidly toward the summit. His strong limbs carried him upward through the tangle of heavy branches and the climbing became slower and more difficult. He was briefly lost from sight upon reaching the topmost branches, then reappeared, hastening down the smooth trunk to rejoin his friends.

Quickly the climbing gear was packed and the group proceeded in a northeasterly direction. Based on Flick's report of the sun's present position, their chosen route should bring them out at a point along the east edge of the Mist Marsh. Menion believed that the forest trek could be completed in one day. It was now early morning, and they were determined to be through the Black Oaks before darkness fell. So they marched steadily, at times rapidly, in single file. The keen-eyed Menion led, picking out the best path, relying heavily on his sense of direction in the semidarkness. Shea followed close behind him, and Flick brought up the rear, glancing occasionally over his shoulder into the still forests. They stopped only three times to rest and once more for a brief lunch, each time quickly resuming their march. They spoke infrequently, but the talk was lighthearted and cheerful. The day wore quickly away, and soon the first signs of nightfall were visible. Still the forest stretched on before them with no indication of a break in the great trees. Worse than this, a heavy graying mistiness was once again seeping into view in gradually thickening amounts. But this was a new kind of mist. It lacked the inconsistency of the lowland mist; this was an almost smokelike substance that one could actually feel clinging to the body and clothes, gripping in its own peculiarly distasteful fashion. It felt strangely like the clutching of hundreds of small, clammy, chilled hands seeking to pull the body down, and the three travelers felt an unmistakable revulsion at its insistent touch. Menion indicated that the heavy, foglike substance was from the Mist Marsh, and they were very close to the end of the forest.

Eventually, the mist grew so heavy that it was impossible for the three to see more than a few feet. Menion slowed his pace to a crawl because of the increasingly poor visibility, and they remained close to each other to avoid separation. By this time, the day was so far gone that even without the mist the forest would have appeared almost black; but with the added dimness caused by the swirling wall of heavy moisture, it was nearly impossible to pick out any sort of path. It was almost as if the three were suspended in a limbo world, where only the solidity of the invisible ground on which they trod offered any evidence of reality. It finally became so difficult to see that Menion instructed the other two to bind themselves together and to him by a length of rope to prevent separation. This was quickly done and the slow march resumed. Menion knew that they had to be very near the Mist Marsh and carefully peered into the grayness ahead in an effort to catch a glimpse of a breakthrough.

Even so, when at last he did reach the edge of the marshland bordering the north fringes of the Black Oaks, he did not realize what had happened until he had already stepped knee-deep into the thick green waters. The chill, deathlike clutching of the mud beneath, coupled with his surprise, caused him to slip farther down, and only his quick warning saved Shea and Flick from a similar fate. Responding to his cry, they hauled in on the rope that bound them together and hastily pulled their comrade from the bog and certain death. The sullen, slime-covered waters of the great swamp covered only thinly the bottomless mud beneath, which lacked the rapid suction of quicksand, but accomplished the same result in a slightly longer time span. Anything or anyone caught in its grip was doomed to a slow death by suffocation in an immeasurable abyss. For untold ages its silent surface had fooled unwary creatures into attempting to cross, or to skirt, or perhaps only to test its mirrorless waters, and the decayed remains of all lay buried together somewhere beneath its placid face. The three travelers stood silently on its banks, looking at it and experiencing inwardly the horror of its dark secret. Even Menion Leah shuddered as he remembered its brief, clutching invitation to him to share the fate of so many others. For one spellbound second, the dead paraded as shadows before them and were gone.

'What happened?' exclaimed Shea suddenly, his voice breaking the silence with deafening sharpness. 'We should have avoided this swamp!'

Menion looked upward and about for a few seconds and shook his head.

'We've come out too far to the west. We'll have to follow the edge of the bog around to the east until we can break free from this mist and the Black Oaks.'

He paused and considered the time of day.

'I'm not spending the night in this place,' Flick declared vehemently, anticipating the other's query. 'I'd rather walk all night and most of tomorrow – and probably the next day!'

Their quick decision was to continue along the edge of the Mist Marsh until they reached open land to the east and then stop for the night. Shea was still concerned about being caught in open country by the Skull Bearers, but his growing dread of the swamp overshadowed even this fear, and his foremost thought was to get as far away as possible. The trio tightened the rope about their waists and in single file began to move along the uneven shoreline of the marsh, their eyes glued to the faint path ahead. Menion guided them cautiously, avoiding the tangle of treacherous roots and weeds that grew in abundance along the swamp's edge, their twisted, knotted forms seemingly alive in the eerie half-light of the rolling gray mist. At times the ground became soft mud, dangerously like that of the marsh itself, and had to be skirted. At other times huge trees blocked the path, their great trunks leaning heavily toward the dull, lifeless surface of the swamp's waters, their branches drooping sadly, motionless as they waited for the death that lay only inches below. If the Lowlands of Clete had been a dying land, then this marsh was the death that waited – an infinite, ageless death that gave no sign, no warning, no movement as it crouched, concealed within the very land it had so brutally destroyed. The chilling dampness of the lowlands was here, but coupled with it was the unexplainable feeling that the heavy, stagnant slime of the swamp waters permeated the mist as well, clutching eagerly at the weary travelers. The mist about them swirled slowly, but there was no sign of wind, no sound of a breeze rustling the tall swamp grass or dying oaks. All was still, a silence of permanent death that knew well who was master.

They had walked for perhaps an hour when Shea first sensed that something was wrong. There was no reason for the feeling; it stole over him gradually until every sense was keyed, trying to find where the trouble lay. Walking silently between the other two, he listened intently, peering first into the great oaks, then out over the swamp. Finally, he concluded with chilling certainty that they were not alone – that something else was out there in the invisible beyond, lost in the mist to their poor vision, but able to see them. For one brief moment the young Valeman was so terrified by the thought that he was unable to speak or even to gesture. He could only walk ahead, his mind frozen, waiting for the unspeakable to happen. But then, with a supreme effort he calmed his scattered thoughts and brought the other two men to an abrupt halt.

Menion looked around quizzically and started to speak, but Shea silenced him with a finger to his own lips and a gesture toward the swamp. Flick was already looking cautiously in that direction, his own sixth sense having warned him of his brother's fear. For long moments they stood motionless at the edge of the marsh, their eyes and ears concentrated on the impenetrable mist moving sluggishly above the surface of the dead water. The silence was oppressive.

'I think you were mistaken,' Menion whispered finally as he relaxed his vigil. 'Sometimes when you are this tired, it is easy to imagine things.'

Shea shook his head negatively and looked at Flick.

'I don't know,' the other conceded. 'I thought I sensed something . . .'

'A Mist Wraith?' chided Menion grinning.

'Maybe you're right,' Shea interceded quickly. 'I am pretty tired and could imagine anything at this point. Let's keep moving and get out of this place.'

They hastily resumed the dreary trek, but for the next few minutes remained alert for anything unusual. When nothing happened, they began to let their thoughts drift to other matters. Shea had just succeeded in convincing himself that he had been mistaken and the victim of an overactive imagination brought about by lack of sleep, when Flick cried out.

Immediately Shea felt the rope that bound them together jerk sharply and begin to drag him in the direction of the deadly swamp. He lost his balance and fell, unable to distinguish anything in the mist. For one fleeting moment he thought he glimpsed his brother's body suspended several feet in the air over the swamp, the rope still tied to his waist. In the next second, Shea felt the chill of the swamp grapple at his legs.

They might have all been lost had it not been for the quick reflexes of the Prince of Leah. At the first sharp jerk of the rope, he had instinctively grasped at the only thing near enough to keep him on his feet. It was a huge, sinking oak, its trunk embedded so far into the soft ground that its upper branches were within reach, and Menion rapidly hooked one arm about the nearest bough and with the other grasped the rope about his waist and tried to pull back. Shea, now up to his knees in the swamp mud, felt the rope go taut on Menion's end and tried to brace himself to aid. Flick was crying out sharply in the darkness above the swamp, and both Menion and Shea shouted encouragement. Suddenly, the rope between Flick and Shea went slack, and out of the gray mistiness emerged the stout, struggling form of Flick Ohmsford, still suspended above the water's surface, his waist gripped by what appeared to be a sort of greenish, weed-coated tentacle. His right hand held the long, silver dagger, which gleamed menacingly as it slashed in repeated cuts at the thing which held him. Shea yanked hard on the rope which bound them, trying to aid his brother in breaking free, and a moment later he succeeded as the tentacle whipped back into the mist, releasing the still-struggling Flick, who promptly fell into the marsh below.

Shea had barely pulled his exhausted brother from the clutches of the swamp, freed him from the rope, and helped him to his feet before several more of the greenish arms shot out of the misty darkness. They knocked the shaken Flick sprawling and one closed about the left arm of an astonished Shea before he could think to dodge. He felt himself drawn toward the swamp and drew his own dagger to strike fiercely at the slime-covered tentacle. As he fought, he caught sight of something huge out in the marsh, its bulk covered by the night and the swamp. To one side, Flick again became entangled in the grip of two more tentacles, and his stocky form was dragged relentlessly toward the water's edge. Valiantly, Shea broke free from the tentacle that held his arm, slashing through the repulsive limb with one great cut; struggling to reach his brother, he felt another tentacle grasp his leg, knocking his feet out from under him. As he fell, his head struck an oak root, and he lost consciousness.

Again they were saved by Menion, his lithe form leaping out of the darkness behind, the great sword flashing dully in a wide arc as it severed in one powerful swing the tentacle which held the unconscious Shea. A second later, the highlander was at Flick's side, cutting and chopping his way past the arms which suddenly reached for him out of the darkness, and with a series of quick, well-placed blows freed the other Valeman. For a moment the tentacles disappeared back into the mist of the swamp, and Flick and Menion hastened to pull the unconscious Shea back from the unprotected edge of the water. But before any of them could reach the safety of the great oaks, the greenish arms again shot out of the darkness. Without hesitation, Menion and Flick placed themselves in front of their motionless friend and struck out at the encircling arms. The fight was silent, save for the labored breathing of the men as they struck again and again, chopping off bits and pieces and sometimes whole ends of the grasping tentacles. But any damage they caused did not seem to affect the monster in the swamp, which attacked with renewed fury at each stroke. Menion cursed himself for not remembering to drag the great ash bow within reach so that he might have taken a shot at whatever it was that lay beyond the mist.

'Shea!' he yelled desperately. 'Shea, wake up, or for the love of heaven, we're done for!'

The silent form behind him stirred slightly.

'Get up, Shea!' pleaded Flick hoarsely, his own arms exhausted from the great strain of fighting off the tentacles.

'The stones!' yelled Menion. 'Get the Elfstones!'

Shea struggled to a kneeling position, but he was knocked flat again by the force of the battle in front of him. He heard Menion shouting, and dazedly felt for his pack, realizing almost immediately that he had dropped it while helping Flick. He saw it now, several yards to the right, the tentacles waving menacingly over it. Menion seemed to realize this at the same moment and charged forward with a wild cry, his long sword cutting a path for the others. Flick was at his side, the small dagger still in his hand. With a final surge of his fading strength, Shea leaped to his feet and launched himself toward the pack containing the precious Elfstones. His slim form slipped between several of the grasping arms, and he threw himself on the pack. His hand was inside, groping for the pouch, when the first tentacle reached his unprotected legs. Kicking and struggling, he fought to keep his freedom for the few seconds he needed to find the stones. For a moment he thought he had lost them again. Then his hand closed over the small pouch, and he yanked it from his fallen pack. A sudden blow from the writhing tentacles almost caused him to drop it, and he clutched it tightly to his chest as he loosened the drawstrings with numbing slowness. Flick had been forced back so far that he stumbled against Shea's outstretched body and fell over backward, the tentacles coming down on top of them both. Now only the lean form of Menion stood between them and the giant attacker, both hands gripping tightly the great sword of Leah.

Almost without realizing it, Shea found the three blue stones in his hand, free from the pouch at last. Scrambling backward, struggling to his feet, the young Valeman let out a wild cry of triumph and held forth the faintly glowing Elfstones. The power locked within flared up immediately, flooding the darkness with dazzling blue light. Flick and Menion leaped back, shielding their eyes from the glare. The tentacles drew back hesitantly, uncertainly, and as the three men risked a second quick glance, they saw the brilliant light of the Elfstones streak outward into the mist above the swamp, cutting through its vapor with the keenness of a knife. They saw it strike with shattering impact the huge, unspeakable bulk that had attacked them as it was sinking sluggishly beneath the slime-covered waters. At that same instant the glare above the disappearing monster reached the intensity of a small sun and the water steamed with blue flames that seared upward into the shrouded sky. One moment the burning glare and the flames were there and the next they were gone. The mist and the night returned, and the three companions were alone again in the blackness of the marshland.

They quickly sheathed their weapons, picked up the fallen packs and dropped back among the huge black oaks. The swamp remained as silent as it had been before the unexpected attack, its dull waters disturbingly placid beneath the gray haze. For several moments, no one spoke as they collapsed silently against the trunks of the great trees and breathed deeply, grateful to be alive. The whole battle had happened quickly, like the passing of a brief, horrible instant in an all-too-real nightmare. Flick was completely drenched by the swamp waters, and Shea was soaked from the waist down. Both shivered in the chill night air; after only a few seconds of rest, they began moving slowly about in an effort to ward off the numbing cold.

Realizing that they had to get free of the marshland quickly, Menion swung his tired body away from its resting place against the rough, bark-covered oak trunk and in one smooth motion swung his pack into place over his shoulders. Shea and Flick were quick to follow, though somewhat less eager. They conferred briefly to decide what direction it would be best to take now. The choice was simple: proceed through the Black Oaks and risk becoming lost and being set upon by the wandering wolf packs or follow the edge of the swamp and chance a second encounter with the Mist Wraith. Neither choice held much appeal, but the battle with the creature from the Mist Marsh was too recent to permit any of them to risk a repeat performance. So the decision was made to stick to the woods, to try to follow a course parallel to the shoreline of the swamp and hopefully gain the open country beyond within a few hours. They now had reached the point where the long hours of traveling with the keen anticipation of danger had chipped and worn away the clear reasoning of the morning. They were tired and frightened by the strange world into which they had journeyed, and the one clear thought left in their numbed minds was to break through this stifling forest that they might find a few hours of welcome sleep. With that dominating their thoughts and overriding the caution that was so desperately needed, they forgot to tie themselves together again.

The journey continued as before, with Menion in the lead, Shea a few paces back and Flick trailing, all walking silently and steadily, their minds fixed on the reassuring thought that ahead lay the sunlit, open grasslands that would take them to the Anar. The mist seemed to have dissipated slightly, and while Menion's form was only a shadow, Shea could make him out well enough to follow.

Yet at times both Shea and Flick would lose sight of the person immediately in front and would find their eyes straining wearily to keep to the path Menion was making for them. The minutes passed with agonizing slowness and the sharpness of each man's eyesight began to lessen with the increasing need for sleep. Minutes lengthened into long, endless hours and still they plodded slowly onward through the misty haze of the great Black Oaks. They found it impossible to tell how far they had traveled or how much time had passed. Soon it failed to matter at all. They became sleepwalkers in a world of half-dreams and rambling thoughts with no break in the wearing march or the never-ending, silent black trunks that came and passed in countless thousands. The only change was a gradual building of the wind from somewhere in the shrouded night, whispering its first faint cry, then growing to a numbing crescendo of sound that gripped the tired minds of the three travelers with spellbinding magic. It called to them, reminding them of the briefness of the days behind and those ahead, warning them that they were mortal creatures of no consequence in that land, crying to them to lie down in the peacefulness of sleep. They heard and fought against the tempting plea with the last of their strength, concentrating mindlessly on putting one foot before the other in an endless succession of footsteps. One minute they were all there in a ragged line; the next, Shea looked ahead and Menion was gone.

At first, he could not accept the fact, his normally keen mind hazy with lack of sleep, and he continued to walk slowly ahead, looking vainly for the shadowy form of the tall highlander. Then, abruptly he stopped as he realized with stabbing fear that they had somehow become separated. He clutched wildly for Flick and grabbed his brother's loose tunic as the fatigued Valeman stumbled into him, dead on his feet. Flick looked unthinkingly at him, not knowing, not even caring why they had stopped, his only hope that he could collapse at last and sleep. The wind in the darkness of the forest seemed to howl in wild glee, and Shea called desperately for the highland prince and heard only the echoes of his own futile cry. He called again and again, his voice rising to a near scream of desperation and fear, but nothing came back except the sound of his own voice, muffled and distorted by the wild whistling of the wind through the great oaks, whisking and wrapping about the silent trunks and limbs, and filtering out among the rustling leaves. Once he thought he heard his own name called; answering eagerly, he dragged himself and the exhausted Flick through the maze of trees toward the sound of the cry. But there was nothing. Dropping to the forest floor, he called until his voice gave out, but only the wind replied in mocking laughter to tell him that he had lost the Prince of Leah.

CHAPTER

7

Whence Shea awoke the following day, it was noon. The bright sunlight streamed into his half-open eyes with burning sharpness as he lay on his back in the tall grass. At first he could remember nothing of the previous night except that he and Flick had become separated from Menion in the Black Oaks. Half awake, he raised himself on one elbow, looked about sleepily, and discovered that he was in an open field. Behind him rose the forbidding Black Oaks, and he knew that somehow, after losing Menion, he had managed to find his way through the dread forest before collapsing in exhaustion. Everything was hazy in his mind after their separation. He could not imagine how he had summoned the strength to finish the march. He could not even recall breaking free of the endless forest to find the grass-covered lowlands he now surveyed. The whole experience seemed strangely distant as he rubbed his eyes and sighed contentedly in the warm sunlight and fresh air. For the first time in days, the Anar forests seemed to be within reach.

Suddenly, he remembered Flick, and looked anxiously about for his brother. A moment later he spotted the stocky form collapsed in sleep several yards away. Shea climbed slowly to his feet and stretched leisurely, taking time to locate his pack. He bent down and rummaged through its

108

contents until he located the pouch containing the Elf-stones, reassuring himself that they were still safely within his possession. Then picking up the pack, he trudged over to his sleeping brother and gently shook him. Flick stirred grudgingly, clearly unhappy that anyone would disturb his slumber. Shea was forced to shake him several times before he at last reluctantly opened his eyes and squinted up sourly. Upon seeing Shea, he raised himself to a sitting position and looked slowly about.

'Hey, we made it!' he exclaimed. 'But I don't know how. I don't remember anything after losing Menion except walking and walking until I thought that my legs would drop off.'

Shea grinned in agreement and clapped his brother on the back. He felt a measure of gratitude when he thought of all they had been through together. So many hardships and dangers, and still Flick could laugh about it. He felt a sudden, keen sense of love for Flick, a brother who, while not related by blood, was even closer for his deep friendship.

'We made it all right,' he smiled, 'and we'll make it the rest of the way, too, if I can get you off the ground.'

'The meanness in some people is unbelievable.' Flick shook his head in mock disbelief and then climbed heavily to his feet. He looked questioningly over at Shea. 'Menion . . .?'

'Lost . . . I don't know where . . .'

Flick looked away, sensing his brother's bitter disappointment, but unwilling to admit to himself that they were not better off without the highland prince. He instinctively distrusted Menion, yet the highlander had saved his life back in the forest and that was not something Flick would forget easily. He thought about it a minute or so longer, then clapped his brother lightly on the shoulder.

'Don't worry about that rouge. He'll turn up – probably at the wrong time.'

Shea nodded quietly, and the conversation quickly turned to the task at hand. They agreed that the best plan was to journey northward until they reached the Silver River which flowed into the Rainbow Lake, and follow it upstream to the Anar. With any luck, Menion would also follow the river and catch up to them within a few days. His skill as a woodsman should enable him to escape the Black Oaks and at some point beyond find their trail and follow it to wherever they were. Shea was reluctant to leave his friend, but was wise enough to realize that any attempt at a search for him in the Black Oaks could only result in their own entanglement. Moreover, the danger they faced if discovered by the searching Skull Bearers far outweighed any risks Menion might encounter, even in that forest. There was nothing for them to do but to continue on.

The pair walked rapidly through the green, quiet lowlands, hoping to reach the Silver River by nightfall. It was already midafternoon, and they had no way of knowing how far they might be from the river. With the sun to serve as a guide, they felt more confident of their position than they had in the misty confines of the Black Oaks, where they had been forced to depend on their own unreliable sense of direction. They talked freely, brightened by the sunlight that had been absent for so many days and by an unspoken feeling of gratitide that they were still alive following the harrowing experiences of the Mist Marsh. As they walked, small animals and high-flying birds scattered at their appearance. Once, in the fading light of the afternoon sun, Shea thought he caught sight of the small, hunched-over form of an old man some distance to the east, moving slowly away from them. But in that light and at that distance he could not be certain and an instant later found he could see no one after all. Flick had seen nothing and the incident was forgotten.

By dusk they sighted a long, ribbon-thin stream of water to the north which they quickly identified as the fabled

Silver River, the source of the wondrous Rainbow Lake to the west and of a thousand firelight tales of adventure. It was said that there was a legendary King of the Silver River, whose wealth and power was beyond description, but whose only concern was in keeping the waters of the great river running free and clean for man and animal alike. He was seldom seen by travelers, the stories related, but he was always there to offer aid, should any require it, or to deal out punishment for violation of his domain. On sighting the river, Shea and Flick could only tell that it appeared very beautiful in the fading light, the sort of faint silver color that the name implied. When they finally reached its edge, the evening had become too dark to permit them to see how clear the waters really were, but upon tasting it they found it clean enough to drink.

They found a small, grass-covered clearing on the south bank of the river, beneath the spreading shelter of two broad, old maple trees that offered an ideal campsite for the night. Even the short journey of that afternoon had tired them, and they preferred not to risk moving about in the dark in this open country. They had just about exhausted their supplies, and after this evening's meal they would have to hunt for food. This was a particularly disheartening thought when they recalled that the only weapons they had between them for killing game were the short and highly ineffectual hunting knives. Menion carried the only long bow. They ate the last of their supplies in silence without the use of a cooking fire, which might have called attention to their presence. The moon was half full and the night cloudless, so that the thousands of stars in the limitless galaxy shone in dazzling white, lighting up the river and the land beyond in an eerie deep-green brightness. After their meal was completed, Shea turned to his brother.

'Have you thought about this trip, about this whole business of running away?' he queried. 'I mean, what are we really doing?'

111

'You're a funny one to ask that!' exclaimed the other shortly.

Shea smiled and nodded.

'I suppose I am. But I have to justify it all to myself and that's not an easy task. I can understand most of what Allanon told us, about the danger to the heirs of the Sword. But what good will it do for us to hide out in the Anar? This creature Brona must be after something besides the Sword of Shannara to go to all this trouble to search for the heirs of the Elven House. What is it he wants . . . what could it be . . .?'

Flick shrugged and tossed a pebble into the swift current of the lapping river, his own mind muddled, unable to offer any sensible answer.

'Maybe he wants to take over,' he suggested vaguely. 'Doesn't everyone who gets a little power, sooner or later?'

'No doubt,' agreed Shea uncertainly, thinking that this special form of greed had brought the races to where they were today, following the long, bitter wars that had nearly destroyed all life. But it had been years since the last war and the appearance of separate and disassociated communities seemed to have provided a partial answer to the long quest for peace. He turned back to a watchful Flick.

'What are we going to do once we get to where we're going?'

'Allanon will tell us,' his brother answered hesitantly.

'Allanon can't tell us what to do forever,' replied Shea quickly. 'Besides, I'm still not convinced that he has told us the truth about himself.'

Flick nodded his agreement, thinking back to that first chilling encounter with the dark giant who had tossed him about like a rag doll. His behavior had always struck Flick as that of a man who was used to having his way and having it when and how he chose. He shivered involuntarily, recalling his first near discovery by the shadowy Skull

Bearer, and found himself confronted with the fact that it was Allanon who had saved him.

'I'm not sure I want to know the truth about any of this. I'm not sure I would understand,' Flick murmured softly.

Shea was startled by the comment and turned back to the moonlit waters of the river.

'We may be only little people to Allanon,' he acknowledged, 'but from now on, I don't move without a reason!'

'Maybe so,' his brother's voice drifted up to him. 'But maybe . . .'

His voice trailed off ominously into the quiet sounds of the night and the river, and Shea chose not to pursue the matter. Both lay back and were quickly asleep, their tired thoughts flowing sluggishly into the bright, colorful dreams of the momentary world of sleep. In that secure, drifting dimension of fantasy, their weary minds could relax, releasing the hidden fears of tomorrow to emerge in whatever form they wished, and there, in that most distant sanctuary for the human soul, be faced privately and overcome. But even with the reassuring sounds of life all about them and the peaceful rushing of the gleaming Silver River to soothe their cares, an inescapable, gnawing specter of apprehension wormed its stealthy way into their dream world and there, in full view of the mind's eye, it perched and waited, smiling dully, hatefully – knowing well the limits of their endurance. Both sleepers tossed fitfully, unable to shake the presence of this frightening apparition entrenched deep within them, more thought than form.

Perhaps it was that same shadow of warning, radiating its special scent of fear, that locked simultaneously in the restless minds of the Valemen and caused both to waken in the same startled instant, the sleep gone from their eyes and the air filled with stark, chilling madness that gripped them tightly and began to squeeze. They recognized it instantly, and panic shone dully in their eyes as they sat motionless, listening to the soundless night. Moments

113

passed and nothing happened. Still they remained immobile, their senses straining for the sounds they knew must come. Then they heard the dreaded flapping of the great wings and together looked to the open river to see the hulking, silent form of the Skull Bearer swoop almost gracefully from out of the lowlands across the river to the north and settle into a long glide, bearing directly toward their place of concealment. The Valemen were frozen with terror, unable even to think, let alone move, as they watched the creature begin to close the distance between them. It did not matter that it had not yet seen them, perhaps did not even know that they were there. It would know in the next few seconds, and for the brothers there was no time to run, no place to hide, no chance to escape. Shea felt the dryness of his mouth and somewhere within his scattered thoughts remembered the Elfstones, but his mind had gone numb. He sat paralyzed with his brother and waited for the end.

Miraculously, it did not come. Just when it seemed that the servant of the Warlock Lord must surely find them, a flash of light from the other bank caught its attention. Swiftly, it winged away toward the light and then there was another a bit farther down and then another – or was it mistaken? It flew swiftly now, searching eagerly, its cunning mind telling it that the search was at an end, the long hunt over at last. Yet it could not find the source of the light. Suddenly the light flashed again, only to disappear in the swiftness of a blinking eye. The maddened creature swooped toward it, knowing it was deeper in the blackness across the river, lost somewhere in the thousands of small gullies and dales of the lowlands. The mysterious light flashed again and then again, each time moving farther inland, taunting, daring the angered beast to follow. On the other bank, the petrified figures of the two Valemen remained concealed in the darkness as their frightened eyes watched the flying shadow move ever more swiftly away from them until it could no longer be seen.

They remained immobile after the departure of the Skull Bearer. Once again they had come close to death and managed to elude its fatal touch. They sat quietly and listened as the mingled sounds of insect and animal returned to the night. Minutes passed and they began to breathe more easily, their stiff poses relaxing into more comfortable slumps as they looked at each other in amazed relief, knowing the creature had gone, but unable to comprehend how it had happened. Then, before they had any chance at all to speak of the matter, the mysterious light that had flashed from across the river reappeared suddenly on a rise several hundred yards in back of them, disappeared for an instant and then flashed again, closer than before. Shea and Flick watched in wonderment as it moved toward them, weaving slightly.

Moments later the figure of an old, old man stood before them, bent with age and clothed in woodsman's garb, his hair silver in the starlight, his face framed by a long, white beard neatly trimmed and combed. The strange light in his hand appeared fiercely bright at this close distance, and there was no hint of a flame in its center. Suddenly it disappeared and in its place was a cylindrical object gripped in the old man's gnarled hand. He looked at them and smiled a greeting. Shea looked quietly at his ancient face, sensing that the strange old man deserved his respect.

'The light,' Shea spoke finally, 'how . . .?'

'A toy of people long since dead and gone.' The voice rolled out in a steady whisper that drifted on the cool air. 'Gone like the evil creature out there . . .' The words trailed off and he pointed in the direction of the departed Skull Bearer with a thin, wrinkled arm that seemed to hang in the night like some brittle stick of dead wood. Shea looked doubtfully at him, unsure of what should be done next.

'We are traveling eastward . . .' Flick volunteered abruptly.

'To the Anar.' The gentle voice cut him short, the elderly head nodding in understanding, the wrinkled eyes sharp in the soft moonlight as they looked from one brother to the other. Suddenly he moved past them to the edge of the swift river and then turned back to them and motioned for them to sit. Shea and Flick did so without hesitation, unable to doubt the old man's intentions. As they sat they felt a great weariness steal over their bodies, their eyes suddenly unable to remain open.

'Sleep, young travelers, that your journey may be shortened.' The voice became stronger in their minds, more commanding. They could not resist the feeling of weariness, so pleasant and welcome, and they stretched out on the soft grassy bank in obedience. The figure before them began to change slowly into something new, and through vague, blurred eyes and half-closed eyelids, it appeared that the old man was growing younger and his clothes were not the same. Shea began to mutter slightly, trying to stay awake, to understand, but a moment later both Valemen were asleep.

As they slept they drifted cloudlike through forgotten days of sunlight and happiness in the peaceful woodland home they had left so many days ago. Once again they roamed the friendly confines of the Duln Forest and swam in the cool waters of the mighty Rappahalladran River, the fears and cares of a lifetime swept away in an instant. They moved through the wooded hills and vales of the countryside with freedom unlike anything they had ever experienced. In their sleep they touched, as if for the first time, each plant and animal, bird and insect with new understanding of its importance as a living thing, however small and insignificant. They floated and drifted like the wind, able to smell the freshness of the land, able to see the beauty of the life nature had placed there. Everything was a kaleidoscope of color and smell, with only gentle sounds reaching their tired minds – sounds of the open air and the quiet countryside. Forgotten were the long, hard days of travel through the mist-covered Lowlands of Clete, the sunless days where life was a lost soul wandering hopelessly in a dying land. Forgotten was the darkness of the Black Oaks, the madness of the endless, giant trees hiding them from the sun and sky. Gone was the memory of the Mist Wraith and the pursuing Skull Bearer, constant, relentless in its search. The young Valemen moved in a world without the fears and cares of the real world and for those hours, time dissipated into peace with the momentary beauty of a rainbow at the end of a sudden, violent storm.

They did not know how long it was that they were lost to the world of dreams nor did they know what it was that had happened to them in that time. They only knew, as they stirred into gentle wakefulness, that they were no longer at the edge of the Silver River. They knew as well that the time was new and somehow different; the feeling was exciting but very secure.

As his vision slowly returned, Shea was aware that there were people all around him, watching and waiting. He raised himself slowly up on one elbow, his hazy vision disclosing groups of small figures standing about, bending over in an anxious manner. From out of the vague background emerged a tall, commanding figure in loose-fitting clothes, leaning down to him, a broad hand on his slim shoulder.

'Flick?' he cried apprehensively, rubbing his sleep-filled eyes with one hand as he squinted to make out the features of the shrouded figure.

'You're safe now, Shea.' The deep voice seemed to roll out of the shadowy figure. 'This is the Anar.'

Shea blinked quickly, struggling to rise as the broad hand held him gently down. His eyes began to clear, and he saw in a glimpse the half-raised figure of his brother next to him, just waking from his deep slumber. Around them were the squat, heavyset figures of men Shea instantly knew to be Dwarfs. Shea's eyes caught the strong face of the figure at his side, and at the moment they came to rest on the gleaming chain mail encasing the hand and forearm stretched out to grasp his shoulder lightly, he knew the journey to the Anar was ended. They had found Culhaven and Balinor.

Menion Leah had not found the last leg of the journey to the Anar quite so simple. When he first realized he had become separated from the two Valemen, panic set in. He was not afraid for himself, but he feared the very worst for the Ohmsfords if left alone to find their way out of the mist-shrouded Black Oaks. He, too, had called hopelessly, futilely, stumbling blindly about in the blackness until his voice was cracked. But in the end he was forced to admit to himself that the search was useless under such conditions. Exhausted, he pushed on through the woods in what he believed to be the general direction of the lowlands, consoling himself slightly with the promise that he would find the others in the daylight. He was in the forest a longer time than he had anticipated, breaking free near dawn and collapsing at the edge of the grasslands. Though he did not know it then, he had emerged at a point south of the sleeping brothers. By this time his endurance had been pushed to the limit and sleep came over him so quickly that he could not remember anything after the slow, feather-light feeling of falling as he collapsed in the tall lowland grass. It seemed to him that he slept a very long time, but in fact he awakened only several hours after Shea and Flick had begun their journey toward the Silver River. Believing that he was a considerable distance south of the point the group had been making for while in the Black Oaks, Menion quickly chose to travel north and try to cut across the trail of his companions before reaching the river. If he failed to find them by that time, he knew he would be confronted with the unpleasant probability that they were still lost in the entanglement of the woods.

Hurriedly, the highlander strapped on his light pack, shouldered the great ash bow and the sword of Leah and began to march rapidly northward. The few hours of afternoon daylight remaining disappeared quickly as he walked, his sharp eyes searching carefully for any sign of human passage. It was almost dusk when he finally picked up the signs of someone traveling in the direction of the Silver River. He found the trail to be several hours old, and he could be reasonably certain that there was more than one person. But there was no way to tell who the travelers were, so Menion pushed on hurriedly in the half-light of dusk, hoping to catch them when they stopped for the night. He knew that the Skull Bearers would also be searching for them, but brushed his fears aside, remembering that there was no reason to connect him with the Valemen. In any event, it was a calculated risk he had to take if he expected to be of any service to his friends.

Shortly thereafter, just before the sun dropped behind the horizon completely, Menion caught sight of a figure to the east of him traveling in the opposite direction. Menion quickly called out to the other, who seemed startled by the highlander's sudden appearance and tried to move away from him. Menion quickly took up the chase, running after the frightened traveler and calling to him that he meant to harm. After several minutes he caught the man, who turned out to be a peddler selling cooking ware to outlying villages and families in these lowlands. The peddler, a bent, timid individual who had been frightened badly by the unexpected pursuit, was now thoroughly terrified by the sight of the tall, sword-bearing highlander facing him at nightfall in the middle of nowhere. Menion hastily explained that he meant no harm, but was looking for two friends from whom he had become separated while traveling through the Black Oaks. This proved to be the worst thing he could have told the little man, who was now thoroughly convinced the stranger was insane. Menion considered telling him that he was the Prince of Leah, but quickly discarded that idea. In the end, the peddler revealed to him that he had seen two travelers fitting the general description of the Valemen from a distance earlier in the afternoon. Menion could not tell if the man had told him that much for fear of his life or to humor him, but he accepted the tale and bade good evening to the little man, who was obviously delighted to be let off so easily, and made a hasty escape southward into the sheltering darkness of evening.

Menion was forced to admit to himself that it was now too dark to attempt to follow the trail of his friends, so he cast about for a likely campsite. He found a pair of large pines that appeared to be the best shelter available and he moved into them, glancing anxiously at the clear night sky. There was sufficient light to enable a prowling Northland creature to find any camped travelers with relative ease, and he inwardly prayed that his friends had sense enough to pick a carefully hidden spot to spend the night. He tossed down his own pack and weapons beneath one of the spreading pines and crawled under the shelter of its low-hanging branches. Famished from the past two days' journey, he devoured the last of his supplies, thinking as he did so that the Valemen would be faced with the same food shortage in the days ahead. Grumbling aloud at the bad luck that had separated them, he reluctantly wrapped himself in his light blanket and was quickly asleep, the great sword of Leah unsheathed at his side, gleaming dully in the moonlight.

Unaware of the events that had transpired that night while he slept soundly several miles south of the Silver River, Menion Leah rose the next day with a new plan in mind. If he could cut across country, traveling northeast, he could catch up with the Valemen much more easily. He was certain that they would be following the edge of the Silver River as it wound its way eastward into the Anar Forests, so their paths had to cross farther up river. Abandoning the faint traces of the trail left the previous day, Menion began to journey across the lowlands in an easterly direction, thinking to himself that if he did not come across some sign of them upriver when he reached the water's edge, he could double back downstream. He also entertained hopes of sighting some small game that would provide meat for the evening meal. He whistled and sang to himself as he walked, his lean face relaxed and cheerful at the prospect of a reunion with his lost comrades. He could even picture the stolid disbelief on old Flick's stern face at the sight of his return. He walked easily with long, loping strides that covered the ground quickly and evenly, the swinging, measured step of the experienced woodsman and hunter.

As he traveled, his thoughts drifted back to the events of the past several days, and he pondered the significance of all that had transpired. He knew little about the history of the Great Wars and the reign of the Druid Council, the mysterious appearance of the so-called Warlock Lord and his defeat by the combined might of three nations. Most disturbing of all was his almost total lack of knowledge of the legend behind the Sword of Shannara, the fabled weapon that for so many years had been a watchword symbolic of freedom through courage. Now it was the birthright of an unknown orphan, half man, half elf. The thought was so preposterous that he still found it impossible to conceive of Shea in that role. He knew instinctively that something was missing from the picture – something so basic to the whole puzzle of the great Sword that, without knowing what it was, the three friends were so many windblown leaves.

Menion also knew that he was not a part of this adventure for the sake of friendship alone. Flick had been right

121

about that. Even now he was unsure exactly why he had been persuaded to undertake this journey. He knew he was less than a Prince of Leah should be. He knew that his interest in people had not been deep enough, and he had never really wanted to know them. He had never tried to understand the important problems of governing justly in a society where the monarch's word was the only law. Yet he felt that in his own way he was as good as any man alive. Shea believed he was a man to be looked up to. Perhaps so, he thought idly, but his life to date appeared to consist of one long line of harrowing experiences and wild escapades that had served little or no constructive purpose.

The smooth, grass-covered lowlands changed to rough, barren ground, rising abruptly in small hills and dropping sharply into steep, trenchlike valleys that made travel slow and almost hazardous in places. Menion looked anxiously ahead for some indication of more level terrain, but it was impossible to see very far, even from the top of the steep rises. He plodded on, deliberately and steadily, ignoring the roughness of the ground and silently berating his decision to come that way. His mind wandered briefly, then suddenly snapped back as he caught the sound of a human voice. He listened intently for several seconds, but could hear nothing further and dismissed it as the wind or his imagination. A moment later he heard it again, only this time it was the clear sound of a woman's voice, singing softly somewhere ahead of him, faint and low. He walked more quickly, wondering if his ears were playing tricks on him, but all the time hearing the woman's mellow voice grow louder. Soon the mesmeric sound of her singing filled the air in a gay, almost wild abandon that reached into the innermost depths of the highlander's mind, bidding him to follow, to be as free as the song itself. Almost in a trance he walked steadily on, smiling broadly at the images the happy song conjured up to him. Vaguely, he wondered what a woman would be doing in these bleak lowlands, miles from any kind of civilization, but the song seemed to dispel all his doubts in its warm assurance that it came from the heart.

At the peak of a particularly bleak rise, somewhat higher than the surrounding hillocks, Menion found her sitting beneath a small twisted tree with long, gnarled branches that reminded him of willow roots. She was a young girl, very beautiful and obviously very much at home in these lands as she sang brightly, seemingly oblivious to anyone who might be attracted by the sound of her voice. He did not conceal his approach, but moved straight to her side, smiling gently at her freshness and youth. She smiled back at him, but made no effort to rise nor to greet him, continuing the gay strains of the tune she had been singing all this time. The Prince of Leah came to a halt several feet away from her, but she quickly beckoned him to come closer and sit next to her beneath the odd-shaped tree. It was then that from somewhere deep within him a small warning nerve twinged, some sixth sense not yet entranced by her vibrant song tugged at him and demanded to know why this young girl should ask a complete stranger to sit with her. There was no reason for his hesitation other than perhaps the innate distrust the hunter has for all things out of place and time in nature; but whatever the reason, it caused the highlander to pause. In that instant the girl and the song disappeared into vapor, leaving Menion to face the strange-looking tree on the barren rise.

For one second Menion hesitated, unable to believe what had just occurred, and then hastily moved to withdraw. But the loose ground about his feet opened even as he paused, releasing a heavy cluster of thick-gnarled roots which wound themselves tightly about the young man's ankles, holding him fast. Menion stumbled over backward trying to break free. For a moment he found his predicament to be ludicrous. But try as he might, he could not work free of those clinging roots. The strangeness of the situation increased almost immediately as he glanced up to see the strange root-limbed tree, previously immobile, approaching in a slow, stretching motion, its limbs extended toward him, their tips containing small but deadly-looking needles. Thoroughly aroused now, Menion dropped his pack and bow in one motion and unsheathed the great sword, realizing that the girl and the song had been an illusion to draw him within reach of this ominous tree. He cut briefly at the roots which bound him, severing them in places, but the work was slow because they were wound so tightly about his ankles that he could not risk broad strokes. Sudden panic set in as he realized he could not get free in time, but he forced the feeling down and shouted his defiance at the plant, which by now was almost on top of him. Swinging in fury as it came within reach, he quickly severed a number of the clutching limbs and it withdrew slightly, its whole frame shuddering in pain. Menion knew that with its next approach he had to strike its nerve center if he expected to destroy it. But the strange tree had other ideas; coiling its limbs into itself, it thrust them toward the imprisoned traveler one at a time, showering him with the tiny needles that flew off the ends. Many of them missed altogether and some bounced harmlessly off his heavy tunic and boots. But others struck the exposed skin of his hands and head and embedded themselves with small stinging sensations. Menion tried to brush them off, while protecting himself from further assault, but the little needles broke off, leaving their tips embedded in his skin. He felt a kind of slow drowsiness begin to steal over him and portions of his nervous system begin to go numb. He realized at once that the needles contained some sort of drug that was designed to put the plant's victim to sleep, to render it helpless for easy disposition. Wildly, he fought the feeling seeping through his system, but soon dropped helplessly to his knees, unable to fight it, knowing that the tree had won.

But amazingly, the deadly tree appeared to hesitate and then to inch slightly backward, coiling again in attack. Slow, heavy footsteps sounded behind the fallen prince, approaching cautiously. He could not turn his head to see who it was, and a deep bass voice warned him abruptly to remain motionless. The tree coiled expectantly to strike, but an instant before it released its deadly needles, it was struck with shattering impact by a huge mace that flew over the shoulder of the fallen Menion. The strange tree was completely toppled by the blow. Obviously injured, it struggled to raise itself and fight back. Behind him, Menion heard the sharp release of a bowstring and a long black arrow embedded itself deep within the plant's thick trunk. Immediately the roots about his feet released their grip and sank into the earth and the main portion of the tree shuddered violently, limbs thrashing the air and showering needles in all directions. A moment later, it drooped slowly to the earth. With a final spasm, it lay motionless.

Still heavily drugged from the needles, Menion felt the strong hands of his rescuer grip his shoulders roughly and force him into a prone position while a broad hunting knife severed the few remaining strands binding his feet. The figure before him was a powerfully built Dwarf, dressed in the green and brown woodsman's clothing worn by most of that race. He was tall for a Dwarf, a little over five feet, and carried a small arsenal of weapons bound about his broad waist. He looked down at the drugged Menion and shook his head dubiously.

'You must be a stranger to do a dumb thing like that,' he reprimanded the other in his deep bass voice. 'Nobody with any sense plays around with the Sirens.'

'I am from Leah . . . to the west,' Menion managed to gasp out, his voice thick and strange to his own ears.

'A highlander – I might have known.' The Dwarf laughed heartily to himself. 'You'd have to be, I suppose. Well, don't

125

worry, you'll be fine in a few days. That drug won't kill you if we get it treated, but you'll be out for a while.'

He laughed again and turned to retrieve his mace. Menion, with his final ounce of strength, grasped him by the tunic.

'I must reach . . . the Anar . . . Culhaven,' he gasped sharply. 'Take me to Balinor . . .'

The Dwarf looked back at him sharply, but Menion had lapsed into unconsciousness. Muttering to himself, the Dwarf picked up his own weapons and those of the fallen highlander. Then with surprising strength, he heaved the limp form of Menion over his broad shoulders, testing the load for balance. Satisfied at last that all was in place, he began trudging steadily, muttering all the while, moving toward the forests of the Anar.

8

Flick Ohmsford sat quietly on a long stone bench in one of the upper levels of the lavishly beautiful Meade Gardens in the Dwarf community known as Culhaven. He had a perfect view of the amazing gardens stretching down the rocky hillside in systematic levels that tapered off about the edges in carefully laid pieces of cut stone, reminiscent of a long waterfall flowing down a gentle slope. The creation of the gardens on this once barren hillside was a truly marvelous accomplishment. Special soils had been hauled from more fertile regions to be placed on the garden site, enabling thousands of beautiful flowers and plants to flourish year round in the mild climate of the lower Anar. The color was indescribable. To compare the myriad hues of the flowers to the colors of the rainbow would have been a great injustice. Flick attempted briefly to count the various shades, a task he soon found to be impossible. He gave up quickly and turned his attention to the large clearing at the foot of the gardens where members of the Dwarf community were passing on their way to or from whatever work they were engaged in. They were a curious people, it seemed to Flick, so dedicated to hard work and a well-guarded order of life. Everything they did was always carefully planned in advance, meticulously thought out to a point where even the cautious Flick was nettled by the time spent in preparation. But the people were friendly and eager to be of service, a kindness not lost on either of the visiting Valemen, who felt more than a bit out of place in this strange land.

They had been in Culhaven for two days now, and still they had not been able to learn what had happened to them, why they were there, or how long their stay would be. Balinor had told them nothing, advising them that he knew very little himself and that all would be revealed in due time, a comment Flick found to be not only melodramatic but aggravating. There was no sign of Allanon, no word of his whereabouts. Worst of all, there was no news of the absent Menion, and the brothers had been forbidden to leave the safety of the Dwarf village for any reason. Flick glanced to the floor of the gardens again to see if his personal bodyguard was still there, and quickly spied him off to one side, his tireless gaze fixed on the Valeman. Shea had been infuriated by this treatment, but Balinor was quick to point out that someone should be with them at all times in case of an attempt on their lives by one of the roving Northland creatures. Flick had acquiesced readily, remembering all too well the close calls he had already had with the Skull Bearers. He put aside his idle thoughts at the approach of Shea on the winding garden path.

'Anything?' Flick asked anxiously as the other reached his side and sat down quietly next to him.

'Not one word,' came the short reply.

Shea felt vaguely exhausted all over again, even though he had had two days to recover from the strange odyssey that had brought them from their home in Shady Vale to the Forests of Anar. Their treatment had been decent if sometimes a bit overdone, and the people seemed genuinely concerned for their welfare. But there had been no word given out as to what was to happen next. Everyone, including Balinor, seemed to be waiting for something, perhaps the arrival of the long-absent Allanon. Balinor had been unable to explain to them how they had reached the Anar. Responding to a mysterious flashing light, he had found them lying on a low riverbank just outside of Culhaven two days ago, and had brought them to the village. He knew nothing of the old man nor of how they had traveled that long distance upstream. When Shea mentioned the legends concerning a King of the Silver River, Balinor shrugged and nonchalantly agreed that anything was possible.

'No news of Menion . . .?' Flick asked hesitantly.

'Only that the Dwarfs are still out looking for him, and it may take some time,' Shea answered quietly. 'I don't know what to do next.'

Flick inwardly conceded that this last admission had proved to be the story of the entire outing. He glanced downward to the foot of the Meade Gardens where a small cluster of heavily armed Dwarfs were congregating around the commanding figure of Balinor, who had suddenly appeared from the woods beyond. Even from their vantage point atop the gardens, the Valemen could tell that he still wore the chain mail beneath the long hunting cloak they had come to recognize so well. He spoke earnestly with the Dwarfs for a few minutes, his face lined in thought. Shea and Flick knew very little about the Prince of Callahorn, but the people of Culhaven seemed to have the highest regard for him. Menion, too, had spoken well of Balinor. His homeland was the northernmost kingdom of the sprawling Southland. Commonly referred to as the borderlands, it served as a buffer zone fronting the southern boundaries of the Northland. The citizens of Callahorn were predominantly Men, but unlike the majority of the people of their race, they mingled freely with the other races and did not pursue a policy of isolationism. The highly regarded Border Legion was quartered in that distant country, a professional army commanded by Ruhl

Buckhannah, King of Callahorn and the father of Balinor. Historically, the entire Southland had relied on Callahorn and the Legion to blunt the initial thrust of an invading army, giving the rest of the land a chance to prepare for battle. In the five hundred years since its formation, the Border Legion had never been defeated.

Balinor had begun a slow ascent to the stone bench where the Valemen sat patiently waiting. He smiled a greeting as he came up to them, aware of the discomfort they felt in not knowing what was to happen to them and of the anxiety they were experiencing for the safety of their missing friend. He sat down next to them and was silent for a few minutes before speaking.

'I know how difficult this must be for you,' he began patiently. 'I have every available Dwarf warrior out looking for your lost friend. If anyone can find him in this region, they will – and they won't give up, I promise you.'

The brothers nodded their understanding of Balinor's efforts to help them in any way possible.

'This is a very dangerous time for these people, though I suppose Allanon did not speak of it. They are facing the threat of an invasion through the upper Anar by Gnomes. There have already been skirmishes all along the border and signs of a huge army massing somewhere above the Streleheim Plains. You may have guessed that all of this is tied in with the Warlock Lord.'

'Does this mean that the Southland is in danger, too?' asked an anxious Flick.

'Undoubtedly.' Balinor nodded. 'That's one reason why I'm here – to arrange a coordinated defensive strategy with the Dwarf nation in case of an all-out assault.'

'But where is Allanon then?' asked Shea quickly. 'Is he going to get here soon enough to help us? What has the Sword of Shannara got to do with all this?'

Balinor looked at the puzzled faces and shook his head slowly.

'I must honestly confess that I cannot give you the answers to any of those questions. Allanon is a very mysterious figure, but a wise man who has been a dependable ally whenever we have needed him in the past. When I saw him last, several weeks before I spoke to you in Shady Vale, we set a date to meet in the Anar. He is already three days overdue.'

He paused in quiet speculation, looking down at the gardens and beyond to the great trees of the Anar Forests, listening to the sounds of the woods and the low voices of the Dwarfs moving about in the clearing below. Then abruptly a shout went up from a cluster of Dwarfs at the foot of the gardens, joined almost immediately by the shouts and cries of others mingled in with a huge clamor swelling from the woods beyond the village of Culhaven. The men on the stone bench rose uncertainly, looking quickly about for some sign of danger. Balinor's strong hand came to rest on the pommel of his broadsword, strapped tightly at his side beneath the hunting cloak. A moment later one of the Dwarfs below came rushing up the path, shouting wildly as he ran.

'They found him, they found him!' he yelled excitedly, almost stumbling in his haste to reach them.

Shea and Flick exchanged startled looks. The runner came to a breathless stop before them, and Balinor gripped his shoulder excitedly.

'Have they found Menion Leah?' he demanded quickly.

The Dwarf nodded happily, his short, stocky frame heaving with the exertion of the dash to reach them with the good news. Without a word, Balinor bounded down the path toward the shouting, Shea and Flick behind him. They reached the clearing below in a matter of seconds and ran along the main path through the woods leading to the village of Culhaven several hundred yards beyond. Ahead of them they could hear the excited shouting of the Dwarf population congratulating whomever it was who had found the lost highlander. They reached the village and, pushing through the throngs of Dwarfs blocking the way, made straight for the center of all the excitement. A ring of guards parted to let them into a small courtyard formed by buildings on the right and left and a high stone wall in the rear. On a long wooden table lay the motionless body of Menion Leah, his face pale and seemingly lifeless. A team of Dwarf doctors bent dutifully over the inert form, apparently treating him for some injury. Shea gave a sharp cry and tried to rush forward, but Balinor's strong arm held him back as the warrior called out to one of the nearby Dwarfs.

'Pahn, what's happened here?'

The solid-looking Dwarf, dressed in armor and apparently one of the returning search party, hastened to their side.

'He'll be all right after he's treated. He was found entangled in one of the Sirens out in the middle of the Battlemound lowlands below the Silver River. Our search party didn't find him. It was Hendel, returning from the cities south of Anar.'

Balinor nodded and looked about for some sign of the rescuer.

'He left for the assembly hall to make his report,' the Dwarf responded to the unasked question.

Motioning the two Valemen to follow him, Balinor made his way out of the courtyard through the crowd and across the main street to the large assembly hall. Inside were the offices of the governing officials of the village and the assembly room, in which they found the Dwarf Hendel sitting on one of the long benches, eating ravenously while a scribe took down his report. Hendel looked up as they approached, glanced curiously at the Valemen and nodded briefly to Balinor, continuing to devour his meal without interruption. Balinor dismissed the scribe, and the three men sat down across from the disinterested Dwarf, who appeared both exhausted and starved.

'What an idiot, tackling one of those Sirens with a sword,' he muttered. 'Got spunk though. How is he?'

'He'll be fine after he's treated,' replied Balinor grinning reassuringly at the uneasy Valemen. 'How did you find him?'

'Heard him yelling.' The other continued to eat without pausing. 'I had to carry him almost seven miles before I ran into Pahn and the search party along the Silver River.'

He paused and looked again at the two Valemen, who were listening intently. The Dwarf appraised them curiously and looked back at Balinor, eyebrows raised.

'Friends of the highlander – and of Allanon,' responded the borderman, cocking his head meaningfully. Hendel merely nodded to them curtly.

'I'd never have known who he was if he hadn't mentioned your name,' Hendel informed them shortly, indicating the tall borderman. 'It might help matters if now and then someone would tell me what was going on – before it's happened, not after.'

He declined to comment further, and an amused Balinor smiled over to the puzzled brothers, shrugging slightly to indicate the Dwarf was irascible by nature. Shea and Flick were a bit uncertain about the fellow's temperament and had purposely kept silent while the other two conversed, though both Valemen were eager to hear the full story behind Menion's rescue.

'What's your report on Sterne and Wayford?' Balinor asked finally, referring to the large Southland cities immediately south and west of the Anar.

Hendel ceased eating and laughed abruptly.

'The officials of those two fine communities will consider the matter and send along a report. Typical bungling officials, elected by the disinterested people to juggle the ball until it can be passed on to some other fool. I could tell five minutes after I opened my mouth that they thought I was crazy. They don't see the danger until the sword is at their own throats – then they scream for assistance from those of us who knew it all along.' He paused and resumed his meal, obviously disgusted with the whole subject.

'I should have expected that, I suppose.' Balinor sounded worried. 'How can we convince them of the danger? There hasn't been a war in so many years that no one wants to believe it could happen now.'

'That's not the real problem, as you well know,' interjected the irate Hendel. 'They simply don't feel they should be involved in the matter. After all, the frontiers are protected by Dwarfs, not to mention the cities of Callahorn and the Border Legion. We've been doing it up to now – why can't we keep doing it? Those poor fools . . .'

He trailed off slowly, finished with his statement and his meal, feeling tired from the long trip home. He had been on the road for almost three weeks, traveling to the cities of the Southland, and it all seemed to have been for nothing. He felt keenly discouraged.

'I don't understand what's happened,' Shea announced quietly.

'Well, that's two of us,' Hendel replied sullenly. 'I'm going to bed for about two weeks. See you then.'

He stood up abruptly and walked out of the assembly room without even a short farewell, his broad shoulders stooped wearily. The three men watched him go without speaking, their eyes fixed on his departing silhouette until it was lost from sight. Then Shea turned questioningly to Balinor.

'It's the age-old tale of complacency, Shea.' The tall warrior sighed deeply and stretched as he rose. 'We may be standing on the brink of the greatest war in a thousand years, but no one wants to accept the fact. Everyone gets in the same rut – let a few take care of the gates to the city while the rest forget and go back to their homes. It becomes a habit – depending on a few to protect the rest. And then one day . . . the few are not enough, and the enemy is within the city – right through the open gates . . .'

'Is there really going to be a war?' Flick asked, almost fearfully.

'That is the question exactly,' Balinor responded slowly. 'The only man who can give us the answer is absent . . . and overdue.'

In the excitement of finding Menion alive and well, the Valemen had temporarily forgotten Allanon, the man who was the reason for their being in the Anar in the first place. The by-now familiar questions again flashed through their minds with new persistency, but the Valemen had learned to live with them over the past few weeks and all doubts were reluctantly shoved aside once more. Balinor caught their attention as he moved toward the open door, and they quickly followed.

'You mustn't mind Hendel, you know,' he reassured them as they walked. 'He's gruff like that with everyone, but he's one of the finest friends you could ask for. He has fought and outwitted the Gnomes along the upper Anar for years, protecting his people and the complacent citizens of the Southland who so quickly forget the crucial role the Dwarfs play as guardians of these borders. The Gnomes would like to get their hands on him, I can tell you.'

Shea and Flick said nothing, ashamed of the fact that the people of their own race could be so selfish, yet realizing that they, too, had been ignorant of the situation in the Anar before hearing of it from Balinor. They were bothered by the thought of renewed hostilities between the races, recalling their history lessons on the old race wars and the terrible hatred of those bitter years. The possibility of a third war of the races was chilling.

'Why don't you two go on back to the gardens,' advised the Prince of Callahorn. 'I'll have a message sent as soon as I hear of any change in Menion's condition.'

135

The brothers reluctantly agreed, knowing they had no other choice in the matter anyway. Before turning in that night, they stopped by the room where Menion was being kept, only to be told by the Dwarf sentry that their friend was asleep and should not be disturbed.

But by the following afternoon, the highlander was awake and being visited by the anxious Valemen. Even Flick was grudgingly relieved to see the other alive and well, though he solemnly intoned that he had correctly predicted their misfortune many days in advance when they first decided to journey through the Black Oaks. Menion and Shea both laughed at Flick's eternal pessimism, but did not argue the point. Shea explained how Menion had been brought to Culhaven by the Dwarf Hendel, and then went on to relate the mysterious way in which he and Flick had been found near the Silver River. Menion was as mystified as they over their strange journey and could offer no logical explanation. Shea carefully refrained from mentioning the legend of a King of the Silver River, knowing full well what the highlander's response would be to any speculation that involved an old folktale.

That same day, in the early hours of the evening, word reached them that Allanon had returned. Shea and Flick were about to leave their rooms to visit Menion when they heard the excited shouts of Dwarfs rushing past their open windows toward the assembly hall where some sort of meeting was about to begin. The anxious Valemen had not taken two steps beyond their doorway when they were surrounded by a team of four Dwarf guards and hustled quickly through the pushing crowds, past the open doors of the large assembly into a small adjoining room, where they were told to remain. The Dwarfs closed the door wordlessly as they exited, slid the lock bolts into place, and assumed positions immediately outside. The room was brightly lit and furnished with several long tables and benches, at which the bewildered Valemen silently seated themselves. The windows to the room were closed and even without checking, Shea knew they would be barred like the door. From the assembly hall they could hear the deep voice of a single speaker.

Several minutes later the door to the chamber opened and Menion, looking flushed but otherwise quite well, was briskly ushered in by two Dwarf guards. When they were left alone, the highlander explained that they had come for him the same as for the Valemen. From snatches of conversation he had heard on the way over, it appeared that the Dwarfs in Culhaven and probably all of the Anar were preparing for war. Whatever news Allanon had brought back with him had thrown matters into a state of confusion in the Dwarf community. He thought he had caught a quick glimpse of Balinor through the open doors of the assembly hall, standing on the platform at the front of the building, but the guards had rushed him past and he couldn't be sure.

The voices from the congregation next door rose in a thunderous roar, and all three paused expectantly. Seconds passed as the shouting continued to roll through the large hall, spreading to the open grounds outside where it was taken up by the Dwarfs there. At the deafening peak of the shouting, the door to their room suddenly burst open to admit the dark, commanding figure of Allanon.

He walked over to the Valemen quickly, shook their hands, and congratulated them on their successful journey to Culhaven. He was dressed as he had been when Flick had first encountered him, his lean face half hidden in the long cowl, his whole appearance dark and foreboding. He greeted Menion courteously and moved to the head of the nearest table, motioning the others to be seated. He had been followed into the room by Balinor and a number of Dwarfs who were apparently leaders in the community, among them the irascible Hendel. Bringing up the rear of this procession were two slim, almost shadowy figures in curious, loose-fitting woodsman garb, who quietly

137

took seats near Allanon at the head of the table. Shea could see them clearly from his position at the other end, and concluded after a quick observation that they were Elves from the distant Westland. Their keen features, from the sharply raised eyebrows to the strange pointed ears, marked them distinctively. Shea turned back and saw that both Flick and Menion were looking at him curiously, obviously appraising his own strong resemblance to the strangers. None of them had ever seen an Elf, and while they knew that Shea was half Elf and had heard descriptions given of the Elven people, none had ever had a chance to compare the Valeman to one.

'My friends.' The deep voice of Allanon boomed out in the slight stir of voices as he rose commandingly to his full height of seven feet. The room was instantly silent as all faces turned in his direction. 'My friends, I must now tell you what I have as yet told no one else. We have suffered a tragic loss.'

He paused and looked at the anxious faces in turn.

'Paranor has fallen. A division of Gnome hunters under the command of the Warlock Lord has seized the Sword of Shannara!'

There was dead silence for about two seconds before the Dwarfs were on their feet, shouting in anger. Balinor rose quickly in an effort to quiet them. Shea and Flick looked at each other in disbelief. Only Menion seemed unsurprised by the announcement, his lean face carefully scrutinizing the dark figure at the head of the table.

'Paranor was taken from within,' Allanon continued after some semblance of order had been restored. 'There is little question as to the fate of those who guarded the fortress and the Sword. I am told that all were executed. No one knows exactly how it happened.'

'Have you been there?' Shea asked suddenly, feeling almost immediately that it was a stupid question.

'I left your home in the Vale so suddenly because I

received word that an attempt would be made to secure Paranor. I arrived too late to help those within and barely escaped detection myself. That is one of the reasons I am so late in reaching Culhaven.'

'But if Paranor has fallen and the Sword been taken . . .?' Flick's whispered question trailed off ominously.

'Then what can we do now?' Allanon finished harshly. 'This is the problem facing us, the one we must provide an immediate answer for – the reason for this council.'

Allanon suddenly left his position at the head of the long table and moved around until he was standing directly behind Shea. He placed one great hand on the slim shoulder and faced his attentive audience.

'The Sword of Shannara is useless in the hands of the Warlock Lord. It can only be raised by a son of the House of Jerle Shannara – this alone prevents the evil one from striking now. Instead, he has systematically hunted down and destroyed all members of that House, one at a time, one after another, even those I tried to protect – all whom I could find. Now they are all dead – all save one, and that one is young Shea. Shea is only half Elf, but he is a direct descendant of the King who carried the great Sword so many years before. Now he must raise it once again.'

Shea would have bolted for the door if it had not been for the strong hand gripping his shoulder. He looked desperately at Flick and saw the fear in his own eyes mirrored in those of his brother's. Menion had not moved, but appeared visibly impressed by this grim declaration. What Allanon seemed to expect from Shea was more than any man had the right to ask.

'Well, I think we have shaken our young friend a bit.' Allanon laughed shortly. 'Do not despair, Shea. Things are not as bad as they may seem to you right now.' He turned abruptly, walked back to the head of the table and faced the others.

'We must recover the Sword at all costs. There is no

other choice left to us. If we fail to do this, the whole of the land will be plunged into the greatest war the races have seen since the near destruction of life two thousand years ago. The Sword is the key. Without it, we must fall back on our mortal strength, our fighting prowess – a battle with iron and muscle that can only result in uncountable thousands dying on both sides. The evil is the Warlock Lord, and he cannot be destroyed without the aid of the Sword – and the courage of a few men, not the least of whom must be those of us in this room.'

Again he paused to measure the force of his words. There was absolute silence as he looked doubtfully at the silent gallery of grim faces staring back. Suddenly Menion Leah rose at the far end of the table and faced the giant speaker.

'What you are suggesting is that we go after the Sword – to Paranor.'

Allanon nodded slowly, a half smile playing over his thin lips as he waited for a reaction from the startled listeners. His deep-set eyes twinkled blackly beneath the great brow, watching carefully the faces about him. Menion sat down slowly, total disbelief showing plainly on his handsome features, as Allanon continued.

'The Sword is still at Paranor; there is an excellent possibility that it will remain there. Neither Brona nor the Bearers of the Skull can personally remove the talisman – its mere physical presence is an anathema to their continued existence in the mortal world. Any form of exposure for more than several minutes would cause excruciating pain. This means that any attempt to transport the Sword north to the Skull Kingdom must be accomplished by use of the Gnomes that hold Paranor.

'Eventine and his Elven warriors were given the task of securing the Druid stronghold and the Sword. While Paranor has been lost to us, the Elves still hold the southern stretch of the Streleheim north of the fortress, and any attempt to travel north to the Dark Lord would require breaking through their patrols. Apparently Eventine was not at Paranor when it was taken, and I have no reason to believe that he will not endeavor to regain the Sword or, at the very least, thwart any attempt to remove it. The Warlock Lord will be aware of this, and I do not think he will risk losing the weapon by having the Gnomes carry it out. Instead, he will entrench at Paranor until his army moves south.

'There is a possibility that the Warlock Lord does not expect us to attempt to regain the Sword. He may believe that the House of Shannara has been exterminated. He may expect us to concentrate on strengthening our defenses against his forthcoming assault. If we act immediately, a small party may be able to slip into the Keep undetected and retrieve the Sword. Such an undertaking would be dangerous, but if there is even the remotest chance of success, the risk is worth it.'

Balinor had risen and indicated he wished to speak to those assembled. Allanon nodded and sat down.

'I do not understand the power of the Sword over the Warlock Lord – that much I freely admit,' the tall warrior began. 'But I do know the threat that we all face if Brona's army invades the Southland and the Anar as our reports indicate it is preparing to do. My homeland will be the first to face this threat, and if I can prevent it in any way, then I cannot do otherwise. I will go with Allanon.'

The Dwarfs leaped up again at this point and enthusiastically shouted their support. Allanon stood up and raised his long arm in a plea for silence.

'These two young Elves at my side are cousins of Eventine. They will accompany me, for their stake in this matter is at least as great as your own. Balinor will go as well, and I will take one of the Dwarf chieftains – no more. This must be a small, highly skilled party of hunters if we are to succeed. Pick the best man among you and let him come with us.'

He looked to the end of the table, where Shea and Flick sat watching in a mixed state of shock and confusion. Menion Leah pondered quietly, looking at no one in particular. Allanon glanced expectantly at Shea, his grim face suddenly softening as he saw the frightened eyes of the young Valeman who had come so far, through so many dangers to this apparent haven of safety, only to be told that he was expected to leave it for an even more perilous trip northward. But there had been no time to break the news to the Valeman in a gentle way. He shook his head doubtfully and waited.

'I think I had better go.' The abrupt declaration came from Menion, who had again risen to his feet to face the others. 'I came with Shea this far to be certain he reached the safety of Culhaven, which he has done. My duty to him is finished, but I owe it to my homeland and to my people to protect them in any way I can.'

'What can you offer then?' asked Allanon abruptly, astonished that the highlander would volunteer without first speaking to his friends. Shea and Flick were clearly dumbfounded by this unexpected announcement.

'I'm the best bowman in the Southland,' Menion answered smoothly. 'Probably the best tracker as well.'

Allanon seemed to hesitate for a moment, then looked to Balinor, who quietly shrugged. For a brief moment Menion and Allanon locked gazes, as if to judge each other's intentions. Menion smiled coldly at the grim historian.

'Why should I answer to you?' he queried shortly.

The dark figure at the other end of the table stared at him almost curiously and a deathly silence settled over the company. Even Balinor stepped back one short pace in shock. Shea knew instantly that Menion was asking for trouble and that everyone at the table except the three companions knew something about the foreboding Allanon they did not. The frightened Valeman shot a quick look at Flick, whose flushed face had gone pale at the thought of a confrontation between the two men. Desperate to avoid any trouble, Shea stood up suddenly and cleared his throat. Everyone looked in his direction, and his mind went blank.

'You have something to say?' demanded Allanon blackly. Shea nodded and his mind raced desperately, knowing what was expected. He looked again to Flick, who managed a barely perceptible nod indicating that he would go along with whatever his brother decided. Shea cleared his throat a second time.

'My special skill appears to be that I was born in the wrong family, but I had better see this matter through. Flick and I – Menion, too – will go to Paranor.'

Allanon nodded his approval and even managed a slight smile, inwardly pleased with the young Valeman. Shea, more than any of the others, had to be strong. He was the last son of the house of Shannara, and the fate of so many would depend on that single, small chance of birth.

At the other end of the table, Menion Leah relaxed quietly in his seat, a barely audible sigh of relief escaping his lips as he silently congratulated himself. He had deliberately provoked Allanon, and in so doing had forced Shea to come to his rescue by agreeing to go to Paranor. It had been a desperate gamble to induce the little Valeman to make up his mind that he was going with them. The highlander had come close to what might have been a fatal confrontation with Allanon. He had been lucky. He wondered if luck would smile on all of them during the journey ahead.

CHAPTER

9

S hea stood quietly in the darkness outside the assembly hall and let the night air wash over his hot face in cool waves. Flick was immediately to his right, the broad face grim in the shadowed moonlight. Menion leaned idly against a tall oak some yards off to their left. The meeting had concluded, and Allanon had asked them to wait for him. The tall wanderer was still inside making preparations with the Dwarf elders to counter the expected invasion from the upper Anar. Balinor was with them, coordinating the defense of the famed Border Legion in distant Callahorn with that of the Dwarf army of the Eastland. Shea was relieved to be out of the stuffy little room – out in the open night where he could consider more clearly his hasty decision to go with the company to Paranor. He knew – and he guessed Flick must have known as well – that they could not expect to stay out of the inevitable conflict centering around the Sword of Shannara. They could have stayed in Culhaven, living almost like prisoners, hoping that the Dwarf people would protect them from the searching Skull Bearers. They could have stayed in this strange land, apart from all who knew them, perhaps forgotten in time by everyone except the Dwarfs. But to alienate themselves that way would have been worse than any imaginable fate at the hands of the enemy. For the first time Shea realized that he must accept the fact finally and forever, that he was no longer merely the adopted son of Curzad Ohmsford. He was a son of the Elven House of Shannara, the son of kings and the heir to the fabled Sword, and though he would have wished it otherwise, he must accept what chance had decreed for him.

He looked quietly at his brother, who stood lost in thought, staring at the darkened earth, and he felt a keen pang of sorrow at the remembrance of the other's loyalty. Flick was courageous and loved him, but he had not bargained for this unexpected turn of events that would take them into the heart of the enemy's country. Shea did not want Flick to be involved in this matter – it was not his responsibility. He knew that the stocky Valeman would never desert him so long as he felt he could help, but perhaps now Flick could be persuaded to remain behind, even to return to Shady Vale to explain to their father what had befallen them. But even as he toyed with the idea, he discarded it, knowing that Flick would never turn back. Whatever else happened, he would see this matter through.

'There was a time,' Flick's quiet voice broke into his thoughts, 'when I would have sworn that I would live out my life in uneventful solitude in Shady Vale. Now it appears that I will be a part of an effort to save mankind.'

'Do you think I should have chosen otherwise?' Shea asked after a moment's silent thought.

'No, I don't think so.' Flick shook his head. 'But remember what we talked about on the trip here – about things being beyond our control, even our understanding? You see how little control we now have over what's to become of us.'

He paused and looked squarely over to his brother. 'I think you made the right choice, and whatever happens, I'll be with you.'

Shea smiled broadly and placed a hand on the other's shoulder, thinking to himself that this was exactly what he had predicted Flick would say. It was a small gesture perhaps, but one that meant more to him than any other could have. He was aware of the sudden approach of Menion from the other side and turned to face the highlander.

'I suppose you think me some sort of fool after what happened in there tonight,' Menion stated abruptly. 'But this fool stands along with old Flick. Whatever happens, we'll face it together, be it mortal or spirit.'

'You caused that scene in there to get Shea to agree to go, didn't you?' an irate Flick demanded. 'That's the lowest trick I have never witnessed!'

'Never mind, Flick,' Shea cut him short. 'Menion knew what he was doing, and he did the right thing. I would have decided to go anyway – at least I'd like to believe I would. Now we've got to forget the past, forget our differences, and stand together for our own preservation.'

'As long as I stand where I can see him,' retorted his brother bitterly.

The door to the conference room opened suddenly and the broad figure of Balinor was silhouetted in the torchlight from within. He surveyed the three men standing just beyond him in the darkness, then closed the door and walked over to them, smiling slightly as he approached.

'I'm glad you decided to come with us, all of you,' he stated simply. 'I must add, Shea, that without you, the trip would have been pointless. Without the heir of Jerle Shannara, the Sword is only so much metal.'

'What can you tell us about this magic weapon?' Menion asked quickly.

'I'll leave that to Allanon,' replied Balinor. 'He plans to speak with you here in just a few minutes.'

Menion nodded, inwardly disturbed at the prospect of encountering the tall man again that evening, but curious to hear more about the power of the Sword. Shea and Flick exchanged quick glances. At last they would learn the full story behind what was happening in the Northland.

'Why are you here, Balinor?' Flick asked cautiously, not wishing to pry into the borderman's personal affairs.

'It's a rather long story – you would not be interested,' replied the other almost sharply, immediately causing Flick to believe he had overstepped his bounds. Balinor saw his chagrined look, and smiled reassuringly. 'My family and I have not been on very good terms lately. My younger brother and I had a . . . disagreement, and I wanted to leave the city for a while. Allanon asked me to accompany him to the Anar. Hendel and others were old friends, so I agreed.'

'Sounds like a familiar tale,' commented Menion dryly. 'I've had some problems like that myself from time to time.'

Balinor nodded and managed a half smile, but Shea could tell from his eyes that he did not consider this a laughing matter. Whatever had caused him to leave Callahorn was more serious than anything Menion had ever encountered in Leah. Shea quickly changed the subject.

'What can you tell us about Allanon? We seem to be placing an unusual amount of trust in him, and we still know absolutely nothing about the man. Who is he?'

Balinor arched his eyebrows and smiled, amused by the question and at the same time uncertain as to how it should be answered. He walked away from them a little, thinking to himself, and then turned back abruptly and motioned vaguely toward the assembly hall.

'I really don't know much about Allanon myself,' he admitted frankly. 'He travels a great deal, exploring the country, recording in his notes the changes and growth of the land and its people. He's well known in all the nations – I think he has been everywhere. The extent of his knowledge of this world is extraordinary – most of it isn't in any book. He is very remarkable . . .'

'But who is he?' Shea persisted eagerly, feeling that he must learn the true origin of the historian.

'I can't say for certain, because he has never confided

completely even in me, and I am almost like a son to him,' Balinor stated very quietly, so softly in fact that they all moved a bit closer to be certain they missed nothing of what was to follow. 'The elders of the Dwarfs and of my own kingdom say that he is the greatest of the Druids, that almost forgotten Council that governed men over a thousand years ago. They say that he is a direct descendant of the Druid Bremen – perhaps even of Galaphile himself. I think there is more than a little truth in that statement, because he went to Paranor often and stayed for long periods, recording his findings in the great record books stored there.'

He paused for a moment and his three listeners glanced at each other, wondering if the grim historian could actually be a direct descendant of the Druids, thinking in awe of the centuries of history behind the man. Shea had suspected before that Allanon was one of the ancient philosopher-teachers known as Druids, and it seemed apparent that the man possessed a greater knowledge of the races and the origins of the threat facing them than did anyone else. He turned back to Balinor, who was speaking again.

'I can't explain it, but I don't believe we could be in better company for any peril, even were we to come face to face with the Warlock Lord himself. Though I haven't one shred of concrete evidence nor even an example to cite you, I'm certain that Allanon's power is beyond anything we have ever seen. He would be a very, very dangerous enemy.'

'Of that, I haven't the slightest doubt,' Flick muttered dryly.

Only minutes later, the door of the conference room opened and Allanon stepped quietly into view. In the half-light of the moon, he was huge and forbidding, almost a replica of the dreaded Skull Bearers they feared so much, the dark cape billowing slightly as he moved toward them, his lean face hidden in the depths of the long cowl about his head. They were silent as he approached, wondering what he would tell them, what it would mean for them in the days ahead. Perhaps he knew their thoughts instinctively as he walked up to them, but their eyes could not pierce the mask of inscrutability that cloaked his grim features and sheltered the man buried within. They could only see the sudden glint of his eyes as he stopped before them and looked slowly from one face to the next. A deep silence settled ominously over the little group.

'The time has come for you to learn the full story behind the Sword of Shannara, to learn the history of the races as only I know it to be.' His voice reached out and drew them commandingly to him. 'It is essential that Shea should understand, and since the rest of you share the risks involved, you should also know the truth. What you will learn tonight must be kept in confidence until I tell you it no longer matters. This will be hard, but you must do it.'

He motioned for them to follow him and moved away from the clearing, drawing them deeper into the darkness of the trees beyond. When they were several hundred feet into the forest, he turned into a small, almost hidden clearing. He seated himself on the worn stub of an ancient trunk and motioned the others to find a place. They did so quickly and waited in silence as the famous historian gathered his thoughts and prepared to speak.

'A very long time ago,' he began finally, still considering his explanation as he spoke, 'before the Great Wars, before the existence of the races as we know them today, the land was – or was thought to be – populated only by Man. Civilization had developed even before then for many thousands of years – years of hard toil and learning that brought Man to a point where he was on the verge of mastering the secrets of life itself. It was a fabulous, exciting time to live in, so expansive that much of it would be totally beyond your comprehension were I empowered to draw you the most perfect picture. But while Man worked all those years to discover the secrets of life, he never managed to escape his overpowering fascination for death. It was a constant alternative, even in the most civilized of the nations. Strangely enough, the catalyst of each new discovery was the same endless pursuit – the study of science. Not the science the races know today – not the study of animal life, plant life, the earth and the simple arts. This was a science of machines and power, one that divided itself into infinite fields of exploration, all of which worked toward the same two ends – discovering better ways to live or quicker ways to kill.'

He paused and laughed grimly to himself, cocking his head in the direction of the attentive Balinor.

'Very strange indeed, when you think about it – that Man should spend so much time working toward two such obviously different goals. Even now nothing has changed – even after all these years . . .'

His voice trailed off for a moment and Shea risked a brief look at the others, but their eyes were fixed on the speaker.

'Sciences of physical power!' Allanon's sudden exclamation brought Shea's head around with a snap. 'These were the means to all the ends of that era. Two thousand years ago the achievements of the human race were unparalleled in earth's history. Man's age-old enemy, Death, could now claim only those who had lived out their natural lifetime. Sickness was virtually eliminated and, given a bit more time, Man would even have found a way to prolong life. Some philosophers claimed that the secrets of life were forbidden to mortals. No one had ever proved otherwise. They might have done so, but their time ran out and the same elements of power that had made life free from sickness and infirmity nearly destroyed it altogether. The Great Wars began, building gradually from smaller disputes between a few peoples and spreading steadily, despite the realization of what was happening – spreading from little matters into basic hatreds: race, nationality, boundaries, creeds . . . in the end, everything. Then suddenly, so suddenly that few knew what happened, the entire world was enveloped in a series of retaliatory attacks by the different countries, all very scientifically planned and executed. In a matter of minutes, the science of thousands of years, the learning of centuries, culminated in an almost total destruction of life.

'The Great Wars.' The deep voice was grim, the glint of the dark eyes watching carefully the faces of his listeners. 'Very apt name. The power expended in those few minutes of battle not only succeeded in wiping out those thousands of years of human growth, but it also began a series of explosions and upheavals that completely altered the surface of the land. The initial force did most of the damage, killing every living thing over ninety percent of the face of the earth, but the aftereffects carried on the alteration and extinction, breaking the continents apart, drying up oceans, making lands and seas uninhabitable for several hundred years. It should have been the end of all life, perhaps the end of the world itself. Only a miracle prevented that end.'

'I can't believe it.' The words slipped out before Shea could catch himself, and Allanon looked toward him, the familiar mocking smile spreading over his lips.

'That's your history of civilized man, Shea,' he murmured darkly. 'But what happened thereafter concerns us more directly. Remnants of the race of Man managed to survive during the terrible period following the holocaust, living in isolated sectors of the globe, fighting the elements for survival. This was the beginning of the development of the races as they are today – Men, Dwarfs, Gnomes, Trolls, and some say the Elves – but they were always there and that's another story for another time.'

Allanon had made exactly the same comment concerning the Elven people to the Ohmsford brothers in Shady

Vale. Shea wanted badly to stop the narration at that point to ask about the race of Elves and about his own origin. But he knew better than to irritate the tall historian by breaking in as he had several times during their first meeting.

'A few men remembered the secrets of the sciences that had shaped their way of life prior to the destruction of the old world. Only a few remembered. Most were little more than primitive creatures, and the few could recollect only bits and pieces of knowledge. But they had kept their books of learning intact and these could tell them most of the secrets of the old sciences. They kept them hidden and secure during that first several hundred years, unable to put the words to practical use, waiting for the time when they might. They read their precious texts instead and then, as the books themselves began to crumble with age and there was no way to preserve them or copy them, those few men who possessed the books began to memorize the information. The years passed and the knowledge was passed down carefully from father to son, each generation keeping the knowledge safely within the family, guarding it from those who didn't use it wisely, who might create a world in which the Great Wars could happen a second time. In the end, even after it once again became possible to record the information in those irreplaceable books, the men who had memorized them declined to do so. They were still afraid of the consequences, afraid of each other and even themselves. So they decided, individually for the most part, to wait for the right time to offer their knowledge to the growing new races.

'The years passed in this way as the new races slowly began to develop beyond the stage of primitive life. They began to unify into communities, trying to build a new life out of the dust of the old – but as you have already been told, they did not prove equal to the task. They quarreled violently over land, petty disputes which soon turned to armed conflict between the races. It was then, when the

152

sons of those who had first kept the secrets of the old life, the old sciences, saw that matters were steadily regressing toward the very thing that had destroyed the old world, that they decided to act. The man called Galaphile saw what was happening and realized that if nothing were done, the races would surely be at war. So he called together a select group of men, all he could find who possessed any knowledge of the old books, to a council at Paranor.'

'So that was the first Druid Council,' murmured Menion Leah in wonder. 'A council of all the knowledgeable men of that era, pooling their learning to save the races.'

'A very praiseworthy effort at explaining a desperate attempt to prevent extermination of life,' laughed Allanon shortly. 'The Druid Council was formed with the best intentions on the part of most, perhaps all at first. They exerted a tremendous influence over the races because they were capable of offering so much to make life considerably better for everyone. They operated strictly as a group, each man contributing his knowledge for the benefit of all. Although they succeeded in preventing on outbreak of total war, and kept peace between the races at first, they encountered unexpected problems. The knowledge that each possessed had become unavoidably altered in small ways in the telling from generation to generation, so that many of the key understandings were different than they had been.

'Complicating the situation was an understandable inability to coordinate the different materials, the knowledge of the different sciences. For many of the council members, the learning passed down to them by their ancestors lacked meaning in practical terms and much of it appeared to be so many jumbled words. So while the Druids, as they called themselves after an ancient group who sought understanding, were able to aid the races in many ways, they found themselves unable to piece together enough out of the texts they had memorized to master readily any of the important concepts of the great sciences, the concepts they felt certain would help the country to grow and prosper.'

'Then the Druids wanted the old world rebuilt on their terms,' spoke up Shea quickly. 'They wanted to prevent the wars that had destroyed them the first time, yet re-create the benefits of all the old sciences.'

Flick shook his head in bewilderment, unable to see what all this had to do with the Warlock Lord and the Sword.

'Correct,' Allanon noted. 'But the Druid Council, for all its vast knowledge and good intentions, overlooked a basic concept of human existence. Whenever an intelligent creature possesses an innate desire to improve its conditions, to unlock the secrets of progress, it will find the means to do so – if not by one method, then by another. The Druids secluded themselves at Paranor, away from the races of the land, while they worked alone or in small groups to master the secrets of the old sciences. Most relied on the material at hand, the knowledge of individual members related to that of the entire Council to try to rebuild and reconstruct the old means of harnessing power. But some were not content with this approach. A few felt that, instead of trying to understand the words and thoughts of the ancient recollections better, such knowledge as could be immediately grasped should be acted upon and developed in connection with new ideas, new rationalizations.

'So it was that a few members of the council, acting under the leadership of one called Brona, began to delve into the ancient mysteries without waiting for a full understanding of the old sciences. They had phenomenal minds, genius in a few instances, and they were eager to succeed, impatient to master the power that would be so useful to the races. But by a strange quirk of fate, their discoveries and their developments led them further and further from the studies of the Council. The old sciences were puzzles

154

without answers for them, and so they deviated into other fields of thought, slowly and relentlessly intertwining themselves in a realm of study that none had ever mastered and none called science. What they began to unveil was the infinite power of the mystic – sorcery! They mastered a few of the secrets of the mystic before they were discovered by the Council and commanded to abandon their work. There was a violent disagreement and the followers of Brona left the Council in anger, determined to continue their own approach. They disappeared and were not seen again.'

He paused for a moment, considering his explanation. His listeners waited impatiently.

'We know now what happened in the years that followed. During his prolonged studies, Brona uncovered the deepest secrets of sorcery and mastered them. But in the process he lost his own identity, eventually even his own soul to the powers he had sought so eagerly. Forgotten were the old sciences and their purpose in the world of man. Forgotten was the Druid Council and its goal of a better world. Forgotten was everything but the driving urge to learn more of the mystic arts, the secrets of the mind's power to reach into other worlds. Brona was obsessed with the need to extend his power – to dominate men and the world they inhabited through mastery of this terrible force. The result of this ambition was the infamous First War of the Races, when he gained domination over the weak and confused minds of the race of Man, causing that hapless people to make war on the other races, subjecting them to the will of the man who was no longer a man, who was no longer even the master of himself.'

'And his followers . . .?' asked Menion slowly.

'Victims of the same. They became servants to their leader, all slaves of the strange power of sorcery . . .' Allanon trailed off hesitantly, as if to add something but uncertain of its effect on his listeners. Thinking better of it, he continued. 'The fact that these unfortunate Druids stumbled onto the very opposite of what they were seeking is in itself a lesson to Man. Perhaps with patience, they might have pieced together the missing links to the old sciences rather than uncovering the terrible power of the spirit world that fed eagerly on their unprotected minds until they were devoured. Human minds are not equipped to face the realities of nonmaterial existence on this sphere. It is too much for any mortal to bear for long.'

Again he trailed off into ominous silence. The listeners now understood the nature of the enemy they were trying to outwit. They were up against a man who was no longer a human, but the projection of some great force beyond their own comprehension, a force so powerful that Allanon feared it could affect the human mind.

'The rest you already know,' Allanon began again rather sharply. 'The creature called Brona, who no longer resembled anything human, was the directing force behind both of the Race Wars. The Skull Bearers are the followers of their old master Brona, those Druids once human in form, once a part of the Council at Paranor. They cannot escape their fate any more than he can. The very forms they take are an embodiment of the evil they represent. But more important for our purposes, they represent a new age for mankind, for all the people of the four lands. While the old sciences have disappeared into our history, forgotten now as completely as the years when machines were the godsend of an easy life, the enchantment of sorcery has replaced them – a more powerful, more dangerous threat to human life than any before it. Do not doubt me, my friends. We live in the age of the sorcerer and his power threatens to consume us all!'

There was a moment of silence. A deep stillness hung oppressively in the forest night as Allanon's final words seemed to echo back with ringing sharpness. Then Shea spoke softly.

'What is the secret of the Sword of Shannara?'

'In the First War of the Races,' Allanon replied in almost a whisper, 'the power of the Druid Brona was limited. As a result, the combined might of the other races, coupled with the knowledge of the Druid Council, defeated his army of Men and drove him into hiding. He might have ceased to be and the whole incident been written off as merely another chapter in history – another war between mortals – except that he managed to unlock the secret of perpetuating his spiritual essence long after his mortal remains should have decomposed and turned to dust. Somehow he preserved his own spirit, feeding it on the power of the mystic forces he now possessed, giving it a life apart from materiality, apart from mortality. He now was able to bridge the two worlds – the world we live in and the spirit world beyond, where he summoned the black wraiths that had for centuries lain dormant, and waited for his time to strike back. As he waited, he watched the races drift apart as he knew they must in time, and the power of the Druid Council wane as their interest in the races grew lax. As with all things evil, he waited until the balance of hatred, envy, greed – the human failings common to all the races – outweighed the goodness and kindness, and then he struck. Gaining easy control of the primitive, warlike Rock Trolls of the Charnal Mountains, he reinforced their numbers with creatures of the spirit world he now served, and his army marched on the divided races.

'As you know, they crushed the Druid Council and destroyed it – all save a few who fled to safety. One of those who escaped was an aged mystic named Bremen, who had foreseen the danger and in vain attempted to warn the others. As a Druid, he was originally a historian and in that capacity had studied the First War of the Races and learned of Brona and his followers. Intrigued by what they had attempted to do, and suspicious that perhaps the mysterious Druid had acquired powers that no one had known about nor could have hoped to combat, Bremen began his own study of the mystic arts, but with greater care and respect for the possible power he felt he might unlock. After several years of this pursuit, he became convinced that Brona was indeed still existent and that the next war upon the human race would be started and eventually decided by the powers of sorcery and black magic. You can imagine the response he received to this theory – he was practically thrown from the confines of Paranor. As a result, he began to master the mystic arts on his own and so was not present when the castle at Paranor fell to the Troll army. When he learned that the Council had been taken, he knew that if he did not act, the races would be left defenseless against the enchantment Brona had mastered, power that mortals knew nothing about. But he was faced with the problem of how to defeat a creature who could not be touched by any mortal weapon, one who had survived for over five hundred years. He went to the greatest nation of his time – the Elven people under the command of a courageous young King named Jerle Shannara – and offered his assistance. The Elven people had always respected Bremen, because they understood him better than even his fellow Druids. He had lived among them for years prior to the fall of Paranor, while studying the science of the mystic.'

'There is something I don't understand.' Balinor spoke up suddenly. 'If Bremen was a master of the mystic arts, why could he not himself challenge the power of the War-lock Lord?'

Allanon's response was somehow evasive. 'He did confront Brona in the end on the Plains of Streleheim, though it was not a battle that was visible to mortal eyes, and both disappeared. It was presumed that Bremen had defeated the Spirit King, but time has proven otherwise, and now . . .' He hesitated only an instant before quickly returning to his narrative, but the emphasis on the pause was not lost on any of his listeners.

'In any event, Bremen realized that what was needed was a talisman to serve as a shield against the possible return of one such as Brona at another time when there was no one familiar with the mystic arts to offer assistance to the peoples of the four lands. So he conceived the idea of the Sword, a weapon which would contain the power to defeat the Warlock Lord. Bremen forged the Sword of Shannara with the aid of his own mystic prowess, shaping it with more than the mere metal of our own world, giving it that special protective characteristic of all talismans against the unknown. The Sword was to draw its strength from the minds of the mortals for whom it acted as a shield – the power of the Sword was their own desire to remain free, to give up even their lives to preserve that freedom. This was the power which enabled Jerle Shannara to destroy the spirit-dominated Northland army then; it is the same power that must now be used to send the Warlock Lord back into the limbo world to which he belongs, to imprison him there for all eternity, to cut off entirely his passage back to this world. But as long as he has the Sword, then he has a chance to prevent its power from being used to destroy him forever, and that, my friends, is the one thing that must not be.'

'But then why is it that only a son of the House of Shannara . . .?' The question formed on Shea's fumbling lips, his own mind reeling confusedly.

'That is the greatest irony of all!' exclaimed Allanon before the question was even completed. 'If you have followed all that I have related about the change of life following the Great Wars, the giving way of the old materialistic sciences to the science of the present age, the science of the mystic, then you will understand what I am about to explain – the strangest phenomenon of all. While the sciences of old operated on practical theories built around things that could be seen and touched and felt, the sorcery of our own time operates on an entirely different principle. Its power is potent only when it is believed, for it is power over the mind which can neither be touched nor seen through human senses. If the mind does not truly find some basis for belief in its existence, then it can have no real effect. The Warlock Lord realizes this, and the mind's fear of and belief in the unknown – the worlds, the creatures, all the occurrences that cannot be understood by men's limited senses – offer him more than enough basis upon which to practice the mystic arts. He has been relying on this premise for over five hundred years. In the same way, the Sword of Shannara cannot be an effective weapon unless the one holding it believes in his power to use it. When Bremen gave the sword to Jerle Shannara, he made the mistake of giving it directly to a king and to the house of a king – he did not give it to the people of the lands. As a result, through human misunderstanding and historical misconception, the universal belief grew that the Sword was the weapon of the Elven King alone and that only those descended of his blood could take up the Sword against the Warlock Lord. So now, unless it is held by a son of the House of Shannara, that person can never fully believe in his right to use it. The ancient tradition that only such a one can wield it will make all others doubt – and there must be no doubt, or it will not operate. Instead, it will become merely another piece of metal. Only the blood and belief of a descendant of Shannara can invoke the latent power of the great Sword.'

He concluded. The silence that followed was hollow. There was nothing left to tell the four that could be told. Allanon reconsidered briefly what he had promised himself. He had not told them everything, purposely holding back the little more that would have proved the final terror for them. He inwardly felt torn between the desire to have it all out and the gnawing realization that it would destroy any chance of success; their success was of paramount importance – only he knew the full truth of that fact. So he sat in silence, bitter in his private knowledge and angered by the self-imposed limits he had set for himself – the limits that forbade a complete revelation to those who had come to depend upon him so very heavily.

'Then only Shea can use the Sword if . . .' Balinor broke the silence abruptly.

'Only Shea has the birthright. Only Shea.'

It was so quiet that even the night life of the forest seemed to have stilled its incessant chatter in sober contemplation of the grim historian's reply. The future came down to each as a simple declaration of existence – succeed or be destroyed.

'Leave me now,' commanded Allanon suddenly. 'Sleep while you can. We leave this haven at sunrise for the halls of Paranor.'

CHAPTER

10

T he morning came quickly for the small company, and the golden half-light of dawn found them preparing to begin their long journey with sleep-filled eyes. Balinor, Menion, and the Valemen waited for the appearance of Allanon and the cousins of Eventine. No one spoke, partly because each was still half asleep and had very little to recommend him in the way of good humor, and partly because each was inwardly thinking about the hazardous trip that lay ahead. Shea and Flick sat quietly on a small stone bench, not looking at each other as they considered the tale Allanon had related to them the previous night, wondering what possible chance they had of recovering the Sword of Shannara, using it against the Warlock Lord to destroy him, and still returning alive to their homeland. Shea, particularly, had passed the point where his chief emotion was fear; now he felt only a sense of numbness that dulled his mind into self-imposed surrender, a robot-like acceptance of the fact that he was being led to the proverbial slaughter. Yet in spite of this resigned attitude toward the journey to Paranor, somewhere in the back of his confused mind was the lingering belief that he could work out all of these seemingly insurmountable obstacles. He could feel it lurking there, waiting for a more opportune moment to arise and demand satisfaction. But for the moment he allowed himself to lapse dutifully into numbed acquiescence.

The Valemen were dressed in woodsman garb provided by the Dwarf people, including warm half-cloaks in which they now wrapped themselves to ward off the chill of the early morning. In addition, they carried the short hunting knives they had brought with them from the Vale, tucked in their leather belts. Their packs were necessarily compact, in accord with the Valeman's small size. The country they would pass through offered some of the best hunting in all the Southland, and there were several small communities friendly to Allanon and the Dwarfs. But it was also the home of the Gnome people, the longtime, bitter enemies of the Dwarfs. There was some hope the little band would be able to maintain an advantage of stealth and secrecy in their travel and avoid any confrontation with Gnome hunters. Shea had carefully packed away the Elfstones in their leather pouch, showing them to no one. Allanon had not mentioned them since he had arrived in Culhaven. Whether this was an oversight or not, Shea was not about to give up the one really potent weapon that he possessed and kept the pouch hidden within his tunic.

Menion Leah stood several yards away from the brothers, pacing idly. He wore particularly nondescript hunting clothes, loose-fitting and colored to blend with the land to make his task as tracker and huntsman as uncomplicated as possible. His shoes were soft leather, toughened by certain oils to enable him to stalk anything without being heard and still travel the toughest ground without injuring the soles of his feet. Strapped to his lean back was the great sword, sheathed now, its strong hilt glinting dully in the early light as he shifted restlessly about. Across his shoulder he carried the long ash bow and its arrows, his favorite weapon on hunting trips.

Balinor wore the familiar long hunting cloak wrapped closely about his tall, broad frame, the cowl pulled up

163

around his head. Beneath the cloak was the chain mail which could be seen glinting sharply ever so often as his arms emerged in brief gestures from beneath the shielding of the garment. He carried in his belt a long hunting knife and the most enormous sword that the Valemen had ever seen. It was so huge that it appeared to them that one sweep of its great blade would cut through a man completely. It was hidden beneath the cloak at the moment, but the brothers had seen him strap it to his side as he came out to them earlier that morning.

Their waiting finally came to an end as Allanon approached from the assembly hall, accompanied by the lithe figures of the two Elves. Without stopping, he bade them all good morning and directed them to fall into line for the trip, warning sharply that once they crossed the Silver River several miles ahead, they would be in country traveled by Gnomes and that conversation must be kept to a minimum. Their route would take them from the river directly north through the Anar Forests into the mountains that lay beyond. There was less chance that they would be detected traveling through this rough country than across the plains that lay farther west, where the terrain was admittedly more even and accessible. Secrecy was the key to their success. If the purpose of their journey became known to the Warlock Lord, they were finished. Travel would be restricted to the daylight hours while they were camouflaged by the forests and mountains, and they would resort to night travel and risk detection by the searching Skull Bearers only when they were forced to cross the plains many miles to the north.

As their representative on the expedition, the Dwarf chieftain had chosen Hendel, the closemouthed Fellow who had saved Menion from the Siren. Hendel led the company out of Culhaven, since he was most familiar with this part of the country. At his side walked Menion, talking only occasionally, concentrating mostly on staying out of the sullen Dwarf's way and trying to avoid drawing attention to his presence, something the Dwarf felt was totally unnecessary. Several paces back from them were the two Elves, their slim figures like brief shadows as they moved gracefully, effortlessly, speaking with each other in quiet musical voices that Shea found reassuring. Both carried long ash bows similar to Menion's. They wore no cloaks – only the strange, close-fitting outfits they had worn at the council the night before. Shea and Flick followed them, and behind the Valemen walked the silent leader of the company, his long strides covering the ground with ease, his dark face lowered to the trail. Balinor brought up the rear. Both Shea and Flick were quick to realize that their position in the center of the company was to assure their maximum protection. Shea knew how valuable the others felt he was to the success of the mission, but he was also painfully aware that they considered him incapable of defending himself in case of any real danger.

The company reached the Silver River and crossed at a narrow spot where the winding thread of gleaming water was spanned by a sturdy wooden bridge. All talking ceased once they had passed over, and all eyes went to the dense forest about them, watching uneasily. The going was still relatively smooth; the ground was level as the path wound sharply through the great forest, leading them steadily northward. The light of the morning sun shone in long streamers through cracks in the heavy branches, occasionally cutting across their path and catching their faces as they walked, warming them briefly in the cool air of the forest. Beneath their feet, the fallen leaves and twigs were soaked with a heavy dew, making a cushion that masked the sound of their footsteps and helped to preserve the quiet of the day. All about them they could hear sounds of life, though they saw only multicolored birds and a few squirrels that scampered eagerly about their treetop domains, sometimes raining the travelers below with torrents of nuts and twigs as they leaped from branch to branch. The trees prevented the members of the company from seeing much of anything, their great girth ranging from three to ten feet in diameter, and their huge roots stretching out from the trunks like mammoth fingers, digging their way relentlessly into the earth of the forest floor. The view from every direction was masked, and the company had to content itself with relying on Hendel's familiarity with the country and the pathfinding knowledge of Menion Leah to guide them through the maze of vegetation.

The first day passed without incident, and they spent the night beneath the giant trees, somewhere north of the Silver River and Culhaven. Hendel was apparently the only one who knew exactly where they were, though Allanon conversed briefly with the taciturn Dwarf concerning their whereabouts and the route they were taking. The company ate its dinner cold, fearing that a fire might attract attention. But the general mood was light and the conversation was enjoyable. Shea took this opportunity to speak with the two Elves. They were cousins of Eventine, chosen to accompany Allanon as representatives of the Elven kingdom and to aid him in his search for the Sword of Shannara. They were brothers, the elder called Durin, a slim, quiet Westlander who gave the instant impression to Shea and the ever-present Flick that he was a man to be trusted. The younger brother was Dayel, a shy, extremely likable fellow who was several years the junior of Shea. His boyish charm was strangely appealing to the elder members of the company, particularly Balinor and Hendel, battle-hardened veterans of so many years of protecting the frontiers of their homelands, who found his youth and fresh outlook on life almost like a second chance for them to regain something that had passed them by years before. Durin informed Shea that his brother had left their Elven home several days prior to his marriage to one of the most beautiful girls in that country. Shea would not have believed Dayel old enough to marry, and found it difficult to understand why anyone would leave on the eve of his marriage. Durin assured him that it had been his brother's own choice, but Shea told Flick later that he believed that his relationship to the king had much to do with that decision. So now as the members of the company sat quietly and spoke in low tones to one another, all save the silent, aloof Hendel, Shea wondered how much the young Elf regretted his decision to leave his bride-to-be to come on this hazardous journey to Paranor. He found himself wishing inwardly that Dayel had not chosen to be a member of their party, but had remained safe within the protective confines of his own homeland.

Later that evening, Shea approached Balinor and asked him why Dayel had been allowed to come on such an expedition. The Prince of Callahorn smiled at the Valeman's concern, thinking to himself that the difference in ages between the two was hardly noticeable to him. He told Shea that in a time when the homelands of so many people were threatened, no one stopped to question why another was there to aid them – it was merely accepted. Dayel had chosen to come because his King had asked it and because he would have felt less of a man in his own mind had he declined. Balinor explained that Hendel had been waging a constant battle with the Gnomes for years to protect his homeland. The responsibility was delegated to him because he was one of the most experienced and knowledgeable bordermen in the Eastland. He had a wife and family at home that he had seen once in the past eight weeks and could not expect to see again for many more. Everyone on the journey had a great deal to lose, he concluded, perhaps even more than Shea realized. Without explaining his final remark, the tall borderman moved off to speak with Allanon on other matters. Somewhat discontented by the abrupt finish to their conversation, Shea moved back to join Flick and the Elven brothers.

'What kind of person is Eventine?' Flick was asking as Shea joined the group. 'I've always heard that he is considered the greatest of the Elven kings, respected by everyone. What is he really like?'

Durin smiled broadly and Dayel laughed merrily at the question, finding it somehow amusing and unexpected.

'What can we say about our own cousin?'

'He is a great King,' responded Durin seriously after a few moments. 'Very young for a king, the other monarchs and leaders would say. But he has foresight, and most important of all, he gets things done before the time for doing them has passed. He holds the love and esteem of all the Elven people. They would follow him anywhere, do anything he asked, which is fortunate for all of us. The elders of our council would prefer to ignore the other lands, to try to remain isolated. Sheer foolishness, but they're afraid of another war. Only Eventine stands against them and that policy. He knows that the only way to avoid the war they all fear is to strike first and cut off the head of the army which threatens. That is one reason why this mission is so important – to see that this invasion is checked before it has time to develop into a full-scale war.'

Menion had sauntered over from the other side of the small campsite and seated himself with them just in time to hear the last comment.

'What do you know of the Sword of Shannara?' he asked curiously.

'Very little actually,' admitted Dayel, 'although for us it's a matter of history rather than legend. The Sword has always represented a promise to the Elven people that they need never again fear the creatures from the spirit world. It was always assumed that the threat was finished with the conclusion of the Second War of the Races, so no one really concerned himself with the fact that the entire House of Shannara died out over the years, except for a few such as Shea whom no one knew about. Eventine's family, our family, became rulers almost a hundred years ago – the Elessedils. The Sword remained at Paranor, forgotten by nearly everyone until now.'

'What is the power of the Sword?' persisted Menion, a little too eagerly to suit Flick, who shot Shea a warning glance.

'I don't know the answer to that question,' Dayel admitted and looked to Durin who shrugged in response and shook his head. 'Only Allanon seems to know that.'

They all looked momentarily toward the tall figure seated in earnest conversation with Balinor across the clearing. Then Durin turned to the others.

'It is fortunate that we have Shea, a son of the House of Shannara. He will be able to unlock the secret of the Sword's power once we have it in our possession, and with that power we can strike at the Dark Lord before he can create the war that would destroy us.'

'If we get the Sword, you mean,' corrected Shea quickly. Durin acknowledged this comment with a short laugh of agreement and a reassuring nod.

'There's still something about all this that doesn't set right,' Menion declared quietly, rising abruptly and moving off to find a place to sleep. Shea watched him go and found himself in agreement with the highlander, but was unable to see what they could hope to do about their dissatisfaction. Right now he felt that there was so little hope of their succeeding in their quest to regain the sword that for the moment he would concentrate on simply completing the journey to Paranor. For now, he did not even want to think about what might happen after that.

The company was awake and back on the winding path with the breaking of the dawn, led by a watchful Hendel. The Dwarf moved them along at a rapid pace through the mass of great trees and heavy foliage that had grown

169

increasingly dense as they penetrated deeper into the Anar. The trail was beginning to slope upward, an indication that they were approaching the mountains that ran the length of the central Anar. At some point farther north they would be forced to cross these broad peaks in order to reach the plains to the west that lay between them and the halls of Paranor. Tension began to mount as they moved more deeply into the domain of the Gnome people. They began to experience the unpleasant sensation that someone was constantly watching them, hidden in the denseness of the forest, waiting for the right moment to strike. Only Hendel seemed unconcerned as he led them, his own fears apparently eased by his familiarity with the terrain. No one spoke as they marched, all eyes searching the silent forest about them.

About midday, the path turned sharply upward and the company began to climb. The trees now grew farther apart and the scrub foliage was less congested. The sky became clearly visible through the trees, a deep blue unbroken by even the faintest trace of a cloud wisp. The sun was warm and bright, shining bravely through the scattered trees to light the whole of the forest. Rocks began to appear in small clusters and they could see the land ahead rise in tall peaks and jutting ridges that signaled the beginning of the southern sector of the mountains in the central Anar. The air became steadily cooler as they climbed and breathing became more difficult. After several hours, the company reached the edge of a very dense forest of dead pines, clustered so closely that it was impossible to see for more than twenty or thirty feet ahead at any one place. On both sides of their path, tall, slab-rock cliffs rose hundreds of feet into the air and peaked against the blueness of the afternoon sky. The forest stretched several hundred yards in either direction, ending at the cliff walls. At the edge of the pines, Hendel called a brief halt and spoke for several minutes with Menion, pointing to the forest and then the cliffs, apparently questioning something. Allanon joined them, then motioned the remainder of the company to gather around in a close circle.

'The mountains we are about to cross into are the Wolfsktaag, a no-man's-land for both Dwarf and Gnome,' Hendel explained quietly. 'We chose this way because there was less chance of meeting up with a Gnome hunting patrol, something that would certainly result in a pitched battle. The Wolfsktaag Mountains are said to be inhabited by creatures from another world – a good joke, isn't it?'

'Get to the point,' Allanon broke in.

'The point is,' Hendel continued, seemingly oblivious of the dark historian, 'we were spotted about fifteen minutes back by one or possibly two Gnome scouts. There may be more around, we can't be certain – the highlander says he saw signs of a large party. In any event, the scouts will report us and bring back help in a hurry, so we'll have to move fast.'

'Worse than that!' declared Menion quickly. 'Those signs said there are Gnomes ahead of us somewhere – through those trees or in them.'

'Maybe so, maybe not, highlander,' Hendel cut back in sharply. 'These trees run like this for almost a mile and the cliffs continue on both sides, but narrow sharply beyond the forest to form the Pass of Noose, the entrance to the Wolfsktaag. That is the way we have to go. To try any other route would cost us two more days, and we would be risking an almost certain run-in with Gnomes.'

'Enough debate,' Allanon said fiercely. 'Let's move out quickly. Once we reach the other side of the pass, we'll be in the mountains. The Gnomes will not follow us there.'

'Encouraging, I'm sure,' muttered Flick under his breath.

The company moved into the thickly clustered trees of the pine forest, following one another in single file, weaving among the rough, disjointed trunks. Dead needles lay in heaps over the whole of the earthen forest floor, creating a soft matting on which the passing of feet made no sound. The white-bark trees rose tall and lean, touching near their skeletal tops like some intricate spider web, lacing the blueness of the clear sky in fascinating designs. The party wound steadily forward through the maze of trunks and limbs behind Hendel, who chose their route quickly and without hesitation. They had not gone more than several hundred yards when Durin brought them up sharply and motioned for silence, looking questioningly about, apparently searching the air for something.

'Smoke!' he exclaimed suddenly. 'They've set fire to the forest!'

'I don't smell any smoke,' declared Menion, sniffing the air tentatively.

'You don't have the sharpened senses of an Elf either,' Allanon stated flatly. He turned to Durin. 'Can you tell where they've fired it?'

'I smell smoke, too,' declared Shea absently, amazed that his own senses were as sharp as those of the Elves.

Durin cast about for a minute, trying to catch the scent of smoke from one particular direction.

'Can't tell, but it appears that they've fired it in more than one place. If they have, the forest will go up in a matter of minutes!'

Allanon hesitated for one brief second, then motioned for them to continue toward the Pass of Noose. The pace picked up considerably as they hastened to reach the other side of the firetrap in which they were encased. A blaze in those dry woods would quickly cut off any chance of escape once it spread through the treetops. The long strides of Allanon and the borderman forced Shea and Flick to run to keep from falling behind. Allanon shouted something to Balinor at one point in the race, and the broad figure dropped back into the trees and was lost from sight. Ahead of them, Menion and Hendel had disappeared, and there were only fleeting glimpses of the Elven brothers dashing smoothly between the leaning pines. Only Allanon stayed clearly in view, a few paces behind, calling to them to run faster. Thick clouds of heavy white smoke were beginning to seep between the closely bunched trunks like a heavy fog, obscuring the path ahead and making it steadily more difficult to breathe. There was still no sign of the actual fire. It had not yet grown strong enough to spread through the intertwining boughs and cut them off. The smoke was everywhere in a matter of minutes, and both Shea and Flick coughed heavily with every breath, their eyes beginning to sting from the heat and irritation. Suddenly Allanon called to them to halt. Reluctantly they stopped and waited for the order to continue, but Allanon appeared to be looking back for something, his lean, dark face strangely ashen in the thick white smoke. Soon the broad figure of Balinor reappeared from the forest behind them, wrapped tightly in the long hunting cloak.

'You were right, they're behind us,' he informed the historian, gasping out the words as he fought for breath. 'They've fired the forest all along our backs. It looks like a trap to drive us into the Pass of Noose.'

'Stay with them,' Allanon ordered quickly, pointing to the frightened Valemen. 'I've got to catch the others before they reach the pass!'

With incredible speed for a man so big, the tall leader leaped away and dashed into the trees ahead, disappearing almost immediately. Balinor motioned for the Valemen to follow him, and they proceeded at a rapid pace in the same direction, fighting to see and to breathe in the choking smoke. Then, with frightening suddenness, they heard the sharp crackle of burning wood and the smoke began to billow past them in huge, blinding clouds of white heat. The fire was overtaking them. In a few minutes it would reach them and they would be burned alive! Coughing furiously, the three crashed heedlessly through the pines, desperate to escape the inferno in which they had been caught. Shea shot a quick glance skyward, and to his horror saw the flames leaping madly fr m the tops of the tall pines above and beyond them, burning their glowing way steadily down the long trunks.

Then abruptly, the impenetrable stone wall of the cliffs appeared through the smoke and the trees, and Balinor motioned them in that direction. Minutes later, as they groped their way along the cliff face, they saw the remainder of the company crouched in a clearing beyond the fringe of the burning trees. Ahead lay an open trail that wound upward into the rocks between the cliffs and disappeared into the Pass of Noose. The three quickly joined the others as the entire forest was enveloped in flames.

'They're trying to force us to choose between roasting in that pine forest or trying to get through the pass,' shouted Allanon over the crackle of burning wood, looking anxiously toward the trail ahead. 'They know we have only two ways to go, but they're facing the same choice and that's where they lose the advantage. Durin, go on ahead into the pass a little way and see if the Gnomes have set an ambush.'

The Elf darted away without a sound, crouching low and keeping close to the cliff wall. They watched him until he had disappeared farther up the trail into the rocks. Shea huddled with the others, wishing that there was something he could do to help.

'The Gnomes are not fools.' Allanon's voice cut into his thoughts abruptly. 'Those in the pass know that they are cut off from those who fired the forest unless they can get by us first. They wouldn't risk having to retreat back through the Wolfsktaag Mountains for any reason. Either there is a large force of Gnomes in the pass ahead, which Durin should be able to tell us, or they've got something else in mind.'

'Whatever it is, they'll probably try it in the section

called the Knot,' Hendel informed them. 'At that point the trail narrows so that only one man at a time can get through the path formed by the converging cliff sides.' He paused and appeared to be considering something further.

'I don't understand how they plan to stop us,' Balinor cut in quickly. 'These cliffs are almost vertical – no one could scale them without a long and hazardous climb. The Gnomes haven't had time to get up there since they spotted us!'

Allanon nodded thoughtfully, obviously in agreement with the borderman and unable to see what the Gnomes had in store for them. Menion Leah spoke quietly to Balinor, then abruptly left the group and moved ahead to the entrance of the pass where the cliff walls began to narrow sharply, scanning the ground intently. The heat of the burning woods had become so intense that they were forced to move farther into the mouth of the pass. Everything was still obscured by the clouds of white smoke which rolled out of the dying woods like a wall and dispersed sluggishly into the air. Long moments passed while the six awaited the return of Menion and Durin. They could still see the lean highlander studying the ground at the entrance to the pass, his tall form shadowy in the smoke-filled air. Finally, he stood up and moved back to them, joined almost immediately by the returning Elf.

'There were footprints, but no other sign of life in the pass ahead,' Durin reported. 'Everything is apparently undisturbed up to the narrowest point. I didn't go beyond.'

'There is something else,' Menion cut in quickly. 'At the entrance to the pass, I found two clear sets of footprints leading in and two sets out – Gnome feet.'

'They must have slipped in ahead of us and then out again by staying close to the cliff walls while we blundered up the middle,' Balinor said angrily. 'But if they were in there ahead of us, what . . .?'

'We won't find out by sitting here and discussing it!'

Allanon concluded in disgust. 'We would only be guessing. Hendel, take the lead with the highlander and watch yourself. The rest stay in formation as before.'

The stocky Dwarf moved out with Menion at his side, their sharp eyes keyed in on every boulder that lined the winding path as it narrowed into the Pass of Noose. The others followed several paces back, casting apprehensive glances at the rugged terrain surrounding them. Shea risked one quick look behind him and noticed that, while Allanon was close on his heels, Balinor was nowhere in sight. Apparently, Allanon had again left the borderman to act as a rear guard at the edge of the burning pine forest, to watch for the inevitable approach of the Gnome hunters lurking somewhere beyond. Shea knew instinctively that they were caught in a trap carefully arranged for them by the furtive Gnomes, and all that remained was to discover what form it would take.

The path ahead rose sharply for the first hundred yards or so, then tapered off gradually and narrowed to such an extent that there was only enough room for one person to pass between the cliff sides. The pass was no more than a deep niche in the face of the cliff, the sides slanting inward and almost closing far above them. Only a thin ribbon of light from the blue sky streamed downward to reach them, faintly lighting the winding, boulder-laden path ahead. Their progress slowed perceptibly as the lead men searched for traps left by the Gnomes. Shea had no idea how far Durin had gone in his scouting mission, but apparently he had not ventured into what Hendel had referred to as the Knot. He could guess where the name had originated. The narrowness of the passage left the sharp impression of being drawn through the knot of a hangman's noose to the same fate as that which awaited the condemned. He could hear Flick's labored breathing almost in his ear and experienced an unpleasant feeling of suffocation at the closeness of the rock walls. The group moved slowly onward, slightly bent to avoid the narrowed cliff sides and their razor-sharp stone projections.

Suddenly, the pace slowed further and the whole line crowded together. Behind him, Shea heard the deep voice of Allanon muttering angrily, demanding to know what had happened, asking excitedly to be let to the front. But in these close quarters it was impossible for anyone to give way. Shea peered ahead and noticed a sharp ray of light beyond the leaders. Apparently the path was widening at last. They were nearly free of the Pass of Noose. But then, just as Shea felt they had reached the safety of the other end, there were loud exclamations and the entire line came to a complete stop. Menion's voice cut through the semi-darkness in surprise and anger, causing Allanon to mutter a low oath of fury and order the company to move ahead. For a moment nothing happened. Then slowly the company began to inch forward, moving into a wide clearing shadowed by the cliff sides as they parted abruptly into a sky of sunshine.

'I was afraid of this,' Hendel was muttering to himself as Shea followed Dayel out of the niche. 'I had hoped that the Gnomes had failed to explore this far into their taboo land. It appears, highlander, that they have us trapped.'

Shea stepped out into the light on a level rock shelf where the others in the company stood talking in hushed tones of anger and frustration. Allanon emerged at almost the same moment, and together they surveyed the scene before them. The rock shelf on which they stood extended out from the opening of the Pass of Noose about fifteen feet to form a small ledge that dropped abruptly into a yawning chasm hundreds of feet deep. Even in the bright sunlight, it appeared to be bottomless. The cliff walls spread outward from their backs to form a half circle around the chasm and then slanted away brokenly, giving way to the heavy forests that began several hundred yards beyond. The chasm, a trick of nature by all appearances, bore the distinct shape of a jagged noose. There was no way around it. On the other side of the fissure dangled the remains of what had previously been some sort of rope and wood bridge which had served as the only means by which travelers could cross. Eight pairs of eyes scanned the sheer walls of the cliffs, seeking a means to scale their slick surfaces. But it was all too apparent that the only way to the other side was directly across the open pit before them.

'The Gnomes knew what they were doing when they destroyed the bridge!' Menion fumed to no one in particular. 'They've left us trapped between them and this bottomless hole. They don't even have to come in after us. They can wait until we starve to death. How stupid . . .'

He trailed off in fury. They all knew they had been foolish in allowing themselves to be tricked into entering such a simple, but effective trap. Allanon moved to the edge of the chasm, peered intently into its depths and then scanned the terrain on the other side, searching for a means to cross.

'If it were a bit more narrow or if I had a little more running room, I might be able to jump it,' volunteered Durin hopefully. Shea estimated the distance across to be easily thirty-five feet. He shook his head doubtfully. Even if Durin had been the best jumper in the world, he would have questioned such an attempt under these conditions.

'Wait a minute!' Menion cried suddenly, leaping to Allanon's side and pointing off to the north. 'How about that old tree hanging off the cliff side on the left?'

Everyone looked eagerly, unable to understand what the highlander was suggesting. The tree of which he spoke grew embedded in the cliff face to the left almost a hundred and fifty yards away from them. Its gray shape hung starkly against the clear sky, its branches leafless and bare, dipping heavily downward like the tired limbs of some weary giant frozen in midstride. It was the only tree that anyone could see on the rock-strewn path that led away from the chasm and disappeared below the cliff sides into the forests beyond. Shea looked with the others but could see no help from that corner.

'If I could put an arrow into that tree with a line tied to it, someone light could go across hand over hand and secure the rope for the rest of us,' the Prince of Leah suggested, gripping in his left hand the great ash bow.

'That shot is over a hundred yards,' replied Allanon testily. 'With the added weight of a line tied to the arrow, you would have to make the world's greatest shot just to get it there, not to mention embedding it in the tree deep enough to hold a man's weight. I don't think it can be done.'

'Well, we had better come up with something or we can forget the Sword of Shannara and everything else,' growled Hendel, his craggy face flushed with anger.

'I have an idea.' Flick ventured suddenly taking a step forward as he spoke. Everyone looked at the stocky Valeman as if they were just seeing him for the first time and had forgotten that he was even along.

'Well, all right, don't keep it to yourself!' exclaimed Menion impatiently. 'What is it, Flick?'

'If there were an expert bowman in the group – ' Flick shot Menion a venomous look ' – he might be able to put an arrow with a line into the wood fragments of the bridge hanging on the other side and pull it back across to this side.'

'That is an idea worth trying!' agreed Allanon quickly. 'Now who . . .'

'I can handle it,' Menion said quickly, glaring at Flick.

Allanon nodded shortly, and Hendel produced a stout cord which Menion Leah fastened securely about the tip of an arrow, tying the loose end to his wide leather belt. He fitted the arrow to the great ash bow and sighted. All eyes peered across the chasm to the length of rope secured at the edge on the other side. Menion followed the length of rope downward into the darkness of the pit until he spotted a piece of wood hanging about thirty feet below, still fastened to the broken bridge tie. The company watched breathlessly as he drew back the great ash bow, sighted quickly, surely, and released the arrow with a sharp snap. The arrow shot into the cavern and embedded itself in the wood, the cord dangling limply from the tip.

'Nice shooting, Menion,' Durin approved at his shoulder, and the lean highlander smiled.

Carefully, the bridge was pulled back across until the severed rope ends were gathered in. Allanon looked in vain for something to secure it, but the spikes that had held it had been removed by the Gnomes. Finally, Hendel and Allanon braced themselves at the edge of the chasm and pulled the bridge rope taut while Dayel worked his way hand over hand across the yawning pit, carrying a second rope at his waist. There were a few anxious moments as the black-robed giant and the silent Dwarf held firm against the strain, but in the end Dayel stood safely on the other side. Balinor reappeared and informed them that the fire was beginning to burn itself out and the Gnome hunters would soon be making their way into the Pass of Noose. Hastily, the rope that Dayel carried was thrown back across after he had finished securing his end, and its longer length was run back into the jutting rocks at the entrance of the pass and fastened in place. The remaining members of the company proceeded to cross the chasm in the same fashion as Dayel, one by one, hand over hand in succession, until all stood safely on the far side. Then the rope was cut and dropped into the pit along with the remainder of the old bridge, to make certain that they could not be followed.

Allanon ordered the company to move out quietly to avoid warning the approaching Gnomes that they had made good their escape from the carefully laid trap. Before they left, however, the tall historian approached Flick, placed a lean, dark hand on his shoulder, and smiled grimly.

'Today, my friend, you have earned the right to be a member of this company – a right above and beyond your kinship for your brother.'

He turned away abruptly and signaled Hendel to take the lead. Shea looked at Flick's flushed and happy face, and clapped his brother warmly on the back. He had indeed earned the right to stand along with the others – a right that Shea had perhaps not yet acquired.

CHAPTER

11

The company journeyed another ten miles into the Wolfsktaag Mountains before Allanon called a halt. The Pass of Noose and the danger of attack by Gnomes had long since been left behind, and they were now deep within the forests. Their travel had been fast and unhindered up to this point, the paths wide and clear and the terrain level even though they were several miles high in the mountains. The air was crisp and cool, which made the march almost enjoyable, and the warm afternoon sun beamed down on the company with a glow that kept their spirits high. The forests were scattered in these mountains, cut apart by jutting ridges of slab rock and peaks which were barren and snowcapped. Although this was historically a forbidden country, even for the Dwarfs, no one could find an indication of anything out of the ordinary which might signal danger for them. All the normal sounds of the forest were there, from the resonant chirping of insects to the gay songs of a huge variety of multicolored birds of all shapes and sizes. It seemed that they had chosen a wise way in which to approach the still-distant halls of Paranor.

'We will stop for the night in several hours,' the tall wanderer announced after he had gathered them about him. 'But I will be leaving you in the early morning to scout ahead beyond the Wolfsktaag for signs of the Warlock Lord and his emissaries. Once we complete our journey through these mountains and through a short stretch of the Anar Forests, we still have to cross the plains beyond to the Dragon's Teeth, just below Paranor. If the creatures of the Northland or their allies have blocked off the entrance, I must know now so that we may quickly decide on a new route.'

'Will you go alone?' asked Balinor.

'I think it safer for all of us if I do. I'm in little danger, and you may need everyone when you reach the central Anar forests again. I have little doubt that the Gnome hunting parties will be watching all the passes leading out of these mountains to be certain that you do not leave them alive. Hendel can lead you through those pitfalls as well as I could, and I will try to meet you somewhere along the way before you reach the plains.'

'Which way out will you be taking?' asked the taciturn Dwarf.

'The Pass of Jade offers the best protection. I'll mark the way with bits of cloth – as we've done before. Red will mean danger. Keep with the white cloth and all will be well. Now let's continue on while we still have some daylight.'

They traveled steadily through the Wolfsktaag until the sun sank beneath the rim of the mountains in the west and it was no longer possible to see the path ahead clearly. It was a moonless night, though the stars cast a dim glow over the rugged landscape. The company made camp beneath a tall, jagged cliffside that rose several hundred feet above them like some great blade cutting sharply into the dark sky. On the open edges of the campsite were tall stands of pines enclosing them against the cliffside in a half circle that provided them with good protection on all sides. They ate a cold dinner for another evening, still unwilling to risk a fire which might draw attention to their presence. Hendel arranged for the posting of a continuous guard throughout the night, a practice he felt to be essential in unfriendly country. The members of the group took turns, each sitting watch for several hours while the rest of the company slept. There was little talk after the meal, and they rolled themselves into their blankets almost at once, tired from the long day of marching.

Shea volunteered to sit the first watch, eager to participate as a member of the company, still feeling that he had contributed little while all of the others were risking their lives for his benefit. Shea's attitude toward the journey to Paranor had altered considerably during the past two days. He was beginning to realize now how important it was that the Sword be obtained, how much the people of the four lands depended on it for protection against the Warlock Lord. Before, he had run away from the danger of the Skull Bearers and his heritage as a son of the house of Shannara. Now he was running toward an even greater threat, a confrontation with a power so awesome that its limits had never been defined – and with little more than the courage of seven mortal men for protection. But even with that knowledge confronting him, Shea felt deeply that to refuse to go on, to hold back what little he had to offer, would be a bitter betrayal of his kinship to both Elf and Man and a callous denial of the pride he felt in caring about the safety and freedom of all men. He knew that if he were told even now that he could not succeed, he would have to try anyway.

Allanon had turned in without a word to anyone and was asleep in a matter of seconds. Shea watched his still form during his own two-hour watch and then retired as Durin took over. It was not until Flick awoke after midnight to take his turn that the tall form of their leader stirred slightly, then rose in a single fluid motion, wrapped ominously in the great black cape, just as he had been when Flick had first encountered him on the road to Shady

184

Vale. He stood for a moment looking at the sleeping members of the company and at Flick sitting motionless on a boulder off to one side of the clearing. Then without a word or a gesture, he turned north on the path leading away from them and disappeared in the blackness of the forest.

Allanon walked for the remainder of the night without pausing in his journey to reach the Pass of Jade, the central Anar, and beyond that, the plain-lands to the west. His dark figure passed through the silent forest with the quickness of a fleeting shadow, touching the land only momentarily, then hastening on. His form seemed substanceless, passing over the lives of little beings that saw him briefly and forgot, neither changing nor yet leaving them quite the same, his indelible print fixed in their uncomprehending minds. Once more he reflected on the journey they were making to Paranor, pondering what he knew that none other could know, and he felt strangely helpless in the face of what was surely the passing of an age. The others only suspected his own role in all that had happened, in all that yet lay ahead, but he alone was forced to live with the truth behind his own destiny and theirs. He muttered half aloud at the thought, hating what was happening, but knowing that there was no other choice for him to make. His long, lean face appeared a black mask of indecision to the silent woods he passed on his lonely march, a face lined deeply with worry, but hard with an inner resolution that would sustain the soul when the heart was gone.

Daybreak found him moving through a particularly dense stretch of woods that ran for several miles over hilly terrain strewn with boulders and fallen logs. He noticed at once that this part of the forest was strangely silent, as if a special kind of death had placed its chill hand upon the earth. The trail behind was carefully marked with small strips of white cloth. He walked more slowly. There had been nothing up to this point to cause him concern, but now a sixth sense reared up within his quick mind, warning him that all was not as it should be. He reached a break in the main path that split into two branches. One, a wide, clear path that looked as if it had once been a major road, ran to the left, downward into what appeared to be a huge valley. It was difficult to tell because the forests had overgrown everything, obscuring from view the trail beyond the first several hundred yards. The second path was choked by heavy underbrush. No more than one person at a time could pass that way without cutting a wider trail. The narrow path led upward toward a high ridge which ran at an angle away from the Pass of Jade.

Suddenly the grim historian stiffened as he sensed the presence of another being, an undeniably evil life form somewhere farther down the trail leading into the invisible valley. There was no sound of movement. Whatever it was, it preferred to lie in wait for its victims along the lower trail. Allanon quickly tore off two strips of cloth, one red and one white, tying the red cloth to the wider trail leading into the valley and the white cloth along the smaller trail leading to the ridge. When he had completed this task, he paused and listened again, but while he could still sense the presence of the creature down the valley path, he could detect no movement. Its power was no match for his own, but it would be dangerous to the men following. Checking the cloth strips one final time, he silently moved upward along the narrow ridge path and disappeared into the heavy underbrush.

Almost an hour passed before the creature that lay in wait on the path leading into the valley decided to investigate. It was highly intelligent, a possibility that Allanon had not considered, and it knew that whoever it was who had passed above had sensed its presence and purposely avoided that approach. It knew as well that this same man had powers far greater than its own, so it lay noiselessly in the forest and waited for him to go away. Now it had waited long enough. Minutes later it gazed intently at the silent fork in the main trail where the two small strips of cloth fluttered brightly in the light forest breeze. How stupid such markers were, thought the creature slyly, and with ponderous footsteps moved its great, misshapen bulk forward.

Balinor had the final watch of the evening, and as the dawn began to break sharply in dazzling golden rays over the eastern mountain horizon, the tall borderman gently awakened the remainder of the company from their peaceful slumber to the chill of the early morning. They turned out hastily, gulped down a short breakfast while attempting to warm themselves in the yet cool air of the sunny day, silently packed their gear, and prepared to begin the day's march. Someone asked about Allanon, and Flick sleepily replied that the historian had departed sometime around midnight but said nothing to him. Nobody was particularly surprised that he had left so quietly, and little more was said about the matter.

Within half an hour, the company was on the path leading northward through the forests of the Wolfsktaag, moving steadily, without conversation for the most part, in the same order as before. Hendel had relinquished his spot as point man to the talented Menion Leah, who moved with the noiseless grace of a cat through the tangled boughs and brush over the leaf-strewn floor. Hendel felt a certain respect for the Prince of Leah. In time he would be unsurpassed by any woodsman. But the Dwarf knew as well that the highlander was brash and still inexperienced, and that in these lands only the cautious and the seasoned survived. Nevertheless, practice was the only way to learn, so the Dwarf grudgingly allowed the young tracker to lead the party, contenting himself with double-checking everything that appeared on the path before them.

One particularly disturbing detail caught the Dwarf's attention almost immediately, although it completely escaped the notice of his companion. The trail failed to reveal any sign of the man who had come this way only hours earlier. Although he scanned the ground meticulously, Hendel was unable to discern even the slightest trace of a human footprint. The strips of white cloth appeared at regular intervals, just as Allanon had promised they would be. Yet there was no sign of his passage. Hendel knew the tales about the mysterious wanderer and had heard that he possessed extraordinary powers. But he had never dreamed that the man was such an accomplished tracker that he could completely hide his own trail. The Dwarf could not understand it, but decided to keep the matter to himself.

At the rear of the procession, Balinor, too, had been wondering about the enigmatic man from Paranor, the historian who knew so much that no one else had even suspected, the wanderer who seemed to have been everywhere and yet about whom so little was known. He had known Allanon off and on for many years while growing up in his father's kingdom, but could only vaguely recall him, a dark stranger who had come and gone without warning, who had always seemed so kind to him, yet had never offered to reveal his own mysterious background. The wise men of all the lands knew Allanon as a scholar and a philosopher without equal. Others knew him only as a traveler who paid his way with good advice and who possessed a kind of grim common sense with which no one could find fault. Balinor had learned from him and had come to trust in him with what could almost be described as blind faith. Yet he had never really understood the historian. He pondered that thought for a while, and then in what came as an almost casual revelation, he realized that in all the time he had spent with Allanon, he had never seen any sign of a change in his age.

The trail began to turn upward again and to narrow as the great forest trees and heavy underbrush closed in like solid walls. Menion had followed the strips of cloth dutifully and had little doubt that they were on the right path, but automatically began to double-check himself as the going became noticeably tougher than before. It was almost noon when the trail branched unexpectedly, and a surprised Menion paused.

'This is strange. A fork in the trail and no marker – I can't understand why Allanon would fail to leave a sign.'

'Something must have happened to it,' concluded Shea, sighing heavily. 'Which route do we take?'

Hendel scanned the ground carefully. On the path leading upward toward the ridge, there were indications of someone's passage from the bent twigs and recently fallen leaves. On the lower trail, however, there were signs of footprints, though they were very faint. Instinctively he knew that something dangerous lay along one and maybe both of the trails.

'I don't like it – something's wrong here,' he grumbled to no one in particular. 'The signs are confused, perhaps on purpose.'

'Perhaps all the talk about this being taboo land wasn't nonsense after all,' suggested Flick dryly, parking himself on a fallen tree.

Balinor came forward and conferred with Hendel briefly concerning the direction of the Pass of Jade. Hendel admitted that the lower trail would be the quickest way, and it clearly appeared to be the main passage. But there was no way to tell which trail Allanon had chosen. Finally Menion threw up his hands in exasperation and demanded that a choice be made.

'We all know that Allanon would not have passed this

way without leaving a sign, so the obvious conclusion is that either something happened to the signs or something happened to him. In either case, we can't sit here and expect to find the answer. He said we would meet at the Pass of Jade or beyond in the forests, so I vote we take the lower road – the quickest way!'

Hendel again voiced his confusion over the signs on the lower trail and his nagging feeling that something dangerous lay ahead, a feeling which Shea had begun to share the minute they arrived at this point without finding the strips of cloth. Balinor and the others debated heatedly for a few minutes and finally agreed with the highlander. They would follow the quickest route, but keep an especially close watch until they were out of these mysterious mountains.

The line of march reformed with Menion leading. They started rapidly down the gently sloping lower trail which appeared to be drawing them into a valley heavily camouflaged by great trees that grew limb to limb for miles in all directions. Remarkably, the road began to widen after only a short distance, the trees and scrub brush to move back, and the geography to level off into a barely perceptible downward slope. Their fears began to dissipate as travel grew easier, and it became readily apparent that in years long since gone, the road had been a major thoroughfare for the inhabitants of this land. They walked for less than an hour's time before reaching the valley floor. It was difficult to tell where they were in relation to the mountain ranges surrounding them. The trees of the forest obscured everything from view but the path immediately ahead and the cloudless blue sky above.

After a short time of traveling across the valley floor, the party caught sight of an unusual structure that rose through the trees like a huge framework. It seemed a part of the forest about it, save for the unusual straightness of its limbs, and within moments they were close enough to see that it was a series of giant girders, covered with rust and framing square portions of the open sky. The company slowed automatically, looking cautiously about to be certain that this was not some kind of trap prepared for unwary travelers. But nothing moved, so they continued their approach, intrigued by the structure that waited silently ahead.

Suddenly the road ended and the strange framework stood completely revealed, the great metal beams decaying with age, but still straight and seemingly as sturdy as they had been in ages past. They were part of what had once been a large city built so long ago that no one recalled its existence, a city forgotten like the valley and the mountains in which it rested – a final monument to a civilization of vanished beings. The metal framework was securely set in huge foundations of something like stone, now crumbling and chipped by the weather and time. In places, remnants of what had once been walls were visible. A large number of these dying buildings were clustered together, pushing out for several hundred yards beyond the travelers and ending where the wall of the forests marked the end of man's feeble invasion into an indestructible nature. Within the structures, and through the foundation and framework, grew brush and small trees in such abundance that the city appeared to be choking to death rather than crumbling with time. The party stood in mute silence at this strange testimonial to another era, the accomplishment of people like themselves, so many years before. Shea felt an undeniable sense of futility at the sight of the grim frames, rusting their weary lives away.

'What place is this?' he asked quietly.

'The remains of some city,' shrugged Hendel, turning to the young Valeman. 'No one has been here for centuries, I imagine.'

Balinor walked over to the nearest structure and rubbed the metal girder. Huge flecks of rust and dirt came off in a shower, leaving beneath a dull steel-gray color that told of the strength still left in the building. The others of the company followed the borderman as he walked slowly about the foundation, looking carefully at the stone-like substance. A moment later he stopped at one corner and brushed away the surface dirt and grime to reveal a single date still legible in the decaying wall. They all bent closer to read it.

'Why this city was here before the Great Wars!' Shea said in amazement. 'I can't believe it – it must be the oldest structure in existence!'

'I remember what Allanon told us of the men who lived then,' declared Menion in a rare moment of dreamy recollection. 'That was the great age, he said, and even so, this is all it has to show us. Nothing but a few metal girders.'

'How about a few minutes' rest before we leave?' suggested Shea. 'I'd like to take a quick look at the other buildings.'

Balinor and Hendel felt somewhat uneasy about stopping, but agreed to a short rest as long as everyone kept together. Shea wandered over to the next building, accompanied by Flick. Hendel sat down and looked warily at the huge frames, disliking every moment they spent in this metal jungle so foreign to his own forest homeland. The others followed Menion to the other side of the building on which they had just found the date, discovering a portion of a name on a fallen chunk of wall. No more than a few minutes had passed when Hendel caught himself daydreaming of Culhaven and his family and jerked into immediate watchfulness. Everyone was in view, but Shea and Flick had moved farther off to the left of the dead city, still looking curiously at the decaying remnants and searching for signs of the old civilization. In the same instant he realized that except for the low voices of his companions, the surrounding forest had gone deathly quiet. Not even

192

the wind stirred through the peaceful valley, not a bird flew over them, not a single insect's vibrant hum was audible. His own heavy breathing was hoarse in his straining ears.

'Something's wrong.' The words came out as he reached instinctively for his heavy battle mace.

At that moment, Flick caught sight of something dull white on the ground off to one side of the building that Shea and he were examining, partially hidden by the foundation. Curiously, he approached the objects which appeared to be sticks of various sizes and shapes scattered aimlessly about. Shea failed to notice his brother's interest and moved away from the building, staring in fascination at the remains of another structure. Flick came closer, but still was unable to tell from even a few feet away what the white sticks were. It was not until he stood over them and saw them shining dully against the dark earth in the noon-day sun that he realized with a sickening chill they were bones.

The jungle behind the stocky Valeman burst apart with a thunderous thrashing of limbs and brush. Forth from its place of concealment emerged a grayish, multilegged horror of monstrous size. A nightmare mutation of living flesh and machine, its crooked legs balanced a body formed half of metal plating, half of coarse-haired flesh. An insect-like head bobbed fitfully on a neck of metal. Tentacles tipped with stingers dipped slightly above two glowing eyes and savage jaws that snapped with hunger. Bred by the men of another time to serve the needs of its masters, it had survived the holocaust that had destroyed them, but in surviving and in preserving its centuries-old existence with bits of metal grafted to its decaying form, it had evolved into a misshapen freak – and worse, an eater of flesh.

It was upon its hapless victim before anyone could move. Shea was closest as the mammoth creature struck his brother with an outstretched leg, knocking him flat and pinning him helplessly to the ground, rasping as its jaws reached downward. Shea never stopped to think; he yelled fiercely and drew his short hunting knife, brandishing the insignificant weapon as he rushed to Flick's rescue. The creature had just grasped its unconscious victim when its attention was directed to the other human charging wildly to the attack. Hesitating at this unexpected assault, it released its deadly grip and took a cautious step backward, its huge bulk poised to strike a second time as its bulging green eyes fixed on the tiny man before it.

'Shea, don't . . .!' yelled Menion in terror as the Valeman struck futilely at one of the creature's twisted limbs. A rasp of fury came boiling out of the depths of the monster's great body, and it swiped at Shea with an extended leg to pin him to the ground. But Shea leaped to safety by scant inches and struck again from another point with his tiny weapon. Then, before the horrified eyes of the other travelers, the nightmare from the jungle rushed the unfortunate Valeman in a flurry of legs and hair. Just as Shea was about to seize Flick to drag him to safety, the creature bowled him over, and for a second everything disappeared in a cloud of dust.

It had all happened so fast that no one else had yet had time to act. Hendel had never seen a creature of this size and ferocity, a creature that apparently had lived in these mountains for untold years, lying in wait for its hapless victims. The Dwarf was the farthest from the scene of the battle, but moved quickly to aid the fallen Valemen. At the same moment, the others reacted as well. The instant the dust settled enough to reveal the hideous head, three bowstrings sounded in harmony and the arrows buried themselves deeply in the black, hair-covered bulk with audible thuds. The creature rasped in fury and raised its body upward, forelegs extended, searching out its new attackers.

The challenge did not go unanswered. Menion Leah discarded the ash bow and drew the great sword from its sheath, gripping it in both hands.

194

'*Leah! Leah!*' The battle cry of a thousand years burst forth as the Prince charged wildly across crumbling foundations and fallen walls to reach the monster. Balinor had drawn his own sword, the huge blade gleaming fiercely in the bright sunlight, and rushed to the aid of the highlander. Durin and Dayel fired volley after volley into the head of the giant beast as it rasped in fury, using its forelegs to brush at the arrows and knock them loose from its thick skin. Menion reached the abomination ahead of Balinor and with one great swing of his sword cut deeply into the closest leg, feeling the iron strike bone with jarring impact. As the monster reared back and knocked Menion aside, it received a powerful blow to the head; Hendel's war mace struck with stunning force. A second later, Balinor stood solidly before the huge creature, the hunting cloak thrown back and billowing out behind the flashing chain mail. With a series of quick, powerful cuts of the great sword, the Prince of Callahorn completely severed a second leg. The beast struck back savagely, trying unsuccessfully to pin one of its attackers to the earth to crush the life out of him. The three men sounded their battle cries and struck ferociously, desperately trying to drive the monster back from its fallen victims. They attacked with precision, striking at the unprotected flanks, and drawing the behemoth first to one side and then to the other. Durin and Dayel moved in closer and continued to rain arrows on the massive target. Many were deflected by the metal plating, but the relentless assault constantly distracted the maddened creature. At one point, Hendel received so severe a blow that he was knocked senseless for a few seconds and the nightmare attacker quickly moved to finish him. But a determined Balinor, mustering every ounce of strength at his command, struck so savagely and relentlessly that it could not reach the fallen Dwarf before he had been pulled to his feet by Menion.

Finally the arrows of Durin and Dayel partially blinded

the creature's right eye. Bleeding profusely from its stricken eye and from a dozen other major wounds, the monster knew that it had lost the battle and would probably lose its life if it did not escape at once. Making a short feint at the closest assailant, it suddenly wheeled about with surprising dexterity and made a quick rush for the safety of its forest lair. Menion gave a brief pursuit, but the creature outdistanced him and disappeared within the great trees. The five rescuers quickly turned their attention to the two fallen Valemen, who lay crumpled and unmoving in the trampled earth. Hendel examined them, having had some experience in treating battle wounds over the years. There were numerous cuts and bruises, but apparently no broken bones. It was difficult to tell if there had been any internal damage. Both had been stung by the creature, Flick on the back of the neck and Shea on the shoulder; the ugly, deep-purple marks indicated penetration of the exposed skin. Poison! The two men remained unconscious after repeated attempts to revive them, their breathing shallow and their skin pale and beginning to turn gray.

'I can't treat them for this,' Hendel declared worriedly. 'We've got to get them to Allanon. He knows something about these matters; he could probably help them.'

'They're dying, aren't they?' Menion asked in a barely audible whisper.

Hendel nodded faintly in the hushed silence that followed. Balinor immediately took command of the situation, ordering Durin and Menion to cut poles to make stretchers, while Hendel and he prepared hammocks to hold the Valemen in place. Dayel was placed on guard in case the creature should return unexpectedly. Fifteen minutes later the stretchers were completed, the unconscious men were securely fastened in place and covered with blankets to protect them from the cold of the approaching night, and the company was ready to march. Hendel took the lead, with the other four carrying the stretchers.

The party quickly crossed through the ruins of the deathly still city and after a few minutes located a trail leading out of the hidden valley. The grim faces of the Dwarf in the lead and the bearers of the unconscious forms strapped tightly to the makeshift stretchers glanced back in futile anger at the still-visible structures rising out of the forest. A bitter feeling of helplessness welled up inside them. They had come into the valley a strong, determined company, filled with confidence in themselves and belief in the mission which had brought them together. But as they left now, their bearing was that of beaten, discouraged victims of a cruel misfortune.

They moved hurriedly out of the valley, up the gentle slopes of the enclosing mountain range, up the broad, winding path shrouded by tall, silent trees, thinking only of the wounded men they carried. The familiar sounds of the forest returned, indicating that the danger of the valley was past. None of them had time to notice now save the taciturn Dwarf, whose battle-trained mind registered the changes of his forest homeland automatically. He thought back bitterly on the choice that had brought them into the valley, wondering what had happened to Allanon and to the promised markers. Almost without considering it, he knew that the tall wanderer must have placed markers before taking the high trail, and that someone or something, perhaps the creature they had encountered, had realized what the markers were for and removed them. He shook his head at his own stupidity in failing to recognize the truth at once and stamped harder on the ground passing beneath his booted feet, grinding his wrath in bits and pieces.

They reached the lip of the valley and continued on, without pausing, through the forests that stretched ahead in an unbroken mass of great trunks and heavy limbs, tangled and woven together as if to shut out the mountain sky. The path grew narrow once more, forcing them to proceed in single file with the stretchers. The afternoon sky was rapidly changing from a deep blue to a mixed bloodred and purple that marked the close of another day. Hendel calculated that they could expect no more than another hour of sunlight. He had no idea how far they were from the Pass of Jade, but he was fairly certain that it could not be far from where they were now. All of them knew that they would not stop at nightfall, could not get any sleep that night or possibly even the next day if they expected to save the lives of the Valemen. They had to find Allanon quickly and have the injuries of the brothers treated before the poison reached their hearts. No one voiced any opinion and no one felt it necessary to discuss the matter. There was only one choice and they accepted it.

As the sun dropped behind the western mountain ridges an hour later, the arms of the four bearers had reached the limit of their endurance, stiff and strained from the uninterrupted haul out of the valley. Balinor called a brief rest and the group collapsed in a heap, breathing heavily in the early evening quiet of the forest. With the coming of night, Hendel relinquished his position as leader of the company to Dayel, who was obviously the most exhausted from carrying Flick's stretcher. The Valemen were still unconscious, wrapped in the layered blankets for warmth, their drawn faces ashen in the fading light and covered with a thin layer of perspiration. Hendel felt their pulse and could barely discern a flicker of life in the limp arms. Menion stormed audibly about the rest area in an uncontrolled fury, swearing vengeance against everything that came to mind, his lean face flushed red with the heat of the past battle and the burning desire to find something further on which to vent his wrath.

The company resumed its forced march after a short ten minutes' rest. The sun had disappeared entirely, leaving them in blackness broken only by the pale light of the stars and a sliver of new moon. The absence of any real light made the traveling slow and hazardous over the winding and often uneven path. Hendel had taken up Dayel's position at the end of Flick's stretcher, while the slim Elf utilized his highly developed senses to locate the trail through the darkness. The Dwarf thought ruefully of the cloth strips Allanon had promised he would leave to guide them out of the Wolfsktaag. Now, more than any time previously, they were needed to mark the proper route – not for himself, but for the two Valemen, whose lives depended on speed. As he walked, his arms not yet feeling the strain of carrying the stretcher, his mind mulling over the situation facing them, he found himself gazing almost absently at two tall peaks which broke the smoothness of the night sky to his left. It was several minutes before he realized with a start that he was looking at the entrance to the Pass of Jade.

At the same moment, Dayel announced to the group that the trail split in three directions just ahead. Hendel quickly informed them that the pass would be reached by following the left path. Without pausing, they moved onward. The trail began to lead them downward out of the mountains in the direction of the twin peaks. Reassured that the end was in sight, they marched faster, their strength renewed with the hope that Allanon would be waiting. Shea and Flick were no longer lying motionless on the stretchers, but were beginning to twitch uncontrollably and even thrash violently beneath the tightened blankets. A battle was waging within the poisoned bodies between the tightening grip of death and a strong will to live. Hendel thought to himself that it was a good sign. Their bodies had not yet given up the struggle to survive. He turned to the others in the company and discovered that they were gazing intently at what appeared to be a light gleaming sharply against the black horizon between the twin peaks. Then their own ears caught the distant sounds of a heavy booming noise and a low hum of voices coming from the location of the light. Balinor ordered them to keep moving, but told Dayel to scout ahead and to keep his eyes open.

'What is it?' asked Menion curiously.

'I can't be sure from this distance,' Durin answered. 'It sounds like drums and men chanting or singing.'

'Gnomes,' declared Hendel ominously.

Another hour's travel brought them close enough to determine that the curious light was caused by the burning of hundreds of small fires, and the noises were indeed the booming of dozens of drums and the chanting of many, many men. The sounds had grown to deafening proportions, and the two peaks marking the entrance of the Pass of Jade loomed like huge pillars in front of them. Balinor felt certain that if the creatures ahead were Gnomes, they would not venture into their taboo land to post guards, so the company would be reasonably safe until they reached the pass. The sound of the drums and the chanting continued to vibrate through the heavy forest trees. Whoever was blocking the pass was there to stay for a while. Only moments later, the group had reached the edge of the Pass of Jade, just beyond reach of the firelight. Moving silently off the path into the shadows, the company held a brief conference.

'What is going on?' Balinor asked anxiously of Hendel, when they were all crouched in the protection of the forest.

'It's impossible to tell from back here, unless you're a mind reader!' the Dwarf growled irately. 'The chanting sounds like Gnomes, but the words are blurred. I had better go ahead and check it out.'

'I don't think so,' Durin advised quickly. 'This is a job for an Elf, not a Dwarf. I can move more quickly and quietly than you, and I'll be able to sense the presence of any guards.'

'Then it had better be me,' Dayel suggested. 'I'm

smaller, lighter, and faster than any of you. Be back in a minute.'

Without waiting for an answer, he faded into the forest and had disappeared before anyone could voice an objection. Durin swore silently, fearing for his young brother's life. If there were indeed Gnomes in the Pass of Jade, they would kill any stray Elf they caught prowling about in the dark. Hendel shrugged in disgust and sat back against a tree to wait for Dayel's return. Shea had begun to moan and thrash more violently, throwing aside his blankets and nearly rolling off the stretcher. Flick was behaving in the same manner, though less forcibly, groaning in low tones, his face frighteningly drawn. Menion and Durin moved quickly to wrap the blankets back around the Valemen, this time tying them securely in place with long strips of leather. The moans continued, but the company had little fear of discovery with all the noise coming from the other side of the pass. They sat back quietly waiting for Dayel, looking anxiously at the bright horizon and listening to the drums, knowing that somehow they would have to find a way past whomever was blocking the entrance. Long minutes slipped by. Then Dayel appeared suddenly out of the darkness.

'Are they Gnomes?' asked Hendel sharply.

'Hundreds of them,' the Elf replied grimly. 'They're spread out all across the entrance to the Pass of Jade and there are dozens of fires. It must be some sort of ceremony from the way they're beating the drums and chanting. The worst of it is that they are all facing right into the pass. No one could possibly go in or out without being seen.'

He paused and looked briefly at the pain-wracked forms of the injured Valemen before turning back to face Balinor.

'I scouted the entire entrance and both sides of the peaks. There is no way out except straight through the Gnomes. They have us trapped!'

CHAPTER

12

ayel's bleak report brought an immediate reaction.
Menion leaped to his feet, reaching for his sword
and threatening to fight his way out or die in the
attempt. Balinor tried to restrain him, or at least to quiet
him, but there was complete bedlam for several minutes
as the others joined the shouting highlander in his vow.
Hendel questioned the somewhat shaken Dayel about
what he had seen at the entrance to the pass, and after a
few brief questions loudly ordered everyone to be silent.

'The Gnome chieftains are out there,' he informed Balinor, who had finally managed to restrain Menion long
enough to listen to the Dwarf. 'They have all the high
priests and members of surrounding villages here for a special ceremony that takes place once each month. They
come at sunset and sing praises to their gods for protecting them from the evils of the taboo land, the Wolfsktaag.
It will last all night, and by morning we can forget about
helping our young friends.'

'Wonderful people, the Gnomes!' exploded Menion.
'They fear the evils of this place, but they align themselves
with the Skull Kingdom! I don't know about the rest of
you, but I'm not giving up because of a few half-wit
Gnomes chanting useless spells!'

'No one is giving up, Menion,' Balinor said quickly.

202

'We're getting out of these mountains tonight. Right now.'

'How do you propose to do that?' demanded Hendel. 'Walk right through half the Gnome nation? Or perhaps we'll fly out?'

'Wait a minute!' Menion exclaimed suddenly and leaned over the unconscious Shea, searching eagerly through his clothing until he produced the small leather pouch containing the powerful Elfstones.

'The Elfstones will get us out of here,' he announced to the others, grasping the pouch.

'Has he lost his mind?' asked Hendel, incredulous at the sight of the highlander eagerly waving the leather pouch.

'It won't work, Menion,' declared Balinor quietly. 'The only one with the power to use the stones is Shea. Besides, Allanon once told me they could only be used against things whose power lies beyond substance, dangers that confuse the mind. Those Gnomes are mortal flesh and blood, not creatures of the spirit world or the imagination.'

'I don't know what you're talking about, but I do know that these stones worked against that creature from the Mist Marsh, and I saw it work . . .' Menion trailed off despondently, reflecting on what he was saying, and finally lowered the pouch and its precious contents. 'What's the use? You must be right. I don't even know what I'm saying anymore.'

'There has to be a way!' Durin came forward, casting about for suggestions. 'All we need is a plan to draw attention away from us for about five minutes and we could slip by them.'

Menion perked up at the suggestion, apparently finding some merit in the idea, but unable to think of a way to distract the attention of several thousand Gnomes. Balinor paced about for a few minutes, lost in thought while the others threw out random suggestions. Hendel suggested in bitter humor that he walk into their midst and let himself be captured. The Gnomes would be so overjoyed at getting their hands on him, the man they had tried so hard to destroy all these years, that they would forget about anything else. Menion thought little of the joke and was all for allowing him to do what he suggested.

'Enough talk!' roared the Prince of Leah finally, losing his temper altogether. 'What we need now is a plan, one that will get us out of here right away, before the Valemen are completely beyond help. Now what do we do?'

'How wide is the pass?' asked Balinor absently, still pacing.

'About two hundred yards at the point the Gnomes are gathered,' Dayel replied, avoiding a confrontation with Menion. He thought a minute longer, and then snapped his fingers in recollection. 'The right side of the pass is completely open, but on the left side there are small trees and scrub brush growing along the cliff face. They would give us some cover.'

'Not enough,' interrupted Hendel. 'The Pass of Jade is wide enough to march an army through, but trying to get past with the little cover offered would be suicidal. I've seen it from the other side, and any Gnome looking would spot you in a minute!'

'Then they'll have to be looking somewhere else,' Balinor growled as the faint glimmer of a plan began to form in his mind. He stopped suddenly, and kneeling on the forest floor drew a crude diagram of the pass entrance, looking to Dayel and Hendel for approval. Menion had stopped complaining long enough to join them.

'From the drawing, it appears that we can stay under cover and out of the light until we reach here,' Balinor explained, indicating a point of ground near the line representing the left cliff face. 'The slope is gentle enough to allow us to remain above the Gnomes and within the cover of the brush. Then there is an open space for about twenty-five or thirty yards until the forests begin against the steeper cliff face beyond. That is the point of diversion, the point where the light will show us clearly to anyone look-ing. The Gnomes will have to be turned another way when we cross that open space.'

He paused and looked at the four anxious faces, wish-ing fervently that he had a better plan, but knowing there was no time to come up with another if they were to pre-serve any chance of recovering the Sword of Shannara. Whatever else was at stake now, nothing was of such para-mount importance as the life of the frail-looking Valeman who was heir to the Sword's power and the one chance left to the people of the four lands to avoid a conflict that would consume them all. Their own lives could be sold comparatively cheaply to preserve that single hope.

'It will take the best bowman in the Southland,' the tall borderman announced quietly. 'That man will have to be Menion Leah.' The highlander looked up in surprise at the unexpected declaration, unable to hide the sense of pride he felt. 'There will be only one shot,' continued the Prince of Callahorn. 'If it is not exactly on target, we will be lost.'

'What is your plan?' interrupted Durin curiously.

'When we reach the end of our cover at the open space, Menion will locate one of the Gnome chieftains to the far side of the pass. He will have one shot with the bow to kill him, and in the confusion that follows, we can slip by.'

'It won't work, my friend,' growled Hendel. 'The minute they see their leader struck by the arrow, they'll be all over that pass entrance. You'll be found in minutes.'

Balinor shook his head and smiled faintly, but uncon-vincingly.

'No, we won't, because they will be after someone else. The minute the Gnome chieftain falls, one of us will show himself back in the pass. The Gnomes will be so incensed and so eager to get their hands on him, that they won't take the time to search for anyone else, and we can slip by in the confusion.'

Silence greeted his appraisal of the situation, and the

anxious faces looked from one person to the next, the same thought in every mind.

'It sounds just fine for everyone but the man who stays behind to show himself,' broke in Menion in disbelief. 'Who gets that suicidal chore?'

'It was my plan,' declared Balinor. 'It will be my duty to stay behind and lead the Gnomes into the Wolfsktaag, until I can circle back and join you later at the edge of the Anar.'

'You must be insane if you think I'm letting you stay behind and claim all the credit,' Menion declared. 'If I make the shot, I stay to take the bows, and if I miss . . .'

He trailed off and smiled, shrugging casually, clapping Durin on the shoulder as the other looked on incredulously. Balinor was about to object further when Hendel stepped forward shaking his broad head in disagreement.

'The plan is fine as it goes, but we all know that the man who stays behind will have several thousand Gnomes attempting to track him down, or at best, waiting for him to come out of their taboo land. The man who stays must be a man who knows the Gnomes, their methods, how to fight and survive against them. In this case, that man is a Dwarf with a lifetime of battle knowledge behind him. It must be me.

'Besides,' he added grimly, 'I told you how badly they want my head. They won't pass up the chance after such an affront.'

'And I've already told you,' insisted Menion again, 'that's my . . .'

'Hendel is right,' Balinor cut in sharply. The others looked at him in amazement. Only Hendel knew that the decision the borderman had made, however distasteful, was the same one he would have made had their positions been reversed. 'The choice has been made, and we will abide by it. Hendel will have the best chance to survive.'

He turned to the stocky Dwarf warrior and extended a

broad hand. The other gripped it tightly for a brief moment, then turned quickly from them and disappeared up the trail at a slow trot. The others watched, but he was gone in a matter of seconds. The booming of the drums and the chanting of the Gnomes rolled deeply out of the lighted sky to the west.

'Gag the Valemen so they cannot cry out,' ordered Balinor, startling the other three with the sharpness of the sudden command. When Menion failed to move, but remained rooted to the spot, looking silently up the path Hendel had taken a moment before, Balinor turned to him and placed a reassuring hand on his shoulder. 'Be certain, Prince of Leah, that your shot is worthy of his sacrifice for us.'

The still-twisting bodies of the two Valemen were quickly secured to the makeshift stretchers and their low cries effectively muffled by tightly bound cloth gags. The four remaining men picked up their gear and the stretchers and moved out of the cover of the trees toward the mouth of the Pass of Jade. The Gnome fires blazed up before them, lighting the night sky in a brilliant aura of yellow and orange flame. The drums crashed out in steady rhythm, the sound deafening in the ears of the four as they drew closer. The chanting grew louder until it seemed as if the entire Gnome nation must be gathered. The overall sensation was one of eerie unreality, as if they were lost in that primitive world of half-dreams traversed by mortal and spirit alike in strange rituals that have no recognizable purpose. The walls of the towering cliffs rose jaggedly into the night sky on either side, distant but ominously huge intruders on the little scene taking place at the high entrance to the Pass of Jade. Rock walls glimmered in a shower of color – red, orange, and yellow blended into an overriding deep green that danced and flickered in the man-made firelight. The color reflected off the hardness of the rock and mirrored softly in the grim-set faces of the four stretcher bearers, touching momentarily the fear they were trying to conceal.

Finally the men stood within the corridor of the pass, just out of sight of the chanting Gnomes. The slopes rose steeply on either side, the northern incline offering little or no cover whatsoever, while the southern fairly bristled with small trees and dense scrub brush that grew so thickly it was choking on itself. Balinor silently signaled the others to make their way up the side of this slope. He took the lead himself, searching out the safest approach, moving cautiously upward toward the small trees that grew higher on the mountain. It took them quite awhile to reach the safety of the trees, and Balinor motioned them slowly ahead into the mouth of the pass. As they inched forward, Menion could look through breaks in the trees and brush to catch quick glimpses of the fires burning below, still ahead of them, their bright flames almost completely masked by the hundreds of small, gnarled figures who moved rhythmically in the light, chanting in a deep, soul-searching drone to the spirits of the Wolfsktaag. His mouth felt dry as he visualized what would happen to them if they were discovered, and he thought grimly of Hendel. He was suddenly very afraid for the Dwarf. The brush and trees began to thin out, rising higher on the slope, and the four crept upward under their cover, but slower now, more hesitantly, as Balinor kept one eye fixed on the Gnomes below. Durin and Dayel walked on cat feet, their light Elven frames moving soundlessly through dry, brittle limbs and twigs, blending into the natural terrain about them. Again Menion peered worriedly at the Gnomes, closer than before, their yellowish bodies weaving to the drums, gleaming with the sweat of hours spent calling on their gods and praying to the mountains.

Then the four reached the end of their cover. Balinor pointed ahead to the yards of open space that lay between them and the dense forests of the Anar standing darkly beyond. It was a long distance, and there was nothing between the men and the floor of the pass but the scrub brush and a few sparse blades of grass, dried from the sun. Directly below were the chanting Gnomes, swaying in the fire's glow and in a perfect position to see anyone attempting to cross the brightly lighted open spaces of the southern slope. Dayel had been correct; it would have been suicide to attempt to sneak past under those conditions. Menion looked up and quickly saw that further efforts to reach higher ground with the two wounded Valemen were effectively prevented by a sheer cliff face that rose abruptly several hundred feet into the air, banking only slightly as it continued upward to its invisible peak. He turned back to look again at the open space. It appeared farther across than before. Balinor motioned the others into a tight circle.

'Menion can move to the edge of the cover,' he whispered cautiously. 'After he picks his target and the Gnome is hit, Hendel will focus their rage by calling attention to himself inside the pass, high on the other slope. He should be in place by this time. When the Gnomes rush him, we move across the open space as quickly as possible. Don't stop to look – keep moving.'

The other three nodded and all eyes rested on Menion, who had unstrapped the great ash bow from his back and was testing its pull. He picked out a single long, black arrow, sighting it for accuracy, and hesitated for a minute, looking downward through the veiled covering of the trees to the hundreds of Gnomes on the valley floor. Suddenly he realized what was expected of him. He was to kill a man, not in battle or in fair combat, but from ambush, with stealth, and that man would never have a chance. He knew instinctively that he could not do it, that he was not the seasoned fighter that Balinor was, that he did not have the cold determination of Hendel. He was brash and even brave at times and ready to stand against anyone in open combat, but he was not a killer. He glanced back momentarily at the others, and they saw it at once in his eyes.

'You must do it!' whispered Balinor harshly, his eyes burning with fierce determination.

Durin's face was averted slightly in the half-light, grim and frozen with uncertainty. Dayel stared directly at Menion, his Elven eyes wide, frightened by the choice the highlander faced, the youthful countenance ashen and ghostlike.

'I cannot kill a man this way,' Menion shook involuntarily at his own words, 'even to save their lives . . .'

He paused and Balinor continued to stare at him, waiting for something more.

'I can do the job,' Menion announced suddenly after a moment's reflection and a second look to the valley below. 'But it shall be done a different way.'

Without further explanation he moved forward through the clump of trees and crouched silently on the fringe, almost beyond its sparse protection. His eyes scanned hurriedly the forms of the Gnomes below, finally coming to rest on a chieftain on the far side of the pass. The Gnome stood before his subjects, his wizened yellow face uplifted, his small hands extended, holding in offering a long bowl of glowing embers. He stood motionless as he led the chanting with the other Gnome chieftains, his face turned toward the entrance to the Wolfsktaag. Menion withdrew a second arrow from the quiver and laid it in front of him. Then on one knee, he inched from the safety of the small tree he had positioned himself behind, fitted the first arrow to the bow and sighted. The other three waited grimly, breathless within the edges of the foliage, watching the bowman. For one split second everything seemed to come to a complete standstill, and then the taut bowstring was released with an audible twang and the arrow flew invisibly to its target. Almost as if a part of the same motion, Menion fitted the second arrow to the string, sighted and fired with blinding rapidity, then dropped motionless into the cover of the closest tree.

It happened so fast that no one saw it all, but each caught glimpses of the bowman's action and the scene that followed in the midst of the unsuspecting Gnomes. The first arrow struck the long bowl in the outstretched hands of the chanting Gnome chieftain and sent it spinning in an explosion of wood splinters. Gleaming red coals flew upward in a shower of sparks. In the next instant, while the astonished Gnome and his still-mystified followers were caught momentarily frozen with uncertainty, the second arrow embedded itself painfully in the half-turned and highly vulnerable posterior of the chieftain, who gave an agonizing howl that could be heard the length and breadth of the firelit Pass of Jade. The timing was absolutely perfect. It happened so quickly that even the unfortunate victim had no time, nor inclination for that matter, to decide where the embarrassing assault had come from or who the deceitful perpetrator might have been. The Gnome chieftain leaped about in terror and pain for several wild moments as his fellow Gnomes looked on in mixed bewilderment and apprehension, emotions that quickly changed. Their ceremony had been rudely interrupted and one of their chieftains had been treacherously struck from ambush. They were humiliated and dangerously angered.

Within seconds after the arrows struck their targets, before anyone had been given a chance to collect his senses, a torch appeared far away inside the pass on the upper reaches of the northern slope, touching off a giant bonfire that blazed into the night sky as if the earth itself had erupted in answer to the cries of the vengeful Gnomes. Before the rising blaze stood the broad, immobile figure of the Dwarf Hendel, his arms raised in challenge, one great hand clutching the stone-shattering mace in menacing defiance of all who looked up at him. His laugh echoed deafeningly off the cliff walls.

211

'Come face me, Gnomes – worms of the earth!' he roared mockingly. 'Stand and fight – it's plain you won't be caught sitting for a while. Your foolish gods cannot save you from the powers of a Dwarf, let alone the spirits of the Wolfsktaag!'

The roar of fury that went up from the Gnomes was frightening. Almost to a man, they surged forward into the Pass of Jade to reach the mocking figure on the slope above them, determined to tear his heart out for the shame and humiliation inflicted upon them. To strike a Gnome chieftain was bad enough, but to insult their religion and their courage in the same breath was unforgivable. Some of the Gnomes recognized the Dwarf immediately and shouted his name to the others, crying out for his instant death. As the Gnomes charged blindly ahead into the pass, their ceremony forgotten, the fires burning untended, the four men on the slope leaped to their feet, clutching tightly the stretchers and their precious cargo, and raced in a low crouch across the open and unprotected southern slope, fully exposed by the glare of the blaze below, their shadows appearing as huge phantoms against the cliffside above their fleeing forms. No one paused to check the progress of the angered Gnomes; they charged madly ahead, eyes glued to the sheltering blackness of the Anar forest looming in the distance.

Miraculously, they made it to the safety of the forest. There they paused, breathing heavily in the cool shadows of the great trees, listening to the sounds in the pass. Below them, the floor of the pass entrance was deserted except for a small cluster of Gnomes, one of whom was engaged in aiding the wounded chieftain by extracting the painful arrow. Menion chuckled inwardly at the sight, a slow smile spreading over his lean face. It quickly vanished, however, as he looked into the pass where the bonfire on the northern slope still burned fiercely. The maddened Gnomes were climbing upward from all directions, an endless number of small yellowish bodies, the foremost of which had almost reached the blaze. There was no sign of Hendel, but from all appearances he was trapped somewhere on the slope. The four watched for only a minute, and then Balinor silently signaled for them to move out. The Pass of Jade was left behind.

It was dark in the heavy forests once the company had gone beyond the light of the Gnome fires. Balinor placed the Prince of Leah in the fore with instructions to move downward from the southern slope to find a trail that would take them west. It did not take long to reach such a trail, and the little band moved into the central Anar. The forests about them shut out most of the dim light of the distant stars, and the great trees framed the path ahead like black walls. The Valemen were thrashing violently on the stretchers again and moaning painfully, even through the heavy gags. The carriers were beginning to lose hope for their young friends. The poison was seeping slowly through their systems and when enough of it reached their hearts, the end would come abruptly. There was no way the four men could know how much time was left the brothers, and no way to estimate how far they might be from any sort of medical assistance. The one man who knew the central Anar was behind them, trapped in the Wolfsktaag and fighting for his life.

Suddenly, so quickly that the four had no time to get off the trail to avoid detection, a group of Gnomes appeared from out of the wall of trees on the path ahead. For a moment everyone stood motionless, each group squinting through the dim light. It only took an instant for each to realize who the other was. The four men quickly put down the cumbersome stretchers and moved forward to stand in a line across the trail. The Gnomes, numbering ten or twelve in all, clustered together for a moment and then one of them disappeared back into the trees.

'They've sent for help,' Balinor whispered to the others.

213

'If we don't get by them quickly, they will have reinforcements here to finish us off.'

He had barely gotten the words out of his mouth before the remaining Gnomes let out a chilling battle cry and charged toward the four, their short, wicked-looking swords gleaming dully. The silent arrows of Menion and the Elf brothers dropped three of them in midstride before the rest swarmed over them like savage wolves. Dayel was completely bowled over by the assault and for a moment was lost from sight to the rear. Balinor stood firm as his huge blade cut two of the unfortunate Gnomes in half with one great sweep. The next several minutes were filled with sharp cries and labored breathing as the fighters battled back and forth across the narrow trail, the Gnomes seeking to get under the long reach of the men before them, the four defenders maneuvering to keep themselves between the fierce attackers and their two injured companions. In the end, the Gnomes all lay dead on the bloodied trail, their bodies small heaps in the dim light of the watching stars. Dayel had received a serious slash in the ribs that had to be bound, and Menion and Durin had received a number of small wounds. Balinor was untouched, his body protected from the Gnome swords by the lightweight chain mail beneath his shredded cloak.

The four paused only long enough to bind up Dayel's rib wound before picking up the stretchers and continuing at an even faster pace along the deserted path. They had further reason to hasten now. Gnome hunters would be quickly on their trail once they found their slain comrades. Menion tried to guess the hour from the position of the stars and by estimating their time of travel since the sun had set back in the Wolfsktaag Mountains, but could only conclude it was somewhere in the early-morning hours. The highlander felt the final signs of fatigue begin to creep through his aching arms and strained back muscles as he walked rapidly behind the broad form of

Balinor, who had taken the lead. They were all close to exhaustion, their bodies worn from the day's travel and their encounters with first the monster in the Wolfsktaag and then the Gnomes. They were kept on their feet primarily because they knew what would happen to the Valemen if they stopped. Nevertheless, thirty minutes after the brief battle with the Gnome rear guard, Dayel simply collapsed in midstride from loss of blood and exhaustion. It took the others several minutes to revive him and get him back on his feet. Even then, the pace slowed noticeably.

Balinor was forced to call a second halt only minutes later to allow them all a much-needed rest. They huddled quietly at the side of the trail and listened in dismay to the growing tumult all about them. Shouting and muffled drums, still distant, had begun again since their encounter on the trail. Apparently the Gnomes were alerted sufficiently to their presence to have called out a large number of hunting parties to track them down. It sounded as if the entire Anar forest were alive with angered Gnomes, stalking the surrounding woods and hills in an effort to find the enemy that had slipped by them on the trail and killed ten or so of their number in avoiding capture. Menion glanced down wearily at the young Valemen, their faces white and covered with a heavy sheet of perspiration. He could hear them moaning through the cloth gags, see their limbs convulse as the poison seeped relentlessly through their failing systems. He looked at them and felt suddenly that he had somehow let them down when they needed him most, and that now they would pay the price for his failure. It angered him when he thought about the whole crazy idea of journeying to Paranor to retrieve a relic of another age on the offhand chance that it would save them, or save anyone for that matter, from a creature like the Warlock Lord. Yet he knew, even as he finished the thought, that it was wrong to question now something they

215

had accepted from the first as little more than a remote possibility. He looked at Flick wearily and wondered why they couldn't have been better friends.

Durin's sudden whisper of warning sent them all scurrying off the exposed path with the cumbersome stretchers to the seclusion of the great trees, flattening themselves against the earth and waiting breathlessly. A moment later the distinct sound of heavy boots reverberated along the deserted trail and, from the direction in which they had come, a party of Gnome warriors marched out of the darkness toward their hiding place. Balinor immediately knew there were too many for them to fight and placed a restraining hand on the excited Menion to keep him from making any sudden movement. The Gnomes marched along the trail in formation, their yellow faces stony in the starlight as their wide-set eyes glanced uneasily about at the dark forest. They reached the point where the company crouched in hiding and moved on up the trail without pausing, unaware that their quarry was within a few feet. When they had disappeared from sight and there was no further sound of them, Menion turned to Balinor.

'We are finished if we don't find Allanon. We won't get another mile carrying Shea and Flick under these conditions unless we have help!'

Balinor nodded slowly, but made no comment. He knew their situation. But he knew as well that stopping now would be worse than capture or a second encounter with the Gnomes. Nor could they leave the brothers in these woods and hope they could find them after they got help – it was clearly too great a risk. He motioned the others to their feet. Without speaking, they picked up the stretchers and resumed the wearing march along the forest path, knowing now that the Gnomes were in front of them as well as behind. Menion wondered again what had befallen the gallant Hendel. It seemed impossible that even the resourceful Dwarf with all his skill in mountain fighting could have managed to evade those enraged Gnomes for any length of time. In any event, the Dwarf could not be in much worse shape than they were, wandering about the Anar with wounded men and no help in sight. If the Gnomes did find them again before they reached safety, Menion had little doubt as to the outcome.

Again Durin's sharp ears picked up the sound of approaching feet and everyone leaped to the safety of the great trees. They had barely gotten clear of the open trail and flattened themselves amidst the brush of the forest when figures appeared through the trees ahead. Even in the faint light of the stars, Durin's sharp eyes immediately picked out the leader of the small party as a giant of a man cloaked in a long black robe wound loosely about his lean body. A moment later the others saw him as well. It was Allanon. But Durin's sudden warning gesture stifled the exclamations of relief that were forming on the lips of Balinor and Menion. They squinted through the darkness and saw that the small, white-cloaked figures accompanying the historian were unmistakably Gnome.

'He's betrayed us!' whispered Menion harshly, his hand instinctively reaching for the long hunting knife at his belt.

'No, wait a minute,' ordered Balinor quickly, motioning them all to lie flat as the party came closer to their hiding spot.

Allanon's tall figure approached slowly along the trail in no apparent hurry, the deep-set eyes turned straight ahead as he walked. His dark brow was furrowed in concentration. Menion knew instinctively that they would be found and tensed his muscles for the leap onto the trail where his first blow would destroy the traitor. He knew he would have no second chance. The white-garbed Gnomes followed their leader dutifully, not marching in any particular order as they shuffled along in apparent disinterest. Suddenly Allanon halted and looked around in startled realization, as if sensing their presence. Menion prepared to spring, but a heavy hand grasped his shoulder, holding him firmly against the earth.

'Balinor,' called the tall wanderer evenly, moving neither forward nor to either side as he looked about expectantly.

'Release me!' demanded Menion furiously of the Prince of Callahorn.

'They have no weapons!' Balinor's voice cut through his anger, causing him to scan again the white-robed Gnomes at the tall man's side. There were no weapons visible.

Balinor stood up slowly and advanced into the clearing, his great sword gripped tightly in one hand. Menion was right behind him, noting the lean figure of Durin just within the trees, an arrow fitted to his bow in readiness. Allanon came forward with a sigh of relief and reached for Balinor's hand, stopping quickly as he saw the faint distrust mirrored in the borderman's eyes and the outright bitterness registered on the face of the highlander. He seemed baffled for a moment, and then looked back suddenly at the small figures standing motionless behind him.

'No, it's all right!' he exclaimed hastily. 'These are friends. They have no weapons and no hatred toward you. They are healers, physicians.'

For a moment no one moved. Then Balinor sheathed the great sword and took Allanon's extended hand in welcome. Menion followed suit, still distrustful of the Gnomes waiting up the trail.

'Now tell me what has happened,' ordered Allanon, once again in command of the weary company. 'Where are the others?'

Quickly Balinor recounted what had befallen them in the Wolfsktaag, their incorrect choice of the trail at the fork, the battle that had followed with the creature in the city ruins, their journey to the pass and the plan that had gotten them past the assembled Gnomes. Upon hearing of the Valemen's injuries, Allanon immediately spoke to the Gnomes who had accompanied him, informing the suspicious Menion that they could treat the wounds his friends had incurred. Balinor continued his tale while the white-robed Gnomes hastened to the side of the injured Valemen and hovered over them in obvious concern, applying a liquid from some vials they carried. Menion looked on anxiously, wondering to himself why these Gnomes were any different from the rest. As Balinor concluded, Allanon shook his head in disgust.

'It was my fault, my miscalculation,' he muttered angrily. 'I was looking too far ahead in the journey and not watching closely enough for immediate dangers. If those two men die, the whole trip will have been for nothing!'

He spoke again to the scurrying Gnomes, and one of them departed at a hasty walk up the trail toward the Pass of Jade.

'I sent one of them back to see what he could learn about Hendel. If anything has happened to him, I'll be the only one to blame.'

He ordered the Gnome physicians to pick up the Valemen and the whole group moved back onto the trail, heading westward, the stretcher bearers in the lead and the weary members of the company trailing behind. Dayel's rib wound had been attended to, and he was able to walk without assistance. As the company traveled along the deserted trail, Allanon explained to them why they would not encounter Gnome hunting parties in this region.

'We are approaching the land of the Stors, these Gnomes that came with me,' he informed them. 'They are healers, separate from the rest of the Gnome nations and all other races, dedicated to helping those in need of sanctuary or medical aid. They govern themselves, live apart from the petty bickerings of other nations – something most men could never manage to do. Everyone in this part of the world respects and honors them. Their land, which we will

219

enter soon, is called Storlock. It is hallowed ground that no Gnome hunting party would dare to cross into unless invited. You may rest assured that invitations are at a premium this night.'

He went on to explain that he had been a friend to these harmless people for many years, sharing their secrets, living with them for as long as several months at a time. The Stors could be counted on, he guaranteed Menion, to cure whatever might be wrong with the young Valemen. They were the foremost healers in the world, and it was no accident that they had come along with the historian when he had returned through the Anar to meet the company at the Pass of Jade. Hearing of the strange events that had taken place from a frightened Gnome runner he had encountered on the trail at the edge of Storlock, who believed the spirits of the taboo land had sallied forth to consume them all, he had asked the Stors to come with him in search of his friends, fearing that they might have sustained injuries at the pass.

'I had no idea that the creature whose presence I detected in that valley in the Wolfsktaag would have the intelligence to remove the trail markers after I had passed,' he admitted angrily. 'I should have suspected, though, and left other signs to be certain that you bypassed that place. Worse still, I passed right through the Pass of Jade in the early afternoon without realizing that the Gnomes would be gathering that evening for the purging of the mountain spirits. It appears I have failed you badly.'

'We were all at fault,' Balinor declared, although Menion, listening silently from the other side, was not so willing to believe he was right. 'Had we all been more alert, none of this would have happened. What matters is curing Shea and Flick and trying to do something about Hendel before the Gnome hunting parties find him.'

They walked on in silence for a while, dejected men too tired to think further on the matter, concentrating only on putting one foot in front of the next until they reached the promised safety of the Stor village. The trail seemed to wind endlessly through the trees of the Anar forest, and after a while the four lost all sense of time and place, their minds dulled into sleepless exhaustion. The night slowly passed away, and finally the first tinges of the dawn's light appeared unexpectedly on the eastern horizon; still they had not reached their destination. It was an hour later when they finally saw the light of night fires burning in the Stor village, reflecting off the trees encircling the tired travelers. All at once they were in the village, surrounded by ghostlike Stors, wrapped in the same white cloaks, looking at the men with sad, unblinking expressions as they helped the exhausted travelers into the shelter of one of the low buildings.

Once within, the members of the company collapsed wordlessly on the soft beds provided, too tired to wash or even undress. All were asleep in seconds except for Menion Leah, whose high-strung temperament fought back the clutches of a soothing sleep long enough to allow his bleary eyes to search silently about the room for Allanon. Upon not finding him, he rose sluggishly from the softness of the bed and stumbled wearily to the closed wooden door, which he dimly recalled led to a second room beyond. Leaning heavily against the door, his ear pressed closely to the crack in the jamb, he listened to snatches of conversation between the historian and the Stors. In a daze of half-sleep, he heard a brief digression concerning Shea and Flick. The strange little people felt that the Valemen would recover with rest and special medication. Then abruptly a door beyond opened to admit several people, and their voices blended meaninglessly in exclamations of dismay and shock. Allanon's deep voice cut through in icy clearness.

'What have you discovered?' he demanded. 'Is it as bad as we feared?'

'They caught somebody in the mountains,' came the timid answer. 'It was impossible to tell who it was or even what it was by the time they were finished. They tore him to pieces!'

Hendel!

Stunned, even in his exhausted condition, the highlander pushed himself upright and stumbled back to his waiting bed, unable to believe he had heard them correctly. Deep within him, a great empty space opened. Helpless tears of anger welled up, unable to reach his still-dry eyes, and hung poised there until the Prince of Leah finally dropped off into comforting sleep.

CHAPTER

13

When Shea finally opened his eyes, it was midafternoon of the following day. He found himself
resting comfortably in a long bed, tucked in with
clean sheets and blankets, his hunting clothes replaced by
a loose white gown tied about his neck. On the bed next to
him lay the still-sleeping Flick, his broad face no longer
drawn and pale, but alive once more with the color of life
and peaceful in slumber. They were in a small, plaster-walled
room with a ceiling supported by long wooden beams.
Through the windows, the young Valeman could see the
trees of the Anar and the shining blueness of the afternoon
sky. He had no idea how long he had been unconscious or
what had happened during that time to bring him to this
unknown place. But he felt certain that the creature of the
Wolfsktaag had nearly killed him, and that Flick and he owed
their lives to the men of the company. His attention was
quickly drawn to the opening door at one end of the small
room and the appearance of an anxious Menion Leah.

'Well, old friend, I see that you've come back to the
world of the living.' The highlander smiled slowly as he
came over to the bedside. 'You gave us quite a scare there
for a while, you know.'

'We made it, didn't we?' Shea grinned happily at the
familiar joking voice.

Menion nodded briefly and turned to the supine figure of Flick, who had stirred slightly beneath the covers and was beginning to awake. The stocky Valeman opened his eyes slowly and looked up hesitantly, seeing the grinning face of the highlander.

'I knew it was too good to be true,' he groaned painfully. 'Even dead, I can't escape him. It's a curse!'

'Old Flick has fully recovered as well.' Menion laughed shortly. 'I hope he appreciates the work it took to carry that cumbersome body of his all this way.'

'The day you do any honest work, I'll be amazed,' mumbled Flick, trying to clear his sleep-fogged eyes. He looked over at a smiling Shea and grinned back with a short wave of greeting.

'Where are we anyway?' asked Shea curiously, forcing himself to sit up in bed. He was still feeling weak. 'How long have I been unconscious?'

Menion sat down on the edge of the bed and repeated the entire tale of their journey after escaping the creature in the valley. He told them of the march to the Pass of Jade and the encounter with the Gnomes there, the plan to get them by, and the results. He faltered a bit retelling of Hendel's sacrifice to the company. Shocked looks registered on the Valemen's faces on hearing of the gallant Dwarf's grisly death at the hands of the enraged Gnomes. Menion quickly continued with the remainder of the story, explaining how they had wandered through the Anar until discovered by Allanon and the strange people called Stors, who had treated their wounds and brought them to this place.

'This land is called Storlock,' he concluded finally. 'The people here are Gnomes who have dedicated their lives to healing the sick and injured. It's really amazing what they can do. They have a salve which, when applied to an open wound, closes it up and heals it over in twelve hours. I saw it work myself on an injury Dayel received.'

Shea shook his head in disbelief and was about to ask for further details when the door again opened to admit Allanon. For the first time he could remember, Shea thought the dark wanderer actually seemed happy, and detected a sincere smile of relief on the grim face. The man walked quickly over to them and nodded in satisfaction.

'I am certainly pleased that you have both recovered from your wounds. I was gravely concerned about you, but it appears the Stors have done their work well. Do you feel recovered enough to get out of bed and walk around a bit, perhaps to have some food?'

Shea looked inquiringly over at Flick, and they both nodded.

'Very well, then, go along with Menion and test your strength,' the historian suggested. 'It is important that you feel well enough to travel again soon.'

Without further word, he left by the same door, shutting it softly behind him. They watched him go, wondering how he could continue to be so coldly formal in his attitude toward them. Menion shrugged, advising them that he would find their hunting clothes which had been taken out and cleaned. He left and quickly returned with their clothing, whereupon the Valemen rose weakly from their beds and dressed while Menion told them a little more about the Stors. He explained that he had mistrusted them at first because they were Gnomes, but his fears had rapidly vanished upon watching them care for the Valemen. The others in the company had slept well into the morning before waking and were scattered now about the village, enjoying their brief respite on the journey to Paranor.

The three left the room shortly thereafter and entered another building that served as a dining hall for the village, where they were given generous portions of hot food to appease their ravenous appetites. Even with their injuries, the Valemen found themselves able to put away several helpings of the nourishing meal. After finishing, Menion led them outside where they encountered a fully recuperated Durin and Dayel, both delighted to see the Valemen back on their feet. At Menion's suggestion, the five walked to the south end of the village to see the wondrous Blue Pond that the highlander had been told about by the Stors earlier in the day. It took only a few minutes for them to reach the small pond, and they sat at its edge beneath a huge weeping willow and gazed in silence at the placid blue surface. Menion told them that the Stors made many of their salves and balms from the waters of that pond, which were said to have special healing elements that could be found nowhere else in the world. Shea tasted the water and found it different from anything he had ever encountered, but not at all displeasing to drink. The others tried it as well and murmured their approval. The Blue Pond was such a peaceful place that for a moment they all sat back and forgot their hazardous journey, thinking about their homes and the people they had left behind.

'This pond reminds me of Beleal, my home in the Westland.' Durin smiled to himself as he ran a finger through the water, tracing out some image from his mind. 'There, you can find the same sort of peace we have here.'

'We'll be back there before you know it,' Dayel promised, and then added eagerly, almost boyishly, 'And I'll be married to Lynliss and we'll have many children.'

'Forget it,' declared Menion abruptly. 'Stay single and stay happy.'

'You haven't seen her, Menion,' Dayel continued brightly. 'She is like no one you have seen – a gentle, kind girl, as beautiful as this pond is clear.'

Menion shook his head in mock despair and slapped the frail Elf on his shoulder lightly, smiling his understanding of the other's deep feeling for the Elven girl. No one spoke for a few minutes as they continued to gaze with mixed feelings at the blue waters of the Stor pond. Then Shea turned to them questioningly.

'Do you think we are doing the right thing? I mean going on this trip and all. Does it all seem worth it to you?'

'That seems funny coming from you, Shea,' remarked Durin thoughtfully. 'The way I see it, you have the most to lose by coming along. In fact, you are the whole purpose of this journey. Do you feel it's worth it?'

Shea considered for a moment while the others looked on silently.

'That's not really a fair question to ask him,' defended Flick.

'Yes, it is,' Shea cut in soberly. 'They are all risking their lives for me, and I've been the only one expressing any doubts about what we're doing. But I can't answer my own question, even to myself, because I feel I still don't know exactly what's happening. I do not think that we have the whole picture before us.'

'I know what you mean,' Menion agreed. 'Allanon hasn't told us everything about what we're doing on this trip. There's more to this business about the Sword of Shannara than we know.'

'Has anybody ever seen the Sword?' Dayel asked suddenly. The others shook their heads negatively. 'Maybe there is no Sword.'

'Oh, I think that the Sword exists, all right,' Durin declared quickly. 'But once we get it, what do we do with it? What can Shea do against the power of the Warlock Lord, even with the Sword of Shannara?'

'I think we must trust to Allanon to answer that when the time comes,' another voice said.

The new voice came from behind the five, and they turned around sharply, breathing an audible sigh of relief when it was Balinor who appeared. Even as he watched the Prince of Callahorn stroll over to them, Shea wondered to himself why it was that they all still felt an unspoken fear of Allanon. The borderman smiled a greeting to Shea and Flick and seated himself with the others.

'Well, it appears that our hardships in coming through the Pass of Jade were worth it after all. I'm glad to see that you're all right.'

'I'm sorry about Hendel.' Shea sounded awkward to himself. 'I know he was a close friend.'

'It was a calculated risk that the situation demanded,' replied Balinor softly. 'He knew what he was doing and what the chances were. He did it for all of us.'

'What happens next?' asked Flick after a moment.

'We wait for Allanon to decide on our route for the last leg of the journey,' replied Balinor. 'Incidentally, I meant what I said about trusting him. He is a great man, a good man, though it may appear otherwise at times. He tells us what he feels we ought to know, but believe me, he does the worrying for us all. Do not be too quick to judge him.'

'You know that he hasn't told us everything,' Menion stated simply.

'I am certain he has told us only part of the tale.' Balinor nodded. 'But he is the only one who realized the threat to the four lands in the first place. We owe him a great deal, and the very least of that is a little trust.'

The others nodded slowly in agreement, more for the reason that they all respected the borderman than because they felt convinced by his reassurances. This was especially true of Menion, who recognized that Balinor was a man of great courage, the kind of man whom Menion looked to as a leader. They spoke no more on the matter, but turned to a further discussion of the Stors, their history as a branch of the Gnome nations and their long, abiding friendship with Allanon. The sun was setting when the tall historian appeared unexpectedly and joined them by the Blue Pond.

'After I am finished with you I want the Valemen back in bed for a few hours' rest. It probably wouldn't hurt the rest of you to get some sleep as well. We will leave this place some time around midnight.'

'Isn't this a little sudden after the wounds Shea and Flick received?' Menion asked cautiously.

'That cannot be helped, highlander.' The grim face seemed black even in the fading sunlight. 'We are all running out of time. If word of our mission, or even our presence in this part of the Anar, reaches the Warlock Lord, he will try to move the Sword immediately, and without it this journey is pointless.'

'Flick and I can make it,' Shea declared resolutely.

'What will be the route?' Balinor asked.

'We will cross the Rabb Plains tonight, a march of about four hours. If we are lucky, we will not be caught out in the open, although I am quite sure the Skull Bearers will still be searching for both Shea and myself. We can only hope they haven't managed to trace us into the Anar. I hadn't told you before, because you had enough to concern you, but any use of the Elfstones pinpoints our position to Brona and his hunters. The mystical power of the stones can be detected by any creature of the spirit world, warning him that sorcery similar to his own is being used.'

'Then, when we used the Elfstones in the Mist Marsh . . .' Flick began in horror.

'You told the Skull Bearers exactly where you were,' Allanon finished with that infuriating smile. 'If you hadn't lost yourselves in the mist and the Black Oaks, they might have had you right there.'

Shea felt a sudden chill sweep over him as he recalled how close they had felt to death at the time, little realizing how much danger they were really in from the creatures they feared the most.

'If you knew that use of the stones would attract the spirit creatures, then why didn't you tell us?' demanded Shea angrily. 'Why did you give them to us to use for protection when you knew what would happen?'

'You were cautioned, my young friend,' came the slow, growling response that always indicated Allanon's temper was shortening. 'Without them, you would have been at the mercy of other equally dangerous elements. Besides, they are protection enough in themselves against the winged ones.'

He waved off further questions, indicating that the subject was closed, causing Shea to become even more suspicious and angered. A watchful Durin saw all the signs and placed a restraining hand on the young Valeman's shoulder, shaking his head in warning.

'If we may return to the matter at hand,' Allanon continued on a more even tone, 'let me explain further the chosen route for the next few days – without interruption. The journey across the Rabb Plains will put us at the foot of the Dragon's Teeth at daybreak. Those mountains offer all the protection we need from anyone searching for us. But the real problem is getting over them and down the other side to the forests surrounding Paranor. All the known passes through the Dragon's Teeth will be closely guarded by the allies of the Warlock Lord, and any attempt to scale those peaks without using one of the passes would get half of us killed. So we'll go through the mountains by a different route, one that they won't be guarding.'

'Wait a minute!' exclaimed Balinor in astonishment. 'You don't plan to take us through the Tomb of the Kings!'

'There is no other alternative open to us if we wish to avoid being discovered. We can enter the Hall of Kings at sunrise and be completely through the mountains and outside Paranor by sundown without the guards at the passes being any the wiser.'

'But the stories say no one has ever gotten through those caverns alive!' insisted Durin, coming quickly to Balinor's aid in discounting the suggested plan. 'None of us is afraid of the living, but the spirits of the dead inhabit those caves and only the dead may pass through unharmed. No living person has ever done it!'

Balinor nodded his head slowly in agreement, while the others looked on anxiously. Menion and the Valemen had never even heard of the place of which the others seemed so deathly afraid. Allanon was actually grinning strangely at Durin's last comment, his eyes dark beneath the heavy brows, his white teeth showing in menacing fashion.

'You are not entirely correct, Durin,' he replied after a minute. 'I have been through the Hall of Kings, and I tell you that it can be done. It is not a journey to be made without risk. The caverns are indeed inhabited by the spirits of the dead, and it is on this that Brona relies to prevent the entry of humans. But my power should be sufficient to protect us.'

Menion Leah had no idea what it was about the caverns that could cause even a man like Balinor to have second thoughts, but whatever it was, he felt there was a good reason to fear it. Moreover, he was through questioning what he had called old wives' tales and foolish legends, since the encounters in the Mist Marsh and the Wolfsktaag. What really concerned him now was what sort of powers the man who proposed to lead them through the caves of the Dragon's Teeth might possess that could protect them from spirits.

'The entire journey has been a calculated risk.' Allanon was speaking once again. 'We all knew what the dangers were before we began it. Are you ready to turn back at this point, or do we see the matter through to the end?'

'We will follow you,' Balinor declared after only a moment's hesitation. 'You knew we would. The risk is worth it if we can lay our hands on the Sword.'

Allanon smiled slightly, his deep-set eyes traveling over the faces of the others, meeting each gaze piercingly, coming to rest at last on Shea. The Valeman stared back unfalteringly, though his heart felt twinges of fear and

231

uncertainty as those eyes bored into his innermost thoughts, seemingly aware of every secret doubt the Valeman had tried to conceal.

'Very well.' Allanon nodded darkly. 'Go now and rest.'

He turned abruptly and walked back toward the Stor village. Balinor hastened after the departing figure, apparently wishing to ask something further. The others watched both until they were out of sight. Then, for the first time, Shea realized it was almost dark, the sun sinking slowly beneath the horizon and the twilight a soft white light in the deepening purple sky. For a moment no one moved, and then silently they climbed to their feet and retired to the peaceful village to sleep until the appointed hour of midnight.

It seemed to Shea that he had just fallen asleep when he felt the rough grip of a strong hand shaking him awake. A moment later, the sharp glare of a burning torch flickered through the darkened room, causing him to squint protectively while his sleep-filled eyes adjusted to this new light. Through a mist of sleep, he saw the determined face of Menion Leah, the anxious eyes telling him that the hour had come for them to depart. He rose unsteadily in the cold night air and, after a moment's hesitation, hastened to dress. Flick was already awake and half dressed, the stolid face a welcome sight in the eerie silence of midnight. Shea felt strong once again, strong enough to make the long march across the Rabb Plains to the Dragon's Teeth and beyond if necessary – anything to reach the end of the journey.

Minutes later, the three companions were making their way through the sleeping Stor village to meet the other members of the company. The darkened houses were black, squarish bulks in the dim light of a night sky which was moonless and screened by a heavy blanket of clouds that moved sluggishly toward some undetermined destination. It was a good night to travel in the open, and Shea felt reassured by the idea that any searching emissaries of the Warlock Lord would have a very difficult time spotting them. As they walked, he found that he could barely detect the tread of their light hunting boots on the damp earth. Everything seemed to be working in their favor.

When they reached the western boundary of Storlock, they found the others waiting, except for Allanon. Durin and Dayel appeared like empty forms in the blackness, their slight figures only shadows as they paced wordlessly, listening to the sounds of the night. Passing close to them at one point, Shea was struck by the distinctive Elven features, the strange pointed ears and the pencil-thin eyebrows arching upward onto the forehead. He wondered if other humans looked at him the way he now looked at the Elven brothers. Were they truly different creatures? He wondered again about the history behind the Elf people, the history that Allanon had referred to once as remarkable, but had never described further. Their history was his own; he knew now what he had always suspected. It was something he wanted to know more about, perhaps if only better to understand his own heritage and the tale of the Sword of Shannara.

He looked over to the tall, broad figure of Balinor standing like a statue to one side, his face featureless in the dark. Balinor was unquestionably the most reassuring thing about the whole expedition. There was something very durable about the borderman, a quality of indestructibility that lent itself freely to all of the members of the company and gave them courage. Even Allanon did not inspire them in quite this way, although Shea felt that he was easily the more powerful of the two. Perhaps Allanon, in his seemingly infinite awareness of all matters, knew what Balinor did for other men and had brought him along for precisely that reason.

'Quite so, Shea.' The soft voice was so close to his ear that the Valeman leaped violently in surprise as the black-cloaked wanderer strolled past him and motioned the others to his side. 'The journey must be made while we have the cover of the night. Stay together and keep your eyes on the men ahead. There will be no talking.'

Without further greeting, the dark giant led them into the Anar Forests along a narrow trail that ran directly west out of Storlock. Shea fell into step behind Menion, his heart still in his throat from the fright he had received, his mind racing madly back over the past encounters with the strange man, wondering if what he had suspected all along were true after all. In any event, he would keep his thoughts to himself any time Allanon was close, however difficult that task might prove to be.

The company reached the western edges of the Anar Forests and the beginning of the Rabb Plains sooner than Shea had expected. Despite the blackness of the night sky, the Valemen could sense the presence of the Dragon's Teeth looming in the distance; without speaking, they looked at one another briefly, then turned back to peer anxiously into the darkness. Allanon led them across the empty plainland without pausing and without slackening the pace. The Plains were completely flat, totally free of natural obstructions and visibly lifeless. The only things growing were small scrub trees and bits of scattered brush that were bare and skeletonlike in appearance. The floor of the plain was hard-packed earth, so dry in parts that it split apart in long, jagged crevices. Nothing moved about the travelers as they marched in silence, their eyes and ears alert to anything out of the ordinary. At one point, when they were almost three hours into the Rabb Plains, Dayel brought them up with a quick gesture, indicating that he had heard something behind them, far back in the blackness. They crouched soundless and immobile for several long minutes, but nothing happened. At last Allanon shrugged and motioned them back into line, and they resumed their march.

They reached the Dragon's Teeth just before daybreak,

the night sky still black and clouded as they halted at the foot of the forbidding mountains that spread upward across their path like monstrous spikes on an iron gate. Both Shea and Flick felt strong, even after the long march, and quickly indicated to the others that they were ready to continue without a rest. Allanon seemed eager to move on immediately, almost as if he were determined to keep an appointment. He took them straight into the treacherous-looking mountains along a pebble-strewn trail that wound gently upward into what appeared to be a pocket in the face of the cliffs. Flick found himself looking up at the peaks on either side of the trail as he walked, craning his stout neck at right angles to catch occasional glimpses of the jagged tips. The Dragon's Teeth seemed an appropriate name.

The mountains on either side began to fold about them as they worked their way toward the cliff pocket. Beyond that shallow pass, they could glimpse other mountains, higher than these and clearly insurmountable by anything that could not fly. Shea paused momentarily at one point, picked up a piece of the loose rock from beneath his feet, and examined it curiously as he resumed walking. To his surprise, it was smooth on its flat surfaces, almost glassy in appearance, and its color was a deep, mirroring black that reminded the Valeman of the coal he had seen burned as fuel in some of the Southland communities. Yet this appeared to be more durable than coal, as if it had been pressured and polished to reach its present state. He handed it to Flick, who glanced at it, shrugged disinterestedly and tossed it aside.

The trail began to twist through huge clusters of fallen boulders, causing the travelers momentarily to lose all sight of the surrounding mountains. They wound about in the tangle of rock for a long time, still climbing toward the pocket, their dark leader apparently oblivious to the fact that no one had any idea where they were going. Finally they reached a clearing in the rocks where they could see enough of the high cliffs about them to tell that they were at the opening to the pocket and evidently close to the summit of the trail, which would then either have to turn downward or level off into the mountains. It was here that Balinor broke the silence with a low whistle, bringing the company to a halt. He spoke momentarily with Durin, who had fallen back with the borderman at the foot of the mountains, then quickly turned to Allanon and the others with a startled look on his face.

'Durin is certain he heard someone following us on the trail up!' he informed them tensely. 'There's no question about it this time – someone is back there.'

Allanon glanced up hurriedly at the night sky. His dark brow furrowed in concern, the lean face revealing that he was deeply worried by this report. He looked at Durin uncertainly.

'I'm sure there is someone back there,' Durin affirmed.

'I cannot stop here to deal with this myself. I have to be in the valley ahead before the break of day,' Allanon declared abruptly. 'Whatever is back there must be delayed until I have finished – it is essential!'

Shea had never heard the man sound so determined about anything, and he caught the looks of consternation on both Flick's and Menion's faces as they glanced quickly at one another. Whatever it was Allanon had to do in the valley, it was critical to him that he not be interrupted until he had finished.

'I'll stay behind,' Balinor volunteered, drawing his great sword. 'Wait for me in the valley.'

'Not alone, you won't,' Menion spoke up quickly. 'I'm staying, too, just in case.'

Balinor smiled briefly and nodded his approval to the highlander. Allanon looked at him for a moment as if to object, then nodded curtly and motioned the others to follow him. The Elven brothers hastened up the trail behind the tall leader, but Shea and Flick hung back uncertainly until Menion motioned for them to get going. Shea waved briefly, reluctant to desert his friend, but realizing that he would be of little help in staying. He glanced back only once and saw the two men positioning themselves among the rocks on either side of the narrow trail, their swords gleaming dully in the faint starlight, their dark hunting cloaks blending with the shadows of the rocks.

Allanon led the remaining four members of the company ahead through the jumbled mass of boulders where the cliff face split apart, climbing steadily upward toward what appeared to be the rim of the mysterious valley. It was only a few short minutes before they stood quietly at its edge, gazing wonderingly at what lay before them. The valley was a barbaric wilderness of crushed rock and boulders strewn about the sides and floor, black and glistening like the rock Shea had examined on the trail; the place was completely covered with them. Nothing else was visible except for a small lake with murky waters that glistened a dull greenish-black and moved in small sluggish swirls as if possessing a life of its own. Shea was immediately struck with the strange movement of the water. There was no wind which might cause the slow rippling. He looked at the silent Allanon and was shocked to see a strange glow radiating from his dark, forbidding face. The tall wanderer seemed momentarily lost in his thoughts as he gazed downward at the lake, and the Valeman could sense a peculiar wistfulness about the man's unbroken study of the slowly churning waters.

'This is the Valley of Shale, the doorstep to the Hall of Kings and the home of the spirits of the ages.' The deep voice rolled suddenly out of the depths of the great chest. 'The lake is the Hadeshorn – its waters are death to mortals. Walk with me to the floor of the valley, and then I must go on alone.'

Without waiting for a response, he started slowly down

the slope of the valley, stepping surefootedly through the loose rock, his gaze fixed on the lake beyond. The others followed in mystified silence, sensing that this was going to be an important moment for them all, that here more than anywhere else in all the lands, Allanon was king. Without being able to explain why, Shea knew that the historian, the wanderer, the philosopher, and the mystic, the man who had brought them through countless dangers on a wild gamble that only he fully understood, the mysterious man they knew as Allanon, had at last come home. Moments later, when they stood together on the floor of the Valley of Shale, he turned to them again.

'You will wait for me here. No matter what happens next, you will not follow me. You will not move from this spot until I have finished. Where I go, there is only death.'

They stood rooted in place as he moved away from them across the rocky floor toward the mysterious lake. They watched his tall, black form walk steadily ahead without variation in either speed or direction, the great cloak billowing slightly. Shea shot a quick glance at Flick, whose tense face revealed his fear of what would happen next. For a split second Shea considered getting out of there, but realized immediately what a foolhardy decision that would be. Instinctively he clutched his tunic, feeling the reassuring bulk of the small pouch that contained the Elfstones. Their presence made him feel safer, even though he doubted that they would be of much use against anything that Allanon could not handle. He glanced anxiously at the others as they watched the diminishing figure, then turning back, saw that Allanon had reached the edge of the Hadeshorn, where he was apparently awaiting something. A deathly silence seemed to grip the entire valley. The four waited, their eyes locked on the dark figure who stood motionless at the water's edge.

Slowly, the tall wanderer raised his black-caped arms to

the sky and the amazed men saw the lake begin to stir rapidly and then churn in deep dissatisfaction. The valley shuddered heavily, as if some form of hidden, sleeping life had been awakened. The terrified mortals looked about in disbelief, fearing they were about to be swallowed by the rock-strewn maw of some nightmare disguised as the valley. Allanon stood firm at the shoreline as the water began to boil fiercely at its center, a spray mist rising toward the darkened heavens with a sharp hiss of relief at its newfound freedom from the depths. From out of the night air came the sound of low moaning, the cries of imprisoned souls, their sleep disturbed by the man at the edge of the Hadeshorn. The voices, less than human and chill with death, cut through the raw edge of sanity of the four who shivered and watched at the valley's edge, straining their frightened minds and twisting with unmerciful cruelty until it seemed the little courage that remained must surely be wrested from them, leaving them stripped completely of all defenses. Unable to move, to speak, even to think, they stood frozen in terror as the sounds of the spirit world reached up to them and passed through their minds, warning of the things that lay beyond this life and their understanding.

In the midst of the chilling cries, with a low rumble that sounded from the heart of the earth, the Hadeshorn opened at its center in the manner of a thrashing whirlpool and from out of its murky waters rose the shroud of an old man, bowed with age. The figure rose to full height and appeared to stand on the waters themselves, the tall, thin body a transparent gray of ghostlike hue that shimmered like the lake beneath it. Flick turned completely white. The appearance of this final horror only confirmed his belief that their last moments on earth were at hand. Allanon stood motionless at the edge of the lake, his lean arms lowered now, the black cloak wrapped closely about his statuesque figure, his face turned toward the shade which stood before him. They appeared to be conversing, but the four onlookers could hear nothing beyond the continual, maddening sound of the inhuman cries that rose piercingly out of the night each time the figure from the Hadeshorn gestured. The conversation, whatever its nature, lasted no more than a few brief minutes, ending when the wraith turned toward them suddenly, raised its tattered skeletal arm, and pointed. Shea felt a chill slice through his unprotected body that seemed to cut to the bones, and he knew that for a brief second he had been touched by death. Then the shade turned away and, with a final gesture of farewell to Allanon, sank slowly back into the dark waters of the Hadeshorn and was gone. As he disappeared from view, the waters again churned sluggishly, and the moans and cries reached a new pitch before dying out in a low wail of anguish. Then the lake was smooth and calm and the men were alone.

As sunrise broke on the eastern horizon, the tall, black figure on the lake's edge seemed to sway slightly and then crumple to the ground. For a second the four men watching hesitated, then dashed across the valley floor toward their fallen leader, slipping and stumbling on the loose rock. They reached him in a matter of seconds and bent cautiously over him, uncertain what they should do. Finally, Durin reached down and shook the still form gingerly, calling his name. Shea rubbed the great hands, finding the skin ice-cold to his touch and alarmingly pale. But their fears were relieved when after a few minutes Allanon stirred slightly and the deep-set eyes opened once more. He stared at them for a few seconds, and then sat up slowly as they crouched anxiously next to him.

'The strain must have been too great,' he muttered to himself, rubbing his forehead. 'Blacked out after I lost contact. I'll be fine in a moment.'

'Who was that creature?' Flick asked quickly, afraid that it might reappear at any moment.

Allanon seemed to reflect on his question, staring into space as his dark face twisted in anguish and then relaxed softly.

'A lost soul, a being forgotten by this world and its people,' he declared sadly. 'He has doomed himself to an existence of half-life that may not end for all eternity.'

'I don't understand,' Shea said.

'It's not important right now.' Allanon brushed the question aside abruptly. 'That sad figure to whom I just spoke is the Shade of Bremen, the Druid who once fought against the Warlock Lord. I spoke to him of the Sword of Shannara, of our trip to Paranor, and of the destiny of this company. I could learn little from him, an indication that our fortunes are not to be decided in the very near future, but that the fate of us all will be decided in days still far away – that is, all but one.'

'What do you mean?' Shea demanded hesitantly.

Allanon climbed wearily to his feet, gazed about the valley silently as if to assure himself that the encounter with the ghost of Bremen was ended, and then turned back to the anxious faces waiting on him.

'There is no easy way to say this, but you've come this far, almost to the end of the quest. You have earned the right to know. The Shade of Bremen made two prophesies on the destiny of this company when I called him up from the limbo world to which he is confined. He promised that within two dawns we would behold the Sword of Shannara. But he also foresaw that one member of our company would not reach the far side of the Dragon's Teeth. Yet he will be the first to lay hands upon the sacred blade.'

'I still don't understand,' Shea admitted after a moment's thought. 'We've already lost Hendel. He must have been speaking of him in some way.'

'No, you are wrong, my young friend.' Allanon sighed softly. 'Upon making the last part of the prophesy, the

241

shade pointed to the four of you standing at the edge of the valley. One of you will not reach Paranor!'

Menion Leah crouched silently in the cover of the boulders along the path leading upward to the Valley of Shale, waiting expectantly for the mysterious being who had been trailing them into the Dragon's Teeth. Across from him, hidden in the blackness of the shadows, was the Prince of Callahorn, his great sword balanced blade downward in the rocks, one big hand resting lightly on the pommel. Menion gripped his own weapon and peered into the darkness. Nothing was moving. He could see for only about fifteen yards before an abrupt twist in the trail concealed the remainder of the pathway behind a cluster of massive boulders. They had been waiting for at least half an hour and still nothing had appeared, despite Durin's assurance that something was following. Menion wondered for a moment if perhaps the creature who had been trailing them was one of the emissaries of the Warlock Lord. A Skull Bearer could take to the air and get behind them to reach the others. The idea startled him, and he was about to signal Balinor when a sudden noise on the trail below caught his attention. He immediately flattened himself against the rocks.

The sound of someone picking his way up the twisting pathway, threading slowly among the great boulders in the dim light of the approaching dawn, was clearly audible. Whoever or whatever it was, he apparently did not suspect they were hidden above, or worse, did not care, because he was making no effort to mask his approach. Scant seconds later, a dim form appeared on the pathway just below their hiding place. Menion risked a quick glance and for one brief second the squat shape and shuffling gait of the figure approaching reminded him of Hendel. He gripped the sword of Leah in anticipation and waited. The plan of attack was simple. He would leap in front of the intruder, barring his path forward. In the same moment, Balinor would cut off his retreat.

With a lightning-quick spring, the highlander shot out of the rocks to stand face to face with the mysterious intruder, his sword held poised as he gave a sharp command to halt. The figure before him went into a low crouch and one powerful arm came up slightly to reveal a huge, iron-headed mace, glinting dully. One second later, as the eyes of the combatants came to rest on one another, the arms dropped in shocked recognition, and a cry of surprise burst from the lips of the Prince of Leah.

'Hendel!'

Balinor came out of the shadows to the rear of the newcomer in time to see an elated Menion leap into the air with a wild shout and charge down to embrace the smaller, stockier figure with unrestrained joy. The Prince of Callahorn sheathed the great sword in relief, smiling and shaking his head in wonder at the sight of the ecstatic highlander and the struggling, muttering Dwarf they had presumed dead. For the first time since they had escaped through the Pass of Jade from the Wolfsktaag, he felt that success was within their grasp and that the company would surely stand together at Paranor before the Sword of Shannara.

The epic quest for The Sword of Shannara *continues in . . .*

THE DRUIDS' KEEP

by Terry Brooks

Shea and Flick Ohmsford have somehow survived the
first stage of their quest. With the aid of their childhood
friend Menion Leah, and new companions, the dwarf
Hendel, Balinor of Callahorn and the elves, Durin
and Dayel, they have successfully evaded capture by
gnomish warriors, and eluded the Warlock Lord's
dread Skull Bearers.

Now, with Allanon to guide them, the company must
continue north, through the vast peaks of the Dragons
Teeth Mountains. It is a route fraught with more danger,
but the only path to their goal – the druid keep at
Paranor, last resting place of Shannara's fabled Sword,
the weapon Shea is destined to wield.

www.atombooks.co.uk

Look out for . . .

THE SECRET OF
THE SWORD

by Terry Brooks

Can the Prince of Leah rally the southern forces to stall
the advancing armies of doom? Is there any hope for
Balinor and his allies, trapped in the dungeons of his
own castle? And can Shea Ohmsford, against all the
odds, recover the fabled Sword of Shannara and fulfil
the prophecy of defeating the Dark Lord and his deadly
Skull Bearers . . .?

Find out in *The Secret of the Sword*, the final volume of
Terry Brooks' classic fantasy trilogy, available from all
good bookshops.

www.atombooks.co.uk

About the Author

Terry Brooks has been a writer since high school and published his first novel, the Sword of Shannara in 1977. It became the first work of fiction ever to appear on the New York Times trade paperback bestseller list, where it remained for more than five months. A practising attorney for many years, Terry Brooks now writes full-time and lives with his wife Judine in the Pacific Northwest and Hawaii.

WWW.ATOMBOOKS.CO.UK